THE BLACK ANGEL

THE BLACK ANGEL

BEN WASSINGER

ISBN-13: 978-1-5004-8639-6
ISBN-10: 1-5004-8639-6

Editor: Carol Weber, http://carolscorrections.weebly.com/
Cover and Formatting: Blue Valley Author Services, http://www.bluevalleyauthorservices.com/

This is a work of fiction. Names, characters, places, and incidents either are the product of the author's imagination or are used fictitiously, and any resemblance to locales, events, business establishments, or actual persons—living or dead—is entirely coincidental.

This book is dedicated to my wife, children, and grandchildren. Their enthusiasm, support, and encouragement were my inspiration.

PART ONE

PROLOGUE

Thursday, May 21, 2009
Council Bluffs, Iowa
5:00 P.M.

T HE PAIN WAS UNBEARABLE. IT just wouldn't quit. *How long has it been?* He wanted it to quit. He had to make it quit! Then there was the God-awful ringing in his ears. It was driving him crazy!

He tried to focus, but his eyes wouldn't cooperate. It was if they had shutters on them that would open and close at will. He had no control. Wait. That's the problem. *I have no control!*

There was a bright light. It appeared to be shining in his eyes. He tried to close them to get rid of it, but he couldn't make his eyelids work. *Somebody do something about that damned light!* He thought he heard voices, but the ringing in his ears drowned them out. He could feel pressure on his body but didn't know where it was coming from. What were they doing to him? *Oh my God. Please just let me die! Or am I already dead? Yes, that's it, I am dead. No, I can't be dead or I couldn't feel the pain. Or could I? Maybe I'm crazy. Yes, that's it. I've gone crazy.* He just wanted it to be over, whatever it was. *Make it stop. Make it stop. Make it stop!*

The light was back again, along with the voices. *Please just go away.* Darkness. And with the darkness came peace.

CHAPTER 1

The Previous Day
Wednesday, May 20, 2009
Grand Island, Nebraska
5:00 P.M.

TED BINGHAM, A TEACHER AT St. John's High School, hurried home from the dedication for the new gymnasium. He was in a rush. Three of his college buddies had made the trip from Omaha for the dedication, and he was planning on doing a little bar-hopping with one of them. The other two, Tom and Jason, were going back to Omaha tonight as they had to work tomorrow. Ted took off his suit and tie, stopping to admire himself in the mirror. Standing in his blue boxers, he ran his fingers through his thick curly brown hair, turned sideways and patted his flat abdomen. He changed into his comfortable jeans, t-shirt , and Nike shoes. A former college athlete, Ted was cocky and proud of the fact he kept in shape after graduating.

A half hour passed and his phone still hadn't rung. He became impatient and called his friend.

"Hey, Nathan, I've been waiting for your call. When're you getting to my apartment so we can hit the bars?"

"Uh...something came up." Nathan hoped his voice didn't tip off the lie. "I had to head back to Omaha."

"Thanks a hell of a lot for calling. Really considerate of you!"

"I got paged during the dedication. A problem surfaced at the car dealership. It needs my attention first thing tomorrow so I left right away."

"You still could have called!"

"I've been on the phone since I got in the car and just forgot. You're right, though; I should have called. I'm sorry."

"Well, guess I'll try and catch up with some of the other teachers. They were all going out to Ed and Nettie's bar since there's no school the next two days. St. John's is having an open house for the general public."

"Yeah, we were all impressed with the gym. It's really nice. Tell you what. We'll get together soon and dinner is on me, okay?"

"Guess that's the way it is," Ted said, his words clipped and sarcastic. He slapped his phone shut and strode out the door, still pissed.

Nathan continued on, sweating as he drove, hoping the man in the trunk of the car he was driving was still alive. *God. What the hell was I thinking? Damn temper of mine! I've got to dump this guy somewhere and get rid of his car. Have to drive carefully, no speeding, and take time to think.* He had pulled onto Interstate 80 and was heading east when a solution popped into his head.

Next Day
Thursday, May 21, 2009
Council Bluffs, Iowa
7:00 A.M.

The cans rattled as the grocery cart jerked along. It was heaped full of aluminum cans, perhaps enough to provide money for an entire week. The tall black man in the long wool overcoat and stocking cap moved slowly. He had graying hair and a beard which made him appear older than his forty years. His size, combined with his dress, made him an ominous figure. He moved along cautiously, as if to guard his treasure. To Sam, it was a treasure. It was the most cans he had ever accumulated. It had taken the better part of a week, but he had hit the jackpot behind Barley's Bar. Wednesday night was happy hour all night at Barley's and drew huge crowds, resulting in massive quantities of beer being consumed. Sam had planned ahead, sleeping in a clump of bushes on the lawn of City Hospital, a few blocks from the bar. He awakened early and pushed his cart down the alley. He found what he wanted. A Dumpster overflowing with aluminum beer cans. He had started the day with only about fifty cans lining the bottom of the cart, but Barley's had proved to be a bonanza. He kept telling himself it was his lucky day as he meticulously crushed each can with the heel of his shoe. It took him almost two hours. For good measure, he filled a black plastic garbage bag with uncrushed cans and put it on the bottom rack of the cart.

The alley was still dark, but the sun was beginning to cast an orange glow on the parking lot behind the bar. It was time to move on. As Sam pushed his cart along, an occasional can slipped out, clanking on the blacktop. Sam would stop the cart, carefully pick up the can and place it back in the cart, never letting go of the handle, as if someone would steal it.

There were a few homeless people still sleeping off the night before in the alley. Sam stepped over and pushed the cart around a few of them. Unmistakable derelicts identified by their clothing and smell. Not unlike his own. He moved on, glancing around nervously, wishing he were clear of the downtown area and people. Sam reached the street and stopped to look both ways. Not for cars, but for police officers. Sam did his best to avoid them. Satisfied it was safe, he hurried across the street and entered another alley. Sam moved slowly down the alley, avoiding the water puddles to keep his feet dry. He maneuvered around a Dumpster, reeking of garbage, and his cart's wheel stuck on something. Sam pushed harder but it wouldn't budge. He cursed, and stooped to see what was in the way. It was a shoe...and it was still on a man's foot!

The man was unconscious, face down. But something was wrong. This man didn't fit. His clothing was dirty and torn, but it wasn't street clothing. It was an expensive suit.

Sam looked around to see if there were any witnesses, then hunched down and edged forward; reaching his hand out to see if the man had a wallet. Sam wasn't a thief by nature, but maybe if the guy was well heeled he wouldn't miss a few dollars. No wallet, no watch, no identification. His head and face were covered with dried blood. Probably a mugging. Sam knew he should do something, but he didn't want to be involved with the police. Fearful they would confiscate his cans, or his name would be listed on the police report, he moved on. *Don't want to be involved with the police. No way. I never took that money they said I did. They wouldn't believe me then, and they won't believe me now. I'm just going to move on. Not going to stay and answer their damn accusing questions.* The recycling center was still almost four miles away. Sam knew it was going to take the rest of the morning to get there, and they closed at 1:00 P.M. on the dot.

Grand Island, Nebraska
11:00 A.M.

Detective Larry Malone ambled along the paved path in the warm spring sunshine. Six feet, two inches tall, one-hundred ninety-five pounds, his muscles were toned from working out every day. His full head of dark hair, pale blue eyes, and perpetual five o'clock shadow gave him a ruggedly handsome appearance. His official title wasn't actually "Detective." He was a "Criminal Investigator" with the CID—Criminal Investigative Division—of the Grand Island Police Department. But the general public understood the title of detective, and use of this term saved Malone time explaining what "Criminal Investigator" meant.

Deep in thought, Malone hardly noticed the fragrant aroma of the lilac bushes bordering the pavement. *Why am I here anyway? Is*

this nostalgia? Or am I just seeking reassurance from my inner self?
He remembered the walks he and his ex-wife used to take through
Pier Park. They had moved to Grand Island when he joined the GI
Police Force in 2005.

Grand Island was close to the middle of the state, situated
about six miles north of the Platte River and Interstate 80. The
Platte River was a brilliant blue jewel that paralleled the interstate,
adding a spectacular beauty to the landscape. It was running deep
and fast this time of year, swollen with the snow runoff from the
mountains of Colorado. By late July it would be a mile wide and
an inch deep.

Grand Island had a population of almost 50,000, enough to
make it the third largest city in Nebraska. It was home to the Stuhr
Museum of the Prairie Pioneer, a gem of the prairie. It also had
a race track, the Heartland Events Center, and was bordered on
the east and west by two corridors of Highway 281, along which
restaurants and strip malls were sprouting up as quickly as the crops
around them. Its downtown was fighting a valiant but losing battle
to remain a viable shopping area. In spite of all the commercialism,
it was still considered an agricultural community, surrounded by
corn and soybean fields in almost every direction. This year's crops
had been planted, and the brown fields were beginning to grow
a blanket of lush green. Center pivots stood alongside the fields,
patiently awaiting the massive diesel engines to roar to life, pulling
the precious water up from the Ogallala Aquifer beneath the earth,
so they could spray the life-giving water on the crops.

Larry thought back to 2003, when he and Carrie first moved
to Grand Island. It was a romantic time in their lives, having been
married only a year, and they looked forward to their walks in the
park. It was safer then. Now the park was overrun with drug dealers
after dark. He remembered picking Carrie a bouquet of lilacs from
the bushes lining the path. She was flattered, but concerned that
a police officer shouldn't be "stealing" lilacs from a city park. That
was Carrie, always worrying about everything.

He hadn't been to the park in the two years since his divorce. Well, not on a personal visit, only for official business. It was too painful. The park held many memories that still pulled at his heart. But he had a date tonight, and had to get over the fact that Carrie was his ex-wife. He knew that would never change, but he needed closure.

This was his first attempt at a real date. He had gone out for dinner with female coworkers, but just on a friendship basis. He was a little nervous, and hoped that this stroll down memory lane would give him a final break from the past and the confidence he needed to begin dating.

He had taken time off work today to buy some new clothes, something comfortable and casual for tonight's date. Larry had always liked the Tommy Bahama look, but a cop's salary didn't justify the price. He saw that Dillard's Department Store was having a sale and purchased some nice khakis and a lavender Nike polo shirt, a welcome change from his drab work clothes. Part of being a detective required him to wear at least a sport coat, but the tie had gone out with the twentieth century. Malone was an easy fit, and remembered when Carrie would have fun picking out clothes for him to try on and buy. The ring of his cell phone jarred him back to the present. It was the Grand Island Safety Center. Malone was needed back at his office. He told the desk sergeant he would be there in ten minutes.

The Safety Center had replaced the old police station three years ago. The GIPD and Hall County Sheriff's Department were now housed in one building, and the Hall County Jail stood on the other side of the street. It was a nice functional building, and Larry had a spacious office with a window, a stark contrast from the old police station where the windows had been covered for security reasons, and he had to close the folding chair to make room to get out from behind his desk.

Malone made it back to the Safety Center in five minutes. He swiped his ID card and the door buzzed to allow him to enter.

He walked down the hall, and went into the communication area where the shift sergeants monitored the daily activity.

"What's up, Sarge?"

"Lady came in to report that her husband is missing."

"How long?"

"Didn't ask. She was really upset, so I just took her back to your office."

"Where's Max?" Max was Malone's partner

"He took the day off."

"Oh yeah, forgot about that. Something with his kids and school. Does this lady have a name?"

"Yeah, Susan Wilson. Says her husband's name is James."

"Okay. Thanks, Sarge."

He had brought his new clothes into the center with him to ask one of the female officers her opinion. He decided it could wait, and put them in his locker on the way to his office.

Susan Wilson was about five feet ten inches tall, blonde, and attractive. Malone guessed she was late twenties or early thirties. Her hair was unkempt, but cut in a fashionable style. It was long on the sides, but had a weird wedge cut out of the back. Malone thought it looked like someone had cut a huge crater out of her hair. *Crater hair? C'mon Malone, this lady is here for your help, not your opinion of her hairstyle.*

She was wearing a light blue hooded workout suit which, despite its loose fit, made him think she had a good figure. *The male brain at its best.* Her eyes were red from crying and rubbing the tears away. He offered her some tissues. She was adamant that something bad had happened to her husband.

He had listened to this same story before. Too many times. Enough to know that most of these cases ended up the same way. After she got home tonight, her husband would eventually show up with some lame excuse.

He asked Susan the obvious questions.

"When did you last see your husband?"

"He was with me at the school yesterday afternoon."

11

"What school?"

"St. John's."

"Does he work there?" Malone asked.

"No, he's a pharmacist. He's half owner of Central Pharmacy," Susan said with pride in her voice.

"Why were you at the school?"

"James made a donation to the new gymnasium and we were invited to the dedication."

"What time did you leave the school?"

"Around 4:30 p.m. I had to leave early to attend a dinner, but James stayed."

"And you haven't heard from him since?"

"No."

Malone rubbed his forehead with his fingers as if in thought. He looked up at Susan and said, "What are his daily habits?"

"If you mean his schedule, he works six days a week, and comes home every evening for dinner. That is, unless he has a meeting or something work-related. Occasionally he goes out with friends or we go out together."

"Could he have had a meeting last night?"

"No, he would have told me yesterday at the dedication."

"Did he work yesterday?"

"Yes, he left for work at 8:30 a.m., and met me at the school about 3:45 p.m. I already told you this," Susan added, appearing irritated.

"What's the make, model, and license of his car?"

"He drives a gray Toyota Camry. I think it's 8-A3246...or 4236...I don't know! I can't think right now!"

Malone could feel the tension, sense her exasperation. "That's all right. I can look it up. Could he have gone on a bender with his guy friends?"

"No. James has never been much of a drinker."

"Could there be someone else?"

The last question got exactly the answer he expected.

"There is nothing wrong with our marriage! We are in love. And how could you even ask that when my husband is missing? You are totally insensitive! Furthermore, I just told James on Wednesday that we are going to have a baby, and he was thrilled!"

Malone nodded as a sign he understood they had a good marriage, but wondered to himself why women always think men are as excited about babies as they are. Sometimes men just have to take a little time to get used to the fact that the sports car is backing out of the garage for the last time, and the family van is just a car payment away. Maybe the poor guy just needed time to think about becoming a father. *Thoughts are wandering again. Stop it, Malone.* Susan Wilson seemed like a nice lady, and he remained attentive, even trying to appear sensitive.

"We have to wait twenty-four hours before we can file a missing persons report," the detective told her as he shrugged his shoulders to indicate his disapproval of the protocol. This was technically untrue. The notion that one had to wait twenty-four hours was mostly urban legend. At the Safety Center it was left to officer discretion, and Detective Malone had already decided it was too early to file a report.

Malone asked her to go over yesterday's events once again, hoping to glean some new information she may have left out the first time.

Susan explained again that she and James had gone to a pep rally/dedication the previous afternoon and basically repeated her former statements.

Malone wondered why they didn't ride together, and asked, "So why did you go in separate cars?"

"Last night was my night out with the girls, so we each drove our own car. A bunch of us girls get together once a month. We go for dinner and then to someone's house to play Bunko. As I said, I left the dedication a little early in order to be on time for dinner."

"Whose house was it at?"

"Sarah Morgan's."

"How late did you stay out?"

"Why is that relevant?"

"It may not be, but I just want to get a feel for the timeline."

"I was home around 10:30 or 11:00 P.M."

"Were you drinking?" Malone knew he was pushing her now, but chose to continue his path.

"I usually have a glass of wine or two, but I didn't have any last evening."

"So two glasses is your usual limit?"

"Yes. I told you we aren't big drinkers. And...I told you I just found out I was pregnant!" Susan said, her eyes narrowing in a glare. Malone chose not to mention that Susan had told him James wasn't a big drinker; she never mentioned her own drinking habits.

Without prompting, Susan continued. "James was still at the dedication when I left. I thought it was strange he wasn't home when I got there. At first I assumed he had gone out with his friends, but he would have called me if that were the case. When he wasn't home by midnight I began to worry. I tried his cell so many times I lost count. This morning I called his partner at the pharmacy to see if James was at work."

"What made you think he would stay out all night, not call, and then show up at work the next day?"

"I don't know. I was just so upset, I guess I wanted some good news!"

"Well, obviously he wasn't at work."

"I wouldn't be here if he were, now would I?" Susan's hands were on her hips and a disgusted look on her face. *Time to back off, Malone; she's getting tired of this questioning.* She got control of herself and said, "No, he was not at work. His partner, Fred Hawthorne, told me that he hadn't seen James since he left for the dedication at St. John's about 3:00 P.M. yesterday. After talking to Fred, I called all of his friends, and none of them had seen him either. He was just gone. I just know something really bad must have happened to him."

Malone had to admit the details were puzzling, and he felt sorry for her, but he was fairly confident her concern would turn out to be unwarranted. To expedite things, he handed her a report to take home, fill out overnight, and bring back in the morning if James was still missing. He assured her that her husband would probably be home by then and the report wouldn't be necessary. Susan took the report, the tears welling up in her eyes. She composed herself, straightened her sweat suit, and said between sobs, "Can you start looking for him right away?"

Malone told her he would do some preliminary checking, but they had to follow department protocol. He walked around his desk, handed her his card and, giving her a reassuring smile, nodded and told her: "Call me as soon as James comes home."

She took the report along with his card and left his office still fighting off tears. Feeling a little guilty, Larry made a call to the hospital emergency room, checked for recent police reports and accident reports. They all turned up negative. He worked on some open cases for a while, got the approval on his new clothes from Michelle, and left the office early. Soon, Susan Wilson was forgotten.

CHAPTER 2

Omaha, Nebraska
11:00 A.M.

NATHAN CALLED JASON TO MEET for lunch. The three friends, Nathan, Jason and Tom , met for lunch at least once a week at the Good Times Brewery. Even though the Good Times no longer brewed beer, the bar still housed the brewing vats behind a wall of glass. This provided a bit of nostalgia to go along with the best Buffalo wings in the area, with a list of sauces as long as your arm.

Tom, Jason, and Nathan were college friends and all had settled in Omaha. Nathan was the only native. Tom was from Fargo, North Dakota, and Jason from Chicago. Their other friend, Ted, from Denver, had taken a teaching job at St. John's High School in Grand Island.

Jason said, "Sure; see you at the brewery at noon."

"No, let's make it Goldbergs. I'm going to be in the Dundee area and that will be closer for me." Nathan said.

"Okay. I may have to leave lunch a little early. I've got a 1:00 appointment back at the office."

"No problem, see you at noon."

Jason was glad for the call. He was concerned about the guy Nathan had beaten yesterday. By the time he got to Goldbergs, he was pretty worked up. He ordered a Bloody Mary and tried to relax. Goldbergs was noted for their Bloody Marys; in fact they were legendary and had won several "Best of Omaha" awards. Jason downed the drink, ate the olives, and ordered another.

Nathan swaggered in about the time the second one arrived.

"Hitting the sauce a little early in the day, aren't you, Jason?"

The two were a study in contrasts, Jason in his best "financial advisor" blue pin-striped suit with a bold striped tie, clean shaven, and dark brown hair perfectly moussed down, Nathan in his usual work attire: jeans, cowboy boots, and a black polo shirt displaying the "Omaha Ford" dealership logo. The shirt was tight, emphasizing his pecs and biceps. Nathan's black hair was loose and unruly, and he sported a two-day growth of dark beard.

"Yeah, why wouldn't I be after yesterday afternoon? I didn't sleep last night. Why did you have to get so carried away, Nathan? Jesus, the guy was just shooting off his mouth!"

"Yeah, and the more he ranted, the more trouble for Ted."

"Well, Teddy-boy probably deserved it," Jason countered. "He was totally out of control...by the way, where's Tom?"

"I didn't call him. He doesn't know what happened and certainly not how things ended up. I want to keep it that way. It's a good thing he just waited for you in the car, or his job could be on the line."

"What about *my* job?" Jason shook his head in disbelief.

"You're not deputy sheriff, Jason. So, did Tom ask you any questions?"

"Well, he asked what took me so long."

"And..."

"And I told him you and I got to talking and looking at the gym."

"That's it?"

"Yeah, we headed back and didn't talk about it again...God, Nathan, I didn't mind talking to this guy, maybe even threatening him a little, but you damn near killed him!"

"No, *we* damn near killed him. You're as guilty as I am." Nathan pointed a finger at Jason to emphasize his point.

The waitress brought water to the table, and asked for their orders. As soon as she was out of earshot, Jason attempted to resume the conversation. "So what *did* you do with him?" Jason asked, lowering his voice.

"I drove to a nearby town. I searched him, took his wallet, watch, phone, and other identification, and left him in an alley. By the time someone finds him, it will just look like another mugging."

"So why did you go to another town?"

"Simple. It will make it more difficult for the police to connect the dots."

"What if he dies?" Jason fretted. "And if he lives, do you think he can identify us?"

Nathan saw that Jason was starting to lose it. "Just don't worry about it." Nathan shrugged. "No one saw us, so it's just our word against his, and that's two to one. Besides, what's the chance that he'll ever run into us again? He knows what I'm capable of, so I don't think he'll want to mess with me again."

"So what do we do now?"

"We just go on with our lives as normal. We keep it to ourselves and no one is any the wiser. Understand?" For emphasis, he repeated, "Do you understand?"

The look in Nathan's eyes almost made Jason fearful of him. "Yes, I understand," Jason nodded in agreement.

Their food arrived and Nathan plowed into his sandwich. Jason picked at his plate and managed to eat some French fries. He was relieved when Nathan said he had to go.

Jason was numb after his lunch with Nathan. His stomach churned and he felt nauseous. He didn't remember walking to his car, opening the door, then throwing up on the pavement. It felt like the whole world was spinning around him. *How can this be? How could Nathan have gotten me into this?*

He always knew Nathan had a hold over him. The first thing he noticed when he met Nathan in college was his charisma. People were drawn to him like metal was drawn to that huge electromagnet in the Science Building at the University of Nebraska. Everyone wanted to be part of Nathan's world, Jason included.

Jason's mind wouldn't stop racing. It was like a runaway train. The Bloody Marys had been a bad idea. The last time he was this worried was when he suspected his high school girlfriend was pregnant. That seemed pretty minor right now. He could be guilty of murder! *My God, only really bad people commit murder. And they go to prison for the rest of their lives—or worse yet, get put to death!*

The night before, when Jason did sleep, he dreamt about Nathan and those steel-capped snakeskin cowboy boots and what he had done to James Wilson.

Jason and Nathan had followed James Wilson to his car. Wilson, along with others, had witnessed the heated exchange between Ted and a student. Then Wilson had gotten vocal about Ted's lack of respect for students, encouraging other school supporters to call the administration to get him fired.

Unfortunately for Wilson, he had parked behind the rectory. The parking spaces there were boxed on three sides by buildings with no windows overlooking them. The three of them were completely alone.

Jason had tried to reason with Wilson, nicely asking him to back off a little with his remarks about Ted, telling him perhaps the kid had it coming. Wilson wasn't buying it; he repeated that Ted needed to be terminated. Jason volunteered to talk to Ted about his behavior.

Wilson wasn't about to slack off. He insisted, "Something needs to be done about that teacher!" Nathan then got in Wilson's face. Wilson pushed him away, and started to get into his car. Nathan hit him, hard, first in the gut, then in the face, as Wilson doubled over. The guy begged him to stop. But Nathan was relentless, like a demon possessed. *Where did that anger come from?* Wilson finally fell to the pavement, nearly unconscious. Nathan started kicking

Wilson in the ribs, back, and then the head. Jason had to pull him off, and was almost afraid Nathan would turn on him.

When Nathan finally settled down, he was matter of fact. "Help me get this guy in his car." He grabbed the keys Wilson had dropped on the pavement, opened the trunk, and found a blanket. "Let's put him in the trunk. Grab him by him arms so you don't get blood on your clothes."

Jason did as he was told, thinking how hard it was to lift a limp body. They put Wilson on the blanket, hoisted him into the trunk and Nathan closed the lid. He told Jason, "Go find Tom before he wonders what's taking so long. I'll take care of dumping this guy."

Fearful, and still in shock, Jason didn't argue. He almost ran back to Tom's car, not wanting to know what Nathan was going to do.

What will my wife think? And my parents? The headlines will read: "Jason Hughes Arrested for Assault." Or murder. A wave of nausea hit him again when he thought about being in prison while his two sons, Jason Jr. and Jeremy, grew up. He fell to his knees and retched again. Breathing became difficult. He began to take deep breaths, afraid he was going to pass out.

His career as a financial advisor had provided a good lifestyle for his family. They lived in a $400,000 home, drove new cars, and his kids attended a private school. And now he might be an accomplice to murder. *What will my friends think? And my clients? Is all this about to come to an abrupt end? How could I be so stupid?*

Jason remembered he had a 1:00 P.M. appointment. He couldn't drive. Hell, he couldn't even stand up. A middle-aged woman stopped and asked if he was all right. "Yes...thank you. Just a little sick...I'll be fine." He stayed on his knees, found his cell phone, and called his office. His receptionist answered. "Sally, this is Jason. Please cancel my appointments for the rest of the day. I'm going home. Think I may be coming down with the flu or something.

Reschedule them for first thing next week." He looked down at his vomit soaked tie, pulled it off, threw it down on the pavement and climbed into his white Lexus.

He started the engine, then just rested his forehead on the top of the steering wheel. He settled down a little, managed to pull away from the curb, almost clipping the rear of a passing car. Two hours later, he had no idea where he'd been. All he realized was that he was now parked in the Old Market outside Barry O's Bar. He went inside the bar and drank a couple of scotches to settle his nerves. He looked at his watch. Time to get home. All the way he kept telling himself, *Act normal.*

Council Bluffs, Iowa
12:45 P.M.

Sam was tired when he arrived at the gravel road leading to the recycling center at 12:45 P.M. He was relieved he was in time to cash in his cans. He pulled on the door, but it was locked. Puzzled, he stepped back and read the sign in the window listing the business hours: 8:00 A.M. TO 1:00 P.M.

Sam saw someone moving inside. He knocked on the door and tried to get his attention. He knocked again. The man inside wouldn't look up. Sam banged loudly on the door. Still no response. Sam became angry. He had walked all morning in order to get here in time, and this asshole wouldn't even look up at him.

He pushed the cart down the walk to the edge of the building and headed through the gravel parking lot to the back, jarring several cans loose. He didn't care about a few cans at this point. Sam saw a loading door in the back and it was still open. He had just pushed his cart through the door when a voice shouted at him.

"What the hell do you think you're doing in here?"

Sam looked in the direction of the voice and saw a short, dumpy man who reminded him of Danny DeVito in the television sitcom *Taxi*, wearing blue work clothes.

"I want to cash in my cans."

"Come back tomorrow!" came the gruff response.

"No, I just walked over four miles and the sign on the door says you're open until 1:00. I want to cash my cans in."

"Get your grungy ass out of here, or I'll throw you out!"

Sam was a former Army ranger, and knew he could crush this little twerp into mincemeat, but had to maintain control. A fight would certainly end up with the police involved, and that was the last thing he needed.

Sam pleaded, "I don't want no trouble. I just want my money."

"You'll leave now," the little man growled.

Sam kept his temper in check, and ventured a threat, "George is going to be very unhappy when I tell him you closed early."

"You don't know George."

"Yes, I do. Mr. Koch helps at the shelter on weekends, and I'll see him at lunch on Saturday. I'll just tell him what happened." Sam spoke with more force this time.

The man grumbled and put the cans on the scale. He paid Sam his money, then spat, "Get here earlier next time."

Sam feigned a weak smile, knowing he had won this battle and wouldn't have any trouble with this guy again. He put his money in his coat pocket. It would last a couple of weeks at least. Sam left a happy man.

Next Day, Friday, May 22
Council Bluffs, Iowa
5:30 A.M.

It was still two hours before daylight when the red Porsche Boxster pulled into the parking lot of City Hospital. The driver wound his way through the lot past most of the open parking spaces. This car was his only extravagance, and he always parked at the far end of the lot to protect it from dings other drivers might inflict on it. Dr. Steve Cantelli would have preferred a covered space in the parking garage, but those spaces were limited. One had to be a senior staff physician or a department head to garner one of those. This would have to do for now. His car was three years old, a gift he had given himself after completing his residency, but he kept it in pristine condition.

Steve grabbed his iPad, exited the car, and noticed the reflection of the full moon off the car's hood. He looked up and watched as wispy clouds floated across the darkened sky, giving the illusion that the moon was moving. Steve savored the moment, feeling this might be the only serene part of his day.

Dr. Cantelli walked across the lot and used his key card to open the door reserved for physicians and other hospital personnel. The cafeteria was on the way to his office, and he stopped to buy a cup of coffee and a bagel. A Bruegger's bagel, no less. The Bruegger's in Omaha supplied the hospital cafeteria. Steve loved their pumpernickel bagels with salmon cream cheese spread. As close to lox and bagels he could get at the hospital, and a minor extravagance. He was addicted to them, and enjoyed the treat every morning. He reminded himself to use some breath mints before he began to see patients. He didn't want to examine anyone with fishy breath.

When he reached his office, Steve balanced his coffee and bagel on his iPad, and used his free hand to unlock the door. He stepped in, kicking the door closed with his heel. Walking to his desk, he emitted a groan when he saw the size of his patient list. It was going to be a long day. Ignoring the patient list, he used his iPad to pull up the *Daily Nonpareil,* the local newspaper, and scanned the news while he finished his bagel and coffee. His daily morning routine complete, it was time to get to work.

Steve stood, brushed the crumbs off his lap, walked across the room and pulled his white lab coat off the coat rack in the corner. He stopped in the restroom, and checked his appearance in the mirror before leaving. He brushed his hand through his curly brown hair and noticed the red in his newly started beard. It was beginning to itch a little, but that would stop in a week or so. Satisfied with his appearance, he headed up to the third floor.

"Morning, Dr. Cantelli," came the greeting from Madeline, the nurse on third floor.

Madeline was about Steve's age, cute and petite. Maybe five feet three inches tall. Her blonde hair was crimped today, hanging loosely over her blue scrubs. Steve found it hard to believe she had four children, all boys. The oldest was in middle school already. He asked about her family. Steve liked to maintain a pseudo-personal relationship with his associates, feeling it inspired teamwork.

"Have you had time to pull my charts for this morning's rounds?"

"That large stack over there. Hope you're ready for a long day."

Steve started to read through his patient charts, all just typical issues until he got to the John Doe. Seeing the extent of his injuries, he asked Madeline, "What happened to the guy in room 313? Car accident?"

"No. They found him in an alley yesterday morning. The police think he was mugged."

"Looks like somebody went out of their way to beat him up."

"Yeah, he's in pretty bad shape. Hope he makes it."

"Well, I think I'll see him first. Come along and fill me in."

Madeline went over the extent of the patient's injuries as they walked down the hall. She told Dr. Cantelli the patient had four broken ribs, a broken clavicle, broken nose, and a skull fracture. He was covered in scrapes and bruises, but somehow none of his internal organs were injured.

"Isn't that unbelievable?" Madeline asked, shaking her head "Anyway, the biggest problem is the swelling and some bleeding in the brain. Dr. Lockwood feels he has the bleeding under control, but he can't guarantee there isn't any irreversible brain damage. He said it's just going to be a 'wait and see' situation."

Dr. Lockwood was a neurological surgeon on staff at the hospital, and Cantelli knew him to be very good at what he did.

Steve did a quick assessment of the patient, noted that the orthopedic and neurological surgeons had left adequate orders, and there was no more he could do at this time. He noted his observations on the chart, and asked Madeline to page him if there was any change in the patient's condition. Steve turned to walk away, looked back at Madeline and asked, "Do we have any idea who he is?"

"No," Madeline replied, "The police are hopeful a family member or a friend will report him missing."

"Let me know. I'll probably be back later in the day. Thanks for filling me in."

Cantelli walked down the hall to see his next patient. He had seen his share of accident and domestic violence victims, but this was over the top. He couldn't help but wonder what sick bastard could do this to another human being?

Back in his office an hour later, Steve called Whitney, the Social Services worker for the hospital, and asked her to come to his office. Whitney had been with the hospital for about ten years, and was the best social worker Steve had ever encountered. She was known to step on some toes if necessary to get help for the underprivileged. She simply saw that as her mission, and never let authority get in her way. The interesting thing about Whitney was her demeanor. No matter how hopeless the situation, she always remained calm and had a smile on her face. He wanted Whitney on board when 313's family showed up. They were going to need someone to hold their hands, and she was just the ticket. *Low salary, works all hours of the day…I wonder if Whitney has time for a life?* A knock sounded on his door.

Grand Island, Nebraska
8:00 A.M.

Detective Malone was in a good mood when he parked at the GISF the morning after his date. It had gone well. He took Mary to Prufrock's martini bar for a drink before dinner. She ordered a Coca-Cola, explaining that she didn't drink alcohol. He hadn't expected that. Larry wanted to ask her why she didn't drink, but he wasn't sure he wanted to hear the answer just yet. He ordered his favorite, an Orgasmartini. After all, this was just a drink and dinner. No sense pretending to be whoever she might want him to be. If this ever led to a relationship, she would have to accept him for who he was.

Malone's female coworkers would be anxious to hear how things had gone. They seemed to take great interest in his lack of a love life. Hardly a week went by without one of them suggesting someone he should date. Unsuccessfully. *Women...Why do they all think they're responsible for my happiness? Hell, it's a woman who is responsible for my misery!*

Malone knew several people who found suitable dates on the internet, but he had vowed not to do that. Partially, it was because he was a police officer and he didn't want to place a target on his back. The last thing he needed was a disgruntled criminal using the Internet to lure him into a trap. Mainly it was because he thought Internet dating was for losers.

He had tried to meet women in the local bars, but most of them were in their early twenties. Larry was thirty-five, and he never had anything in common with them. He finally gave in, out of desperation, and signed up for a local singles site on the web. He had been conversing with Mary for a couple of weeks. She was divorced, no children, and worked at the Chamber of Commerce office as a secretary. Her off the wall sense of humor intrigued him, and she had a great smile. Mary was also as attractive as her photo, but her hair was now auburn, instead of blonde. Bright blue eyes, and best of all, she was tall, probably five feet ten inches at least. They seemed to have a lot in common and, before the night was over, Larry had already decided he wanted to see her again.

Malone strolled into the Safety Center and greeted the desk sergeant, "Morning, Stan."

"Morning, Larry. Your friend from yesterday afternoon is back. Here bright and early. She's waiting outside your office."

Guess her husband didn't show up after all. Wrong call. Normally he would grumble, as he hadn't had his morning coffee, but his contentment from last night kept him in tow.

"Thanks, Stan. I better get in there and see what's up."

A mile away Ted was just waking up. Ted and some fellow teachers had a tee time for 9:00 A.M. He heard the rumble of thunder before his alarm went off. The raindrops pinged against his windowpane. He looked out the window at the dark sky. *No golf today. Might as well go to the school and get some paperwork done.*

He dressed, grabbed a hat, his Gore Tex jacket, and ran through what was now a downpour to his car.

In addition to teaching Business Administration, Ted was the head basketball coach and an assistant football coach. St. John's, being a parochial school, couldn't afford to hire full-time coaches, and they found their coaches from among the teaching staff. Ted loved coaching, and he didn't care that it paid little; he would have coached for free. The parking lot and horseshoe drive leading to the front doors of the school were filled with cars as Ted pulled up. *What's going on? There isn't any school today…Oh, yeah, the community open house. Duh.*

The parking spaces reserved for teachers were all filled, so Ted had to park almost a block away. He gave a mental shrug and sprinted for the door.

Ted walked into the lobby, shaking the excess water from his jacket, greeted a couple of teachers, and waved a hello to Harlan Jensen, the superintendent. Harlan was talking with Nancy Ursted, the science teacher, and barely noticed him. It was understandable why Harlan was totally immersed in his conversation. Ted had never seen Nancy in anything other than the business suits she normally wore to school. Today, her long blonde hair was pulled back in a ponytail; she had on a pink tee top, and tight jeans. It was difficult to take his gaze off of her, and he stopped just short of walking smack into a pillar.

She is hot! Also very married, he reminded himself. Ted pushed his fantasies aside and walked down the hall to his homeroom and began grading papers.

Thirty minutes later, Harlan strode into Ted's room and put his hands on his hips. "We have to talk."

One thing about Harlan Jensen, he was all black and white. No gray could enter his life. Other than the patch of gray halfway around his head, that is. He was completely bald on top and spent a lot of time grooming the little hair he had with his hands. Harlan was in his early fifties, and always impeccably dressed in a suit and tie. Ted thought he was a real pain in the ass from the moment they met.

"Talk about what?" Ted didn't bother to hide his annoyance.

"Your little outburst the other day."

"He deserved it. Do you have any idea what a slacker he is? And always making cute little remarks. I just had my fill of it!"

"Wrong answer, Ted." Harland planted his feet and put his hands on his hips, pulling his suit coat back. "You publicly berated a student in front of his peers, parents, and several school supporters. I've had calls from parents, and to make it worse, the Monsignor had a complaint from James Wilson, our largest donor for the gym. Where *your* basketball team plays...need I remind you?"

"Just because a guy donates money, it gives him a right to criticize me?" Ted's voice grew louder with each word in angry indignation.

"No," Harlan frowned. "The issue is that this isn't the first time I've had complaints about you demeaning students. I understand this may be a part of your coaching tactics, but it doesn't carry over to the classroom or beyond. It seems to be a pattern, and this time it went too far. I'm putting a letter in your file, and you can consider this a warning." Harlan pointed a finger at Ted. "One more complaint and you will not be coming back to St. John's next fall. You are dealing with high school students and your job is to teach and act as a role model. You are the professional, and I expect you to act like one. Now, this discussion is over and I will not have it again!"

Harlan turned on his heel and stormed out of the room. Anger flashed in Ted's eyes as he raised his middle finger in defiance, and mouthed, "Asshole."

CHAPTER 3

Same Day
Grand Island, Nebraska
8:05 A.M.

MALONE WALKED TOWARD HIS OFFICE and immediately saw his visitor. She sat on one of the wooden armchairs outside his office. He took time to stop at the coffee pot and poured himself a cup. He hated station coffee. It was too strong and reminded him of the stuff his ex-wife used to drink. She had lived in the South for a while, and liked chicory coffee, a combination of swamp water and mud left over from Hurricane Katrina. Since his divorce he had gotten used to Dunkin Donut coffee; the shop was on his route to work. He had absentmindedly driven right past it this morning.

A couple of sips and he was ready for Susan Wilson. He strolled over to her chair. "Good morning, Mrs. Wilson. May I get you a cup of coffee?"

"No, thank you."

Very wise decision, Malone thought, as he took another sip.

Susan didn't say anything, just handed him the missing persons report completely filled out, and extra notes on the back side of some of the pages.

"Let's step into my office," Larry said, opening the door for her. He offered her the only chair and walked around and sat behind his desk.

"I stayed up all night waiting, but James never showed up."

He knew this was true. She was wearing the same blue workout suit, and it had obviously been slept in. In spite of her appearance, she did seem more composed today. *Wonder if there's any significance in that?*

He read the report. James was thirty years old, a pharmacist, and owned a pharmacy in downtown Grand Island. He had a partner, Fred Hawthorne, who was also a pharmacist. *If James made a substantial donation to the school, just how lucrative is this pharmacy business?* Police work was a lot of paperwork, filled with little details. The good officers could sort out those details and key in on the ones of importance. They never jumped out at you. You had to dig deep and it took lots of time. Malone laughed at the cop shows on television. He had never solved a case in the twenty-four hours it took the actors.

What else was her husband involved in? Illegitimate drugs as well as legal ones? Maybe that was why he went missing? Larry shook his head and reminded himself not to jump to conclusions too quickly. He had almost convicted the wrong man once, thinking he had the case all neatly tied together. *Sometimes it's just too easy to make assumptions and then fit the facts into your own little scenario. Just write down the information and let the facts dictate the conclusion.* Even so, he made a mental note to check the amount of the donation and the Wilsons' bank accounts.

Malone went over the information he had garnered from Susan the day before. He drilled down a little deeper this time, grabbing a yellow legal pad and making notes.

Susan watched Malone making notes. She sat, wringing her hands, and finally asked, "What are you writing?"

"Just things from your report that I think may be pertinent. I'm adding them to my notes from yesterday when you gave me the timeline."

"Do you think you are going to find him from your notes, or should you be out looking for him?"

Malone ignored her remark. "Where did James and Fred get the money to buy the pharmacy?"

"Fred's father sold them the pharmacy with no money down. They have a contract to make monthly payments to him."

"Does the pharmacy make money?"

"Well...yes. It provides us with a living."

"So, not a lot of money?"

"I guess not."

"So just how much does it gross in a year?"

"I don't know. I don't even know what gross is."

"Let me word it this way. How much does it earn in a year?"

"I don't know. I already told you on the back of the report that James does all the bookkeeping for the pharmacy because Fred is a good pharmacist but doesn't have a head for the finances."

"I understand that. But you're telling me you don't know how much money James makes?"

"Isn't that what I said?"

"It just seems a little odd, that's all. Did the pharmacy earnings support the donation to the gym?"

"I don't know. You have to ask James that."

"Since that seems to be impossible right now, I'm asking you."

"You know, Detective, I'm getting a little tired of your insinuations!" The anger flashed in her eyes.

"The report says you work at St. Francis Medical Center as a nurse. How much do you make?"

"I think it's around $28.00 an hour."

"So roughly $1000.00 per week?"

"I'm not the one missing!"

She was almost shouting now. Malone decided to tone it down a little.

"Please, Mrs. Wilson, bear with me. I know this is difficult." Malone's tone was sympathetic, masking his current thought: *And your job gives you access to drugs, too.* "We're going to find your husband, but I need to ask you questions which you may think have no bearing on the situation. I have to get to know your husband. What about his family?"

"I am his only family. His parents were killed in a car accident when he was fourteen, and he was raised by his uncle, Chuck Wilson. Oh, and an aunt who lives in Wichita. She's a Catholic nun and in a retirement home. We only see her maybe once a year."

"Where does Chuck live?"

"He died about ten years ago."

Malone went on to question Susan about James's habits, haunts, normal routine, friends, etc. He wrote down names and places, but could find no discrepancies in her answers from the previous day.

"We'll get this worked up right away. I've already contacted the hospital and checked the police reports. No one matching James' description shows up either place. I've notified the sheriff's department and the state patrol as well as our own officers. We have an APB out on his car and license number.

"I thought you had to wait twenty-four hours."

"We do to file the missing persons report. That didn't stop me from looking in the meantime."

"Oh, I guess I just assumed..." and her voice dropped off.

"What I want you to do now, Susan—may I call you by your first name?"

No answer.

Malone's voice was gentle. "I want you to go home and wait for a phone call, or better yet, wait for James to show up. Do you have someone to stay with you?"

"My parents will be here tomorrow. I'll be all right until then."

Susan looked back at Malone as she left, and said: "You know, James was a passenger in a horrible car accident when we were in college. The driver was killed, but James escaped without a scratch. I was hysterical when I heard, but he just laughed, and said he had a guardian angel watching over him. I want desperately to believe his guardian angel is still protecting him. Please call me as soon as you hear any news, Detective."

"I will," he assured her.

The minute Susan Wilson was gone, Malone yelled out to his partner, "Max, get into my office. Think we've got a live one."

Detective Max Worthy was five years Larry's junior. He had traded his uniform for a suit a year ago when he made detective. A college degree in Criminal Justice contributed highly to his promotion. Max was the complete opposite of Malone, both physically and mentally. Max was short, had a little belly hanging over his belt, unkempt sandy hair, dimples and rosy cheeks. Larry felt his wife should either buy wrinkle-free shirts or learn to iron, as his appearance always tended to be rumpled and would never strike fear in the hearts of criminals. Putting all that aside, he was a good detective; a little green around the edges, but learning every day. Malone had taken Max under his wing, and was determined to make him his equal. Malone was serious by nature, and Max was a clown. Despite Malone's attempts to get Max to mimic his serious side, Max continued to keep the department in stitches with his wit and humor. Malone wouldn't admit it, but Max had actually been helping him lighten up a little with his wisecracks. Malone's biggest problem with Max was keeping their car free of fast food sacks and candy bar wrappers. Max not only had no regard for his health, he managed to keep the car looking like a McDonald's dumpster.

Larry filled Max in on the Wilson situation, and handed him the report along with his notes.

"Get this read. We need to start working on it right away. For some reason I've got a bad feeling about this one."

"Why's that?"

"I don't know. Call it gut instinct. Actually, you can read it in the car. Let's get going. First stop, St. John's High School. Either something bad has really happened, or this guy is involved in something bigger than it appears."

CHAPTER 4

Same Day
Council Bluffs, Iowa
10:00 A.M.

D R. CANTELLI EXPECTED THE KNOCK on his door to be Whitney, the Social Services worker. He said, without looking up, "Come in, I've been expecting you."

"And why is that?"

Dr. Cantelli raised his head from his paperwork and saw Helen, the charge nurse on the third floor. She had held that position as long as anyone in the hospital could remember. In fact, she ran the floor. Helen was from another era in which nurses dressed like professionals. She still wore a stiffly starched white dress uniform, complemented by white nylon stockings and stiff white leather shoes. At least she had discarded the funny little hat. In spite of her 1950s dress, she was a great nurse with modern skills. Petite, gray haired, and in her early sixties, she didn't take a back seat to anyone, especially the physicians. She clashed with their egos and usually came out on top. Steve wasn't that way. She got a little pushy at times, but he adopted the E. F. Hutton philosophy: when she talked, he listened.

"Sorry, Helen," he smiled, "I was expecting Whitney. Have to get her involved with the patient in 313."

37

"Actually, that's why I'm here. He sometimes appears to be floating in and out of consciousness, and I'm afraid if he comes around he may have a lot of anxiety. He probably doesn't have a clue where he is, and may mentally be back in that alley or wherever it was he was beaten. I don't want him to harm himself, or any of my nurses when he wakes up. I need something on hand to sedate him if necessary."

"Good idea, Helen. I'll write an order for Lorazepam, 1 mg IM every four to six hours as needed for anxiety."

"Thank you, Doctor." And whoosh, Helen was gone.

Steve didn't think 313 would be capable of harming anyone due to the extent of his injuries, but it didn't hurt to have the order. Also, Helen was happy.

The light was back. It was shining in his eyes. And the voices. One was loud. Even with the ringing in his ears. He couldn't make out the words. It was as if they were speaking some foreign language. *What the hell is going on?* He tried to move. It was too painful. His eyes scanned the room but everything was fuzzy. *Why can't I focus? And where am I? Hospital? An emergency room? Got to relax. Got to think!* But thinking was impossible with the roaring in his head. And then everything went black again.

Same Day
Grand Island, Nebraska
11:00 A.M.

Ted couldn't concentrate after his chewing out. He was pissed. Really pissed. After he calmed down a bit, he pulled out his cell phone.

"Hey, Nathan, Ted."

"What's up, bro?"

"I just got my butt chewed out by that jackass, Harlan Jensen. You know, the prissy fagot I've got for a superintendent."

"What for?"

"An argument I got into with a student day before yesterday. I'm surprised you didn't see it. Man, I need to unwind. How about I come to Omaha and we go out and hit some bars tonight? Then I can collect on that meal you owe me."

"Works for me. In fact, Audrey is out of town visiting her sister in Minneapolis and you can just crash at my place."

"Sounds great! What about Jason and Tom? Let's all go out."

"No can do. Tom is doing a bicycle ride this weekend and Jason is going to SAG for him. It's in Des Moines, and they won't be back until Sunday afternoon. So just me and you." The truth was, he wanted to get Ted alone.

"Okay. I've got to get some paperwork done, so I'll be there late afternoon. Your place or the dealership?"

"My place. I'm taking off early today."

"Okay."

Ted hung up and thought about it. *Why do I care about the damned paperwork anyway?* He grimaced. *Because I need my job and this is the most upset I have ever seen Harlan. Plus, he definitely has the ear of Monsignor Kelly.* This gave Harlan the ability to ruin Ted's career as a teacher. Ted settled in and got his papers graded before leaving for Omaha.

As soon as Ted hung up, Nathan called Tom and Jason and told them he was leaving town for the Memorial Day weekend and would call them next week. The last thing he wanted was Jason showing up and opening his stupid mouth about what had happened. Besides, he wanted to know if Ted had heard anything about this James Wilson guy. Nathan knew his name from the ceremonies at the gym. Also from his wallet. He had burned the wallet in his fireplace and shredded the credit cards and other identification. His watch and cell phone were on the bottom of the

Missouri River, probably several miles downstream getting covered with mud and silt.

Same Day
Council Bluffs, Iowa
11:00 A.M.

Whitney Weston knocked on Dr. Cantelli's door. Whitney was a very attractive black woman. She was tall, wore her hair long over her shoulders, and had a graceful walk that almost made her appear to be gliding. Her best feature was her perpetual smile. She entered the office, flashed that smile, and asked Dr. Cantelli, "What's so urgent on a Friday morning?"

"Sorry about that. As dedicated as you are, Whitney, I didn't expect you even knew it was Friday."

"Oh, yeah. As soon as I get off, I'm going camping with my family for a long weekend."

So that's how she gets away from all the stress.

"David got a camping spot at Mahoney State Park for the Memorial Day weekend a year ago."

"You've had it reserved for a year?" asked Steve, puzzled.

"Have to for Memorial Day if you want a spot. It's the most popular park in Nebraska, and it's only about thirty miles from here."

"What makes it so special?"

"It's right on the Platte River, has a great water park for the kids, and David and I can just sit back and relax. Lily, our oldest, takes the two boys swimming in the afternoon and we all go to the melodrama in the evening. Actually, we love the melodrama. You boo and hiss the villain, and can even throw popcorn at him!"

Steve chuckled. "Sounds like you are in for a good time. So how old are your kids now?"

"Lily is sixteen, and the boys are eight and ten." Whitney laughed and said, "I'm sure you didn't call me to ask about my family and weekend plans."

"Actually I wanted to see how you were coming on our John Doe in room 313."

"Not much to go on, Steve." Whitney felt comfortable calling him Steve, although not in front of their colleagues. Hospital policy dictated he be referred to as "Doctor," but they had worked together long enough to drop the formalities when alone. Besides, she had her doctorate degree and everyone just called her Whitney. "No missing persons reports, car accidents, or other information. Is he out of his coma yet?"

"No, but Helen was in earlier and she thinks he may be coming out of it soon."

"That's great news! It not only means he may recover, but maybe now we can find out who he is."

"Right. We can contact his family and take the weight off the shoulders of the hospital's bean counters all at the same time."

"Oh, yes. Admissions have called me a couple of times to see how the bill will be handled. Guess we all have our priorities."

"Well, right now, mine is to see he recovers."

"And mine is to ensure that you can continue to provide him care until we find out his name."

"At least two of us are on the same page," Dr. Cantelli chuckled. "I promised Helen I would look in on him. Why don't you come along and then you can get started on your weekend."

Whitney fell into step beside Steve as they headed for the elevator as she answered, "It's a nice idea, but I've got lots to do yet before 5:00. Besides, David will have a drink and dinner waiting for me when I get there."

"He cooks, too?"

"With my hours, he either cooks or starves." She laughed.

Same Day
Grand Island, Nebraska
11:30 A.M.

When Malone and Worthy arrived at St. John's, they stopped at the office as directed by the sign on the door. They showed their badges to the secretary and exchanged a few pleasantries.

"So where are all the students?" asked Max.

"Our open house for the new gymnasium is today, so school has been dismissed until Tuesday," the secretary said.

Malone got down to business. "Could we speak to the superintendent or principal, please?"

"That would be Mr. Jensen. He's conducting a tour right now, but I will inform him you are here. He should be done in about ten minutes. I'll tell him you are waiting in his office." She ushered them through the door.

Both officers looked around the office, noticing how sparsely it was furnished. Concrete block walls painted a pale green, a metal desk from the 1960s, a small metal table, and two plastic cafeteria chairs for visitors comprised all its contents.

"Must be on a tight budget." Max offered.

Malone let out a sigh. "This is a parochial school, Max. They get no tax support, and rely totally on tuition and private donations to provide an education. They can't afford to spend money on fancy furniture."

"Yeah, but I hear good things about the school. In fact, the newspaper said it was ranked as one of the highest college prep schools in the state."

"True," Malone nodded, surprised that Max read the newspaper. He thought all people Max's age got their news off the Internet. "But you have to understand that these teachers have a fundamental belief in a Catholic education. Some of them are the best in their field, but they choose to work in an environment which combines religious beliefs and education. These teachers work for less money than in a public school, but their reward is the satisfaction of knowing they have fulfilled a need in our society."

"Spoken like the product of a Catholic education." a voice behind them said. Max and Larry turned their heads and saw a man very tall in stature, broad shoulders, and a bald head ringed by gray hair. His eyes were bright and alive, and he was smiling.

"I assume you are detectives Malone and Worthy."

Malone was impressed. The secretary had remembered their names.

"We are," Malone replied. "I'm Detective Malone and this is my partner, Detective Worthy."

"I am Harlan Jensen, and I am the superintendent at St. John's. How may I assist you gentlemen?"

Malone explained that the conversation had to be kept confidential for the time being, and told Harlan about the possible disappearance of James Wilson.

"James has disappeared?" Harlan's astonishment was apparent.

"I said possible disappearance," Malone answered. "This is just preliminary and that's why we really can't open an investigation."

"That's terrible," Harlan shook his head, "but how can I help?"

"For starters," Max said, "you can tell us about his donation to the gym. Specifically, how much it was, and also how you know James."

"James has been a school supporter since coming to Grand Island. He and his partner, Fred Hawthorne, own a pharmacy downtown. I only know him from finance meetings for the school, but he seems to be a solid citizen. He impresses me as a bright young man and an asset to the community. As for the donation, rumor has that it was in the neighborhood of fifty thousand dollars, but you would have to ask Monsignor Kelly about that. I am not privy to that information."

"Where can we find the monsignor?" Malone asked.

"Ordinarily I would not bother him, as he has a full schedule today, but let me make a quick phone call."

Maybe the badge does carry some weight after all? A minute later, Harlan hung up the phone, and turned to Malone. "Monsignor Kelly will see you in the rectory right away." Harlan escorted them down the hallway.

Harlan took them out a side door of the school, and led them across a well-manicured courtyard to a two-story brick home.

"This is our rectory," Harlan said as they walked up the steps of the house. "Monsignor Kelly and our two parish priests live here." He opened the door without knocking, and greeted Mrs. Murphy, a petite gray-haired lady, wearing a print dress and apron. She was busy dusting an ornate antique table in the hallway and regarded the detectives with a jaundiced eye. Malone guessed she didn't like police officers on her turf.

Harlan led them down the hall, stopped at the third door on the left and rapped his knuckles on the partially open ancient oak door. He walked in, motioning them to follow. In contrast to the school, the rectory was richly furnished. High ceilings, ornate oak moldings, and rich tapestries told Malone the parish had spared no expense when building the rectory.

A handsome gentleman, wearing a royal blue shirt with a Roman collar, sat behind the desk. He appeared to be in his middle fifties, had curly brown hair, broad shoulders, appeared a little portly, and had a twinkle in his blue eyes. He rose, walked around the desk, and greeted Max and Larry. He was taller than he had appeared when sitting. He was also wearing jeans and cowboy boots. He must have noticed Malone's surprise, and after shaking hands, winked and said, "Casual Friday." He laughed at his own attempt at a joke. "Seriously, I grew up on a farm fifty miles north of here, near Greeley. I still feel more comfortable in a shirt and jeans. Some people expect me to wear a cassock with a Roman collar, red buttons and trim. Even when I do, I've got my jeans and boots on underneath."

Malone liked him immediately.

"So you are here about James?" The monsignor sighed heavily.

"Yes," Malone replied. "His wife came to the Safety Center and told us he hadn't returned home since the dedication on Wednesday. We are hoping you might be able to shed some light on his whereabouts."

"This is dreadful news," Monsignor Kelly frowned, "but I don't have any idea where he might be. Do you think foul play is involved?"

"We don't know at this point," Max said. "His wife is very concerned, and quite frankly, we are too, now. It's too early to make assumptions, but we want to check a few things out. Oh, and please keep this confidential for the time being. It may turn out to be nothing."

Larry said, "Tell us about James Wilson."

"Well, I've known him about three years. He is very active in the church, and serves on our finance committee. In fact he was the chairperson for our fund drive. Very bright young man. And very generous too. I know his wife, Susan, of course, but I know little of his personal life."

"Speaking of generous, Monsignor, how much was the donation he made to the gym?" Larry ventured.

"James wanted to keep the amount confidential, but under the circumstances, I will tell you it was sixty thousand dollars. His original donation was fifty, but when pledges began to lag, James offered to donate one dollar for each new dollar pledged, and ended up with a total donation of sixty. We are very fortunate to have a few parishioners, James included, who believe in contributing so that we may continue to offer a good Catholic education."

Malone had to ask the obvious question. "Do you know if Wilson has any enemies—or of anyone who might have a grudge against him?"

"Once again, Detective, I really know little of his personal life. That might be a better question for Susan or his business partner, Fred Hawthorne."

Malone thanked him for his time as he shook his hand. The monsignor added, "I will keep James in my prayers."

Malone thought, *He may need more than prayers!*

CHAPTER 5

H ARLAN WALKED THE DETECTIVES OUT, bid them goodbye, and promised to let them know if anything came up concerning James Wilson.

On the way to the car, Max asked, "What do you think of the cowboy priest?"

"I like the guy." Malone shrugged. "He is who he is, and doesn't put on any airs. My kind of guy."

"Do you think he was hiding anything?"

"About what? Other than the sixty thousand dollar donation, he really doesn't know anything!" Larry gave the rookie a little shove. *Hiding anything?!? Max, you're watching too many cop shows on TV. Or is this just one of your funnies, trying to get into my head?*

"Okay, let's visit his banker."

"Mind if I drive?" Max said and headed for the driver's seat without waiting for an answer, a wide grin on his face.

Malone gave in and let the rookie drive across town to Community Bank. He generally hated letting Max drive. Not that he was a bad driver, but Larry liked being in charge. And that meant holding the wheel of the car, too. Larry had been a cop for ten years, and the fact that he had been shot on a traffic stop gave him an edge over some older officers when he took the detective exam.

Larry looked over at Max behind the wheel, and a strong memory washed over him. *He was on patrol at 2 A.M., and noticed a car with a broken tail light. He played it by the book and put on the red and whites and pursued. The car went about a block, before pulling over. Larry radioed dispatch, gave them his location at the intersection of Seventh and Cedar, told them he had a "10-52, white light on rear," (so other officers wouldn't respond), "gray Buick 4-door sedan, license NE 8-2043." He exited his cruiser, and walked to the driver's side of the vehicle. He approached with appropriate caution and stood slightly behind the driver, forcing him to twist back to see him. The intersection was well lit, and he could see he had a white male, probably early twenties, with unkempt brown hair and wisps of facial hair that didn't quite qualify as a beard.*

"What'd I do?" the driver asked.

"License and registration please, sir."

"What'd I do?" he repeated, a little louder this time.

Larry held back his irritation, knowing he had to focus on a cop's number one rule: get their license and registration so you know who you're talking to, so that dispatch can tell you if they have a criminal record, and you can find them if they flee.

"I need to see your license and registration. Then I'll tell you why I pulled you over."

A flash and the sound of a shot, and Larry was propelled back and found himself lying on the pavement. It hurt like hell. He was glad he'd worn his Kevlar vest, thinking it had stopped the bullet. The car tore off.

Larry called it in from his half-sitting position. "10-89, officer needs assistance, corner of Seventh and Cedar, vehicle fleeing the scene east on Seventh, am pursuing." He tried to get up, but he couldn't move his left arm. He looked down, saw his blood-soaked sleeve, managed to tell dispatch, "Officer down," and passed out.

The room was spinning and he was nauseous. He thought he heard Carrie's voice, but didn't know where he was, and knew he was going to be sick. He was, then the nausea subsided and his mind began to clear up.

Carrie was by his side, and he realized he was in a hospital. The doctor came in and told him how lucky he was. The bullet had just missed his carotid artery, and had broken his collarbone, but that had been repaired and he would be fine.

"What about my arm?" he had demanded. "When can I go back to work?"

"How can you even think about that?" Carrie blurted out. "You almost get killed and all you can ask is when you can go back to work?!?"

"Let's take one step at a time," the doctor said, ushering Carrie out of the room, "He needs his rest now."

Larry was relieved to see her walk out the door, and hoped the doctor could feel his appreciation.

Officer Trent Hildegard stopped in to visit Larry. "You heard we got him?"

"No...No one told me anything."

"Well, he crashed his car into a tree when he tried to turn onto Sycamore Street. Higher than a kite, man. Another meth head. You ended up riding to the hospital in the same ambulance.

"Good thing I didn't know that. I would have shot his ass!"

Six months later, Larry accepted the medal the department presented for "Bravery Under Fire," or some bullshit name like that. Larry really didn't care. He thought he should have been given a medal for stupidity. Anyway, his career remained on the fast track and here he was, riding with a rookie detective.

Larry shook his head. What's the matter with me? Why am I reliving something that happened six years ago? Max must be getting to me. Got to let it go. He's a decent cop and I can't be his protector and his partner both. Max's voice interrupted his thoughts. "Hey Lar, where's that bank again?"

"What?" Larry's mind was jarred back to the present.

"Wilson's bank. What's the address?"

"It's downtown. Right off of Third Street on Pine or Locust."

"Got it. Right around the corner, man."

"Hey, Max, when we're done I'm treating for lunch."

They walked into the bank and the receptionist referred them to a Dave Person. That was his real name, Dave Person. Max rolled his eyes at Malone as the receptionist dialed Mr. Person. Dave greeted them nervously. He was young, probably about Max's age. He was wearing a smart, pinstriped blue suit, matching blue shirt and striped tie, looking like the stereotypical banker.

Wonder if he thinks we look like the stereotypical cops? Malone mused.

Max began. "We're investigating Mr. James Wilson, a customer of the bank and would like access to his accounts."

"What are you investigating him for?" Dave inquired with a raised eyebrow.

"We can't divulge that information at this point," Max countered. "The investigation is still in the preliminary stages."

Dave punched some keys on his computer keyboard, and scanned the screen.

"There's a problem. Mrs. Wilson is listed as a joint account holder. We will need her permission to give you access to their financial information."

"We are here on behalf of Mrs. Wilson," Malone interjected.

"Let me ask Mr. Groninski," Dave said as he rose to leave the office. He returned a few minutes later.

"I'm afraid I have bad news. Mr. Groninski, our bank president, backs my earlier statement. Mrs. Wilson must give her permission in writing for the bank to allow you access to their financials."

Malone resented the smug look on his face, and heard himself saying, "I can get a warrant." Dave didn't bite. He simply said, "Fine. Get your warrant and I will provide you with whatever you need. Now, if you will excuse me, I have a meeting."

Meeting, my ass. Malone and Worthy stood and left the office.

"How are you going to get a warrant without probable cause?" Max asked, pausing to stare at Larry.

"I'm not. That cocky son of a bitch just pissed me off. The problem is, I have a gut feeling about this situation, and it's not good. But I'm starved and I promised you lunch. Pull around the corner to the Coney Island.

"You're taking me there for lunch?"

"Hey, it's a great place. You're going to love it. Trust me."

They went in the 1930s vintage café, and were greeted by Gus and George, the owners.

"Hey, Larry, long time, no see."

"Yeah, been busy, Gus. Meet my partner, Max. He's a first-timer."

Max scanned the café. It was about twenty feet wide and sixty feet deep, long and narrow. There were booths the length of the wall to the left, and a counter with stools to the right. They took a booth. Max commented on the color. Dark red walls, dark red wooden booths. "This Gus guy have a thing for red?"

"Ambience isn't everything," Malone said.

Larry ordered a Coney, fries, and chocolate malt.

Max, not seeing a menu, said, "I'll have the same."

Without writing anything down, Gus yelled "two fries" and went back behind the counter.

A few minutes later George walked over and slid two plates with Coney dogs on their tabletop. Max looked at the steamed bun, dog inside, with mustard and onions, covered in meaty sauce. By the time the fries and malts—thick individually mixed malts, and fries made from real potatoes cut the same morning—arrived, Max had ordered two more Coneys.

Gus came by, wiping his hands on his once-white apron. He asked Max about his family, wanted to know when Malone was going to get married again, commented about the city council, and everything in general. Then he moved on to the next booth. Same friendly chatter.

They got up to leave. At the register, George said, "What'd we have today?"

Larry answered, "four Coneys, two fries, and two malts."

George rang it up and Larry paid the bill.

When they got outside, Max exclaimed, "Wow, that was weird." He shook his head.

"What was that?" Malone cocked his head as he asked.

"No bill. He trusted us to tell him what we ate."

Malone smiled with satisfaction. "Yeah, well, that's how they do it at the Coney."

"Okay, it's a great place."

"It took three Coneys to convince you."

"Yeah, they were pretty good. Want a Snickers for dessert?" He held one up for Malone.

Malone just shook his head with a small shudder as he got into the car and called the Safety Center to see if Susan Wilson had called in to report her husband was home. He got a negative answer, so he and Max headed for the pharmacy to talk to his partner, Fred Hawthorne. The relief pharmacist on duty told them Fred had taken Memorial Day weekend off, and wouldn't be back until Tuesday. They talked to some of the other employees in the pharmacy but no one seemed to think James had any enemies, and thought this was very bizarre behavior for him.

"Apparently Fred's not too worried about Wilson if he's leaving town," Max said, "and his hired help doesn't know anything."

"Yeah, makes you wonder just what the hell is going on?" Malone nodded. "I'm telling you, Max, we've got something really weird here." They decided to work on some other cases for the balance of the day.

Susan Wilson had left the Safety Center in despair that soon turned to near-hysteria. James's disappearance terrified her, and she was angry with Detective Malone for taking so long to file a missing persons report, and didn't understand why he couldn't have done it the day before. She returned home and waited all morning hoping James would call. By noon, she was frantic. She called the Safety Center.

"No, Detective Malone is not in his office," the desk sergeant said perfunctorily. "He's out on some cases."

"When do you expect him back?"

"He didn't say. He may not be back at all, since he has the weekend off."

This only fueled her anger. Susan gritted out a thank you and slammed her phone shut. She decided to pursue it on her own. One thing about Susan Wilson, she was a woman of action. If Malone wasn't going to get the job done, she would take the matter into her own hands.

Susan looked up the number to St. John's. "Mr. Jensen, this is Susan Wilson, James's wife. I would like to talk to you about James. I need to find out if you know anything about his whereabouts."

"No, I don't, Mrs. Wilson. The last time I saw him he was leaving the dedication with the rest of the crowd. I am very sorry about his disappearance, and I'm sure he will show up with a logical explanation."

"How did you know he was missing?"

"Two detectives were here earlier this morning. They spoke with me and Monsignor Kelly."

"Oh…I wasn't aware of that," Susan said, surprised. "Thank you for your time, Mr. Jensen."

Susan dialed again. "Monsignor Kelly, please. This is Susan Wilson."

"Hello, Susan." The Monsignor was immediately solicitous. "I am so sorry to hear about James. All of us at St. John's are praying for his safe return."

"Thank you, Monsignor. I really need to know if you can shed some light on his disappearance."

"I wish I could. After the dedication, I thanked James once again for his generosity and his attendance, and then to my knowledge he left with the other folks. That was the last time I saw him. You might visit some other people who were at the school that day. He might have indicated his plans to one of them."

"No, I seriously doubt it. He would have told me. I was just hoping you might have some information that would help me."

"I'm sorry, I wish I did…I should probably mention that when I returned to the rectory after the dedication, I had voice mail from James. He expressed concern over the actions of a teacher who he witnessed publically chastising a student after the dedication."

"Do you think this teacher may have something to do with James?"

"Not really," the Monsignor said, dismissing the idea. "The teacher wasn't even aware of the complaint until this morning."

"Thank you for your time, Monsignor. If you hear anything, please call me right away."

"You can be assured I will."

Susan hit her speed dial. "Sarah, this is Susan. I need your help."

The posters had a picture of James beneath one word: "MISSING." The poster listed a physical description of James, a description of the suit he was wearing when he disappeared, and Susan's phone number to call. Susan felt a little strange. Like she was putting his picture on a milk carton. But something had happened to him, and she decided that every minute she wasted just delayed finding him. She had asked her friend, Sarah, who worked at CopyCat Printing, if she would make a flyer about James. Sarah had talked her boss into letting her make 500 copies at no cost, and they were ready to be picked up within an hour. Susan and Sarah had called friends, and by the time they were printed, fourteen housewives had divided the city into sections and were tacking up posters all over town. Light poles, fences, business windows; within another hour, it was hard to find a block without a poster.

Malone and Worthy were headed back to the Safety Center. Without warning, Max hit the brakes, throwing Malone forward in his seat.

"What the hell?" Larry exclaimed as the seat belt tightened around his chest, jerking his head forward.

"Look at that!" Max shouted, pointing at the light pole as he backed the car up.

Larry, still miffed at Max, finally saw the poster. "She's gone wacko!"

He grabbed his phone and called Susan's cell.

"Mrs. Wilson, this is Detective Larry Malone. What's going on with all the posters?"

"I decided to get pro-active."

"Don't you think this is a little premature?"

"No, I don't. While you take the weekend off, I am going to continue to search for my husband."

"Who said I was taking the weekend off?"

"I called the Safety Center."

"I'm not scheduled to work, but I was planning on spending some time on the case this weekend anyway."

"That's comforting to know. Now I must get back to my posters." The phone went dead.

"Jesus, the nerve of that woman!" Malone banged his fist on the dash. "The sooner I can clock out the better. Not even two days and she's driving me nuts!" Max pulled into the lot of the Safety Center. Malone got out of the unmarked car, and as he walked away, Max yelled with a big grin, "Hey, Larry, have a nice weekend. Bet she's back Tuesday morning bright and early! Sure you don't want a Snickers?"

Malone gave him a one finger salute.

CHAPTER 6

Same Day
Council Bluffs, Iowa

S TEVE AND WHITNEY EXITED THE elevator, and saw Helen
nose-to-nose with two police officers. Helen saw Steve coming
her way, and said, "Here's Dr. Cantelli now. Doctor, would you
please explain to these officers that they are not to be in room 313
trying to interview our patient?"

"Have they been in his room?" Dr. Cantelli frowned.

"Yes, the medication aide told me they were in his room when
she checked on him. She came and got me. I have been explaining
to them that he is in critical condition, a coma, and not allowed
visitors, especially visitors who may upset him."

Seeing his chance to jump in, the senior-appearing officer said,
"Your patient is the victim of a crime, Doctor, and we need to find
out any details about his mugging as soon as possible. The more
time that passes, the less our chance of finding the person who did
this to him."

"I'm sure that's true, Officer Valdez," Dr. Cantelli said, reading
his name tag, "but until Helen or I sign off on visitors, our patient
is off limits, even to the police."

"Doctor, I respect you protecting your patient, but this is a
criminal investigation, and we need to speak to him as soon as
possible."

"And you will. Helen or I will call you as soon as he is able to talk."

"Maybe we'll just hang around for a while. He might wake up and we want to be here."

Dr. Cantelli felt that Sgt. Valdez was just stalling so he could get back in John Doe's room.

"Sergeant, do you know Melvin Marlowe?"

"Sure, he's the Chief of Police."

"Yes, he is. And that would make him your boss, right?"

"Ah...right."

"Then you will leave now, or I will call him on his cell and he will tell you himself to wait for my or Helen's call."

Valdez looked puzzled for a moment, as if he were working out whether he should call Dr. Cantelli's bluff. A shadow crossed his face, a blend of irritation and resignation, and he handed the doctor his card. "Call me as soon as he wakes up. Day or night. My cell number is on the back." The two officers walked into the elevator and the doors closed.

"That was pretty good, Doctor," Helen said, "They really believed you would do it."

Cantelli laughed. "I would have. Melvin's son is my best friend. I'm usually at the chief's house for Sunday dinner once a month." He turned to Whitney, and said, "Let's look in on our patient now." Finding no change in his condition, Steve told Whitney she may as well get on with her weekend, and he would fill her in when she got back on Tuesday.

Same Day
Omaha, Nebraska
5:00 P.M.

Nathan and Ted went to the Fox and Hound, a bar in west Omaha. It was miles from the places he hung out at with Tom and

Jason. Ted was still worked up over his conversation with Harlan Jensen.

"Prissy fagot," he said, then repeated his side of the story for the third time. "The kid is just plain lazy. And a smart-ass to boot."

Nathan let him talk, trying to find out any news he could. After a few beers, James Wilson's name came up. Nathan was all ears.

"That rotten SOB called Monsignor Kelly and complained about me." Ted said as he jabbed his finger at Nathan. "Just because he gave some money to the school he has no right to condemn my behavior!"

"You may have been a little out of line, Ted. It didn't seem like the right time or place to light into a student."

"He made a wise crack when I walked by, and I just lost my temper."

"Well, it's over and sometimes it's just best to let sleeping dogs lie."

"Yeah, well it still pissed me off!" Ted huffed, to get the last word in on the issue.

Nathan decided to segue way the conversation to Wilson. "So what happened to this Wilson guy?" he asked. Too late, he realized he shouldn't know anything was up. He heaved a sigh of relief when Ted didn't notice.

"No one knows," Ted said. "Weird thing. Rumors all the way from an abduction to a mob hit. The best guess is he just took off to get away from his wife. Word is she's a piece of work. He'll probably think it over and end up coming back."

"Yeah, we all feel the need to get away from our wives once in a while," Nathan said as he rolled his eyes. At this moment Nathan felt like a duck cruising on the lake. Smooth on the surface, but paddling like hell under the water. If Wilson lived, he could make a definite tie to Nathan and Jason, since they told him they were friends of Ted. The police would be on Ted's doorstep in a heartbeat and he and Jason would be toast. He didn't need this.

Nathan decided to change the subject. Ted was Nathan's eyes and ears at St. John's. When Ted first got his job at the school, he told Nathan about kicking a couple of kids off the basketball team for drinking. Nathan took advantage of this information, figuring that an alcohol user is a potential drug user. He had his people contact the kids and soon they were dealing drugs for him. Nathan liked Ted, and he had every intention of remaining friends. But Nathan used everyone, even his friends, to get what he wanted. Ted didn't have a clue, and Nathan wanted to keep it that way.

And Tom. When Tom was with the Hall County Sheriff's Department in Grand Island, Nathan utilized information gleaned from Tom to eliminate his competition. Meth labs blew up every day. It was easier to facilitate the explosion if one knew the address. Tom would talk to Nathan, as friends often do, and reveal just enough information about drug activity to alert Nathan about a raid on his own people. All Nathan had to do was make a phone call and the lab would be gone before morning. Tom, of course, had no knowledge about Nathan's involvement in the drug trade. Now Tom was in Omaha and Ted was Nathan's only source of information in Grand Island.

Ted was feeling the effect of the alcohol, and Nathan soon found out everything he needed to know.

"Let's get back to my house while we're still able to drive." Nathan suggested. He was troubled. Ted didn't have any solid news about Wilson, and Nathan had to make sure he was dead. If he were by some chance still alive, he could identify Nathan. Nathan used the men's room before leaving the bar. *Damn. Why did I let myself get involved?* He slammed his fist against the stall in fury and frustration.

Nathan thought things over during the drive back to his house. Ted crashed right away when they arrived, and Nathan started dialing. It was time to get his people busy.

"This is Nathan...Yes, I know what time it is. I need you to do something...Find out if they found a body behind the Fiddlin' Monkey Bar the other night. I need to find out if the guy's still alive, and if he is, where he's at. I'll be at this number. Be discrete, but be quick."

Same Day
Council Bluffs, Iowa
10:00 P.M.

Visiting hours were over. The hospital was all but deserted. The tall black man in the smelly wool overcoat took the stairs to the third floor. It was safer than the elevator. Less chance of being seen.

Sam's conscience had gotten the best of him. When he'd found the victim behind the Fiddlin' Monkey, he finally had to tell someone. He'd pushed his cart to the Thrift Store and Food Pantry at the next intersection. He told the girl on duty that a man was in the alley badly hurt and to call an ambulance.

He had waited to make sure the ambulance came and then headed on. Sam wasn't exactly sure why he was here now, but he felt some odd kind of tie to this guy. Maybe it was just his imagination.

He looked around and saw that there were no nurses visible, and went into room 313. He had found out the room number from an all-too-helpful maintenance man, who had forgotten about privacy rules.

There was a low light on in the room. The patient was in bed, sleeping. The tubes and monitors made Sam uneasy. At least he was still alive. Sam wasn't sure what to do, so he just stood at the foot of the man's bed, watching his chest rise and fall. The line on the monitor rose and fell. After about ten minutes, Sam decided he had best move on before someone saw him and started asking questions. He took the stairs back down and headed for the shelter, buttoning his overcoat and putting on his stocking cap. The temperature had begun to drop, and the cold wind-driven rain stung his face.

At the same time, Dr. Cantelli was pulling into the parking lot. He had been to a movie, *The Sorcerer's Stone*. A local theater was running all the movies in the Harry Potter series. Few people knew he was a Harry Potter fan. Three chapters through the first book in the series, he was hooked. He was so caught up in the saga, he had even attended a "Harry Potter Rally" in Las Vegas a couple years earlier. It was an eye-opener. He had no idea there were so many adults dedicated to Harry Potter. Doctors, lawyers, construction workers, executives, almost any walk of life. Many of them were in costume: Professor Dumbledore, Severis Snitch, Mad Eye Moody, Lord Voldemort, and on and on. Steve didn't wear a costume. He did buy a replica of Harry's wand, however. He wasn't sure what he would do with it, except maybe use it on a difficult patient. He hadn't done that yet. Anyway the movie was good, and he decided to stop by the hospital and look in on the patient in 313.

He went to the third floor, and as he got off the elevator, the nurse stopped him as he went past the nurses' station.

"I'm sorry, sir, but visiting hours are over."

"I know; I'm here to see the patient in room 313."

"Are you a relative? Do you have power of attorney?"

Steve suddenly realized he was wearing jeans, sneakers, and a t-shirt—hardly typical doctor attire. "I'm Dr. Cantelli, a hospitalist here, and 313 is my patient. I just stopped by to check on him."

"I'm so sorry, Doctor." The nurse flushed. "I didn't recognize you without your white coat."

Funny you would say that. I've never seen you and I doubt you have ever seen me. It would be really easy to have free reign anywhere in the hospital if all you require is my say-so, Cantelli thought with more than a little concern.

He looked at the chart on the way to the room. He examined the patient. Not much change, but his vitals were okay. *What is that smell? It smells horrible in here!*

Steve asked the nurse about the smell in room 313. She wasn't aware of any strange odor.

"Well, check his dressings for abscesses, purulent drainage, or anything that could be causing that smell. If you find anything, call my cell." He went home.

The nurse went into the room and checked on the patient. She examined his dressings but couldn't find any cause for the odor lingering in the air, so went back to her charting.

The poking and prodding had caused the patient to drift into and out of consciousness. *What is happening?* Nothing made any sense. *Why can't I move?* It was black, then the light came back. The pain was better. Until someone moved and poked him. *How much time has gone by? Days? Weeks?* He just wanted to scream. Maybe that would get somebody's attention? He tried to scream. His dry, cracked lips resisted his attempt to open them wide. Finally, a long blood-curdling scream emerged that seemed to go on forever! At least he thought he had screamed. *I didn't hear it. Did anyone hear it?* He began to cry. And he knew he was crying because he could feel the warm tears rolling down his cheeks. He sobbed for a long time, then it all went black again.

CHAPTER 7

Saturday, May 23
Omaha, Nebraska
8:00 A.M.

T HE PHONE CHIRPED. *WHAT TIME is it?* Nathan looked at his watch. *8:00* A.M. He had slept late. It was a text with a phone number for him to call.

Ted was still on the sofa. He had passed out there and Nathan had just let him be. Nathan shook him awake.

"C'mon, Ted, time to get moving."

"Oh man...I can't move. My head feels like a basketball."

"You're already dressed. I'll find you some Tylenol, then let's get some coffee and food in our stomachs. That ought to sober you up."

Nathan and Ted each drove to a nearby Denny's. As soon as the last pancake was gone, Nathan told Ted he had to get going. "Have a safe drive back to GI, and stay out of trouble."

Ted's car had barely exited the drive when Nathan dialed the number he had been texted.

"Well, what have you got?"

"He's in City Hospital. He's alive, in a coma, and they think he will probably live."

"Get over there and keep tabs on him."

"I'll do the best I can, but I don't want to be conspicuous."

"Use your imagination. That's why I pay you so well." He hit the "end" button and got in his car.

Nathan needed to settle down. There was still some time before his wife's flight arrived and he had to think this through. *Damn, why hadn't the guy just died? Or why didn't I just finish it? Hindsight.*

Nathan went to the dealership, but couldn't concentrate, so he decided he may as well go to the airport and wait. On the way he passed the Quest Center, and noticed the Bob Kerry Pedestrian Bridge in the background. He had never been on the bridge. Maybe a walk would clear his mind.

The bridge is a 3000 foot long span across the Missouri River between Omaha and Council Bluffs. Named for the former senator from Nebraska, the bridge is supported by two 200 foot towers surrounded by suspension cables. Fifty-two feet above the water, the bridge presents a spectacular view of the surrounding area. He strolled across the bridge and looked around at the park-like area on the Council Bluffs side. He sat on a bench and watched the clusters of people passing by. The crisp air and brisk walk had cleared his mind. *Wonder if they have problems like I do?* He thought about the events of the past three days. *Why did I get involved in the first place? And why did I let my temper take over?*

He decided to head back over the bridge, but stopped at the halfway point and looked south along the river. From the height he could see the bridge, about a mile away, he had driven over with Wilson in the trunk of his own car.

Originally, Nathan had never intended to drive the victim to Council Bluffs. After he left the parking lot behind the rectory, his intention was to dump him in a ditch outside of town. When he opened the trunk, Wilson was unresponsive. Too many loose ends. Best to make him disappear; he was going to die anyway. Nathan called a friend and told him he wanted to meet at his friend's body shop in Council Bluffs at 2:00 A.M.

"Two in the morning? You've got to be kidding!"

"Trust me. I'll make it worth your time...Oh, and show up alone."

"Who would I find dumb enough to come with me at that hour?" his friend said.

Nathan wasn't in the mood for snide comments. "Just be there!"

Nathan drove to Council Bluffs and dumped Wilson in the alley behind the Fiddlin' Monkey bar. Nathan was sure he would be dead by the time anyone found him in the morning. He took the plates off of Wilson's car, cleaned out all the papers and other items that might identify the owner, and met his friend at the body shop. He drove the car inside and his friend gave him a ride back to the dealership. The body shop doubled as a "chop shop." Wilson's car had been disassembled the same night and by now had been assumed into inventory by several different body shops. Nice to know the right people.

Nathan never intended to become a drug dealer. His goal was to get a college degree, return to Omaha and run his family's car dealership. He did exactly that. Right after college, he moved back to Omaha, married Audrey, and now was in charge of the dealership. He was well-respected in Omaha, a pillar of the community. He and Audrey associated with the right people, were invited to all the right parties, and were known for their community support and generosity. It was easy for Nathan. He had always loved Omaha, and giving back to the city he cared so much about gave him a great deal of satisfaction.

When Nathan was in college, he had a roommate who was dealing drugs. Nathan stayed away from them, and insisted no drugs be in their room, and no dealing out of the room. His roommate complied. He kept Nathan out of it completely.

The situation made Nathan nervous, however, so he moved out. About the same time, he had a temporary falling out with his father, and the money dried up. Nathan was used to a new car, nice clothes, and money to spend. But the old man cut him off. He went back to his former roommate, knowing there was easy money if one didn't get caught. He started dealing, and soon had all the money he needed. His old roommate wasn't so lucky. He got busted and was sent to jail.

This was the first opportunity Nathan had used to sacrifice other people for his personal gain, and he played it well. Nathan was called in for questioning regarding his former roommate. Nathan made sure that his statements led the police to the people whose testimony would seal the deal. The result was twenty years in the Nebraska State Penitentiary for his friend and former roommate.

Within a month, the entire business was Nathan's. Nathan and his father patched things up, and he purchased the dealership from his father after graduation. The drug business had proven to be more profitable than the car business, so Nathan kept it going. He had expanded his drug operation into Omaha, Grand Island, and Council Bluffs was next.

No one had a clue Nathan was involved with drugs. He kept himself distanced from his subordinates and maintained a very low profile. They did his dirty work, and he paid them well. But now he had gotten involved. Nathan stood on the bridge, and made a decision. A loose end could be his downfall. He opened his cell.

"This is Nathan. I want you to finish the job. Call me when it's done." He closed his phone, walked to his car, and headed for the airport.

Same Day
Grand Island, Nebraska

Susan Wilson was continuing her crusade to find her husband. Malone had called her house, and her mother answered. She told him Susan was at the shopping mall handing out brochures about James. Malone thanked her and headed for the mall.

Seeing Malone, Susan came over with an attitude.

"Working on your day off, or shopping?"

"I'm working. And let's stop sparring here, Mrs. Wilson. I want to find your husband as much as you do. But you need to understand, I can do a much better job if you drop the comments and cooperate."

"Dave Person called me. I'm not giving you access to our bank accounts."

"We need more than that. We need the list I asked you to make of anyone who might have reason to harm James. And remember, it doesn't have to be anything major. Sometimes a minor disagreement or seemingly innocuous incident can set people off."

"I guess I've been so busy getting the word out, I haven't had time to make a list. I'm going home at two o'clock. I promise I will start working on it."

"Thank you. I see your parents are here in town. That should give you some much-needed support. Let me know if anything comes up." Malone left.

Council Bluffs, Iowa

Dr. Cantelli had finished his rounds and gone home. He had just finishing washing the supper dishes when the phone rang.

"Dr. Cantelli, this is Sergeant Valdez with the Council Bluffs Police Department."

How in the hell did he get my home number? I need to talk to the nurses about this. "What can I do for you sergeant?"

"We would like to photograph and fingerprint your patient. We'll get his picture out to other law enforcement agencies, and maybe someone will recognize him, or there will be a report of a missing person we can trace."

"Sounds like a good idea. I only have one condition."

"What's that?"

"You have the nurse in the room with you when you take the picture."

"Why? Don't you trust us?"

"I trust you. I just don't want a camera flash or anything to frighten the patient. He doesn't know where he is, and he may be extremely anxious when he wakes up."

"No problem, Doctor. We'll be there first thing in the morning."

"Okay. I'll leave word to expect you at the nurses' station. And by the way, thanks for calling ahead of time."

"Hey doc, can I ask you a question?"

"Sure."

"Would you really have called Chief Marlowe?"

"Are you a poker player, sergeant?"

"I play a little."

"Then you know a good poker player never shows his hand unless someone calls."

"Goodnight, doc."

"Night, sergeant."

Both of them hung up smiling.

Sunday, May 24
Council Bluffs, Iowa
8:00 A.M.

Officer Valdez was explaining to the nurse blocking the door—all of it—that he had phoned Dr. Cantelli and obtained permission to photograph and fingerprint the patient in room 313. "I told him we'd be here first thing in the morning, and Dr. Cantelli told me he would leave word at the nurses' station; his only condition was that we were to ask a nurse to accompany us into the room."

"I didn't see any such order."

"He said to call his cell if there was a problem."

"Well, you better call him then, cuz I'm not letting you past me."

Valdez decided not to argue. Not only did she look like Godzilla, she was built like him, too. She stood firm, her arms crossed in defiance, while he called Dr. Cantelli.

When the doctor answered, the other officer started to chuckle, and Valdez heard Cantelli also laughing.

"What's so funny?" Valdez asked, a puzzled look on his face. The other officer just pointed behind him. When Valdez turned his head around, Dr. Cantelli was standing there, phone in hand, sharing the joke.

The nurse didn't appreciate the humor, and took over from there. She breezed past Valdez, almost knocking him over, and launched her attack at Dr. Cantelli.

"These cops wanted to take a patient's picture. I told them it was not allowed under any circumstances." Her defiance and crossed-arms were all for Cantelli this time.

"Now Mildred, just settle down. You know we need to locate his family and these nice officers are just doing their job. They intend to send his picture to other law enforcement agencies and the media to see if anyone can identify him. I would appreciate it if you would assist them."

"That's against hospital policy, Doctor, and I can't allow it."

"Sorry, Mildred, not your call. If you won't go in the room and watch over the patient I'll do it myself."

The indignant nurse glowered at him. "You haven't heard the end of this, Doctor."

As she huffed her way down the hall, Cantelli said, "Unfortunately, she's probably right. It may be against hospital policy. But then, she isn't happy unless she's making someone miserable. The hospital has been trying to get her to retire for years, but they are afraid of a lawsuit." He grinned at the officers. "Her nickname is 'Nurse Ratched,' but I don't advise calling her that to her face."

The officers looked blank.

"You know, Nurse Ratched in the movie *One Flew Over the Cuckoo's Nest*, with Jack Nicholson?"

They looked at each other and shrugged. *Where have these guys been the last twenty years?*

"Hey, Doc," Valdez said, "I've got a job for her. Why doesn't the hospital use her fat ass to land their helicopter on?"

Suppressing a groan, Cantelli said, "Enough with Nurse Ratched; let's get this done before she comes back with the cavalry."

That Evening

The figure was dressed in blue scrubs. He exited the elevator and checked the nurses' desk. No one there. He had watched the floor the prior evening and noted that both nurses took their break around 11:30 P.M. He was back tonight to see if they followed the same routine. So far, so good. He walked the hall looking for the other personnel: nurse aides, physicians, cleaning crews. He was wearing a stolen hospital ID badge clipped to his pocket. The picture didn't match but he knew no one paid much attention to the badges anyway. He entered room 313. He checked out the monitors. There appeared to be no way to turn them off without activating the backup batteries. Besides, the entire hospital had generators in case of a power failure. He would have to do it the old-fashioned way, but not tonight; the nurses would be back from their break soon. His method was clear. The reconnaissance had paid off. He walked the twenty paces to the stairwell and headed down. He would double-check the exits and be back tomorrow.

Monday, May 25
Memorial Day
Omaha, Nebraska

Jason told his wife he had a migraine and she should take the kids to the Memorial Day picnic without him.

"No, if you're not feeling well, we'll all stay home."

"The kids will be disappointed. You go on and I'm just going to lie on the sofa and try and shake this headache."

"I know, but I feel sorry for you."

"The peace and quiet will be good for the headache."

"You're probably right. I'll get the kids out of your hair. Love you, and I'll bring you some chicken and potato salad."

As soon as the car pulled away from the house, Jason got out a bottle of scotch. He hadn't slept since his lunch with Nathan. He knew booze wasn't the answer, but he wanted—no, needed—to chase away the nightmares. It worked, for today at least. When his wife came home that evening, she found him sound asleep on the sofa. He'd had the foresight to put the bottle away. She left him sleeping on the couch and took the kids upstairs for bed.

Nathan was at a get-together at his father's house. He hated these family gatherings. His two brothers barely spoke to him, as he was very successful with the family business. It didn't matter that neither of them had ever wanted any part of it. He chalked it up to sibling jealousy.

While the wives chatted it up amicably, and the kids played games, he continued to parry with his brothers. The old man had a little too much to drink and Nathan told him to go in the house and take a nap. One of his brothers asked Nathan if he was on drugs. Barbs began flying back and forth like a Badminton shuttle. Luckily, his phone rang before things got out of hand.

Nathan went to the back of the yard and answered when he saw the number.

"Is it done?...What do you mean, not yet?... I'm not paying you to scout the situation out; I'm paying you to finish the job!...If that guy wakes up?...Okay, okay. You've done your homework. Now, do your job!"

Nathan closed his phone and looked for something to kick. The only thing close was his father's dog, and that didn't seem like a good idea. He walked back to the picnic table. He was really in the mood for a fight right now. After five minutes of watching Nathan spar with his brothers, Audrey decided it was time to leave, and practically dragged him to the car.

Across town, Tom went to brunch with Julie and Timmy at his mother-in-law's home. He hated family dinners. His mother-in-law was a good cook, but she just couldn't stay out of his and Julie's business. Tom had married Julie right after college, when they found out she was two months pregnant. He knew that , with a baby coming, money was going to be tight, so he put his plans for law school on the back burner.

After Julie had gotten a teaching job in Grand Island, and Tom had signed on with the Hall County Sheriff's Department, the tension escalated.

Julie's dad had been a stabilizing influence, but shortly after Timmy was born, he passed away. Julie spent so much time running to Omaha to visit her mother, Tom figured they may as well move there. At least he got to see more of his family. Unfortunately he spent a lot of time listening to her mother's comments.

"I was so looking forward to having a lawyer in the family. When are you going to quit that dreadful deputy's job and go back to school?"

She didn't have a clue. Tom was grateful that Julie hadn't gotten pregnant earlier and the two of them had been able to stay in college long enough to graduate. They were both content for the time being. Tom didn't want to make the customary Memorial Day visit to the cemetery, so he excused himself to go into work for a while. It had been a busy weekend and he needed to catch up on paperwork anyway. He arrived at his office, picked up his stack of faxes, and went to his desk. He flipped through them, stopping when he saw the picture of James Wilson. He studied it for a minute, thinking he looked familiar. It was hard to tell with the bandages and tubes. He put it aside. an action that would later come back to haunt him.

Council Bluffs, Iowa
Same Day

It was time to change shifts at City Hospital. The afternoon shift nurses were in the break room giving patient reports to the night shift coming on duty.

The report droned on as a figure emerged from the elevator. The man moved purposely and entered room 313. The patient was asleep, or still in a coma, the intruder didn't know or care which. He reached into the closet and grabbed the spare pillow. No need to get fancy. This method was quick, effective, and sure. Beads of perspiration ran down his forehead and collected on the lenses of his glasses. He had to hurry. This would take five minutes and the nurses would be returning soon after that. He approached the bed, pulled the plastic bag out of his pocket, placed it over the patient's face and pushed it tight with the pillow. The patient didn't offer any resistance at first, but then his body began to tense. He pushed harder on the pillow as the patient began to thrash around, fighting for air. He glanced at his watch: three minutes. The patient's body was offering less resistance. One more minute and it would be over. He continued to hold the pillow firmly in place, until the body was perfectly still.

CHAPTER 8

T HE DOOR SQUEAKED AS IT opened. The figure pulled the
pillow away from the patient, patting it as if he were fluffing
it up.

"I'm sorry. I didn't know anyone else was on duty." It was an
orderly.

Jesus, where did this guy come from? The intruder placed the
pillow under 313's head, careful to conceal the plastic bag covered
with sweat as he balled it into his hand, hoping he wouldn't have
to use it on this unsuspecting orderly.

"I was going back to second floor after my break and heard a
moan. I looked in. This guy was twisting and jerking, looking very
uncomfortable. I thought another pillow might help."

"That was considerate of you," the orderly said.

"Well, best get going and let him sleep. He looks comfortable
now." The brown-skinned figure tried to appear casual as he took
one last glance back at the patient. No rising or falling of his chest;
he wasn't breathing. He left the room, put the bag in his pocket
and walked directly to the stairs. *Thank God I had foresight to wear
a disguise.* He reached the lobby, quickly exited the building, and
headed for his car. He decided to wait until he got home before he
called Nathan. Right now he just wanted to be as far away from the
hospital as possible when the orderly realized the patient was dead.
He reached the safety of his home and texted Nathan: "Project
completed."

Tuesday, May 26
Grand Island, Nebraska
9:00 A.M.

The sun was trying to break through the clouds, but the darkening sky was winning the battle. Thunderstorms were in the forecast for the next two days. Malone looked out the door of the Safety Center and decided to grab his raincoat. He and Max had just finished discussing the Wilson case and were heading out to start some more interviews.

"Okay, here's the plan," Malone said. "I'll start with Fred Hawthorne at the pharmacy, you question the list of acquaintances, then we'll meet up and visit Susan Wilson. Any questions?"

"Nope," Max replied. "It works for me."

"Let's go." Malone leaned into the wind.

The rain started halfway to the pharmacy. It soon escalated into a full-blown thunderstorm. The raindrops splattered off the hood of the car, while lightning lit up the black clouds. It came down so hard and fast, water was already flowing along the curbing into the gutters. Larry pulled into a parking place in front of the pharmacy, but decided to stay in the car until the rain subsided. It took five minutes before it let up enough for him to get out and hurry into the pharmacy. It was a typical small town corner drugstore. It even had a soda fountain.

Larry was impressed. He wondered why he had never been in here before. He made his way past cosmetics, gifts, and seemingly hundreds of medicines. A middle-aged clerk, wearing a blue smock, approached and asked if she could help him. Malone flashed his badge, and asked to see Fred.

"Is this about James?" the clerk asked.

"Yes," Malone replied. "Do you have any information that can help us?"

"No, but this is just terrible. He's such a nice guy."

"Yes, I need to talk to Fred."

"He's back in the dispensing area."

Malone walked to the back of the store, and saw two women and a man wearing a white coat standing behind the counter. The man was about five feet ten, had brown curly hair, a slight build, and looked frenzied.

"Fred Hawthorne?" Malone asked.

"Yes."

Malone introduced himself and said he needed to talk to him.

"Can you come back later...say mid-afternoon?" Fred asked abruptly.

"We really need to talk." Malone said, perturbed.

"I understand." Fred said, holding up one hand while grabbing the phone with the other. After the call, he apologized. "I want to help. But I'm the only one here today and you can see how busy it is...I'm up to my ass in alligators and there isn't time to drain the swamp right now. Please come back around two o'clock or so."

Malone stopped and talked to the rest of the employees on the way out of the pharmacy, but garnered no new information. Same song, second verse. Nice guy, no one would ever want to hurt him.

Larry figured he may as well join up with Max, and pulled out his cell to call him and see where he was. Before he could dial, the cell rang.

"Malone."

"Detective Malone, this is Sergeant Michalski. We just got a 911 call that someone found a body on Potash Road near Heartland Shooting Park. I thought you and Max would want to know."

"Thanks, Sarge. Got an exact location?"

"No, but the black and whites are already there, so you should see plenty of lights."

"Okay."

Larry called Max as he headed for the location.

"What's going on?"

"Someone found a body along Old Potash Highway. We better check it out in case it's Wilson."

"Oh, shit! I'm on my way."

They both arrived at the scene in five minutes. There were already units from the GIPD, State Patrol, and Sheriff's Department. Larry and Max approached the scene carefully, not wanting to destroy any evidence, although the rain had probably taken care of that. They found the officer in charge, Captain Brookfield of the Hall County Sheriff's Department. He was standing with his hands on his hips, seemingly oblivious to the downpour around him. Soaked to the skin, the Captain looked up and greeted Larry.

"What do you have?" Larry asked.

"Male, probably been here a week or so, decomposition has already started." Larry didn't need to be told that. His nose had already picked up the smell, hanging like a putrid fog in the rain.

"Any ID?"

"No. No wallet, no watch, nothing."

Larry said, "I need to see the body. We're working a missing person's case and this may be our guy."

"Come on over and take a look. Just watch where you step."

Larry covered his nose wondering if the rain made the smell worse. He noticed the body was partially immersed in water. He looked at the body, frowned, nodded at the Captain, and started to slosh back toward Max. It was then that the KGIN-TV news van arrived.

Stephanie Green, the news reporter, and her cameraman, both clad in black hooded rain jackets were hurriedly setting up. She sloshed toward Larry, carrying her high heels in her hands to avoid ruining them in the water and mud.

She was talking into her microphone when she reached Larry.

"This is Stephanie Green reporting from a scene near the Heartland Shooting Park, where a body has been found. Detective Malone, do you have anything you can share with me at this time?"

"Yes." Malone replied, looking grim, as the microphone was pushed into his face. "The wind has blown your hood off and the rain has ruined your perfect hairdo."

Larry saw that he had flustered Stephanie, gave Max a wide grin, and said, "We better get to Susan Wilson's house before she sees the news. C'mon, ride with me."

CHAPTER 9

Same Morning

T HE WILSONS LIVED IN AN older part of town on Charles Street. In days gone by, this was where the elite of the community lived. Large two- and three-story homes filled the neighborhood, although no particular style of architecture dominated. The most impressive thing about the area was the trees. Many of them had to be over a hundred years old, oaks, elms, and maples so thick they formed a canopy over the street. Local runners favored the street for the shade on hot days.

They pulled up in front of the house. Malone noticed it was a three story, Tudor style, with arched wooden trim accenting the brick front. Not an extravagant home, but nice. It was probably a fixer-upper when they purchased it. He noticed a Buick Electra with out-of-state plates parked in the drive. It was one of the larger ones from the late eighties that could hold a family of six plus most of their furniture.

The trees gave Larry and Max some protection from the rain as they hurried to the door. Malone knocked on the door, only to be by a gray-haired lady, perhaps in her late sixties. She was dressed in a light blue sweat suit. He had to hide a grin as he wondered if it were a family trait. He introduced himself, showing her his ID.

"Oh, thank heavens," she said. "Was it James?"

"You must have your television on?"

"Yes, we just saw where they found a body outside of town."

"Can we see Susan?"

"Come right in. She's in the living room with her father," Susan's mother said, apprehension written all over her face.

The two officers checked the place out as they walked in. Nothing spectacular. Standard furniture, a few old tables, mismatched chairs. Perhaps antiques, maybe not. Neither of them would know a real antique from a fake.

They followed Susan's mother into the living room. Susan and her father were sitting on the sofa, watching the developing news. Malone noticed that Susan was crying uncontrollably.

"Susan, dear, these officers are here to talk to you."

Her father stood immediately, almost at attention. His handshake was firm. He was tall and very handsome, with not a gray hair in his head.

"Her mother and I came as soon as we could," he explained. "We'll step out so you can talk to Susan privately."

Susan interjected, "That won't be necessary, Dad. I want you and Mom to stay." She looked Malone in the eye and said, "It's James they found, isn't it?"

"I'm sorry you had to see the news. We tried to get here before they got on air."

"I don't give a damn how long it took you. Was it James?"

"No." Malone replied.

Susan collapsed into her father's arms, sobbing with relief. Larry and Max stepped into the hallway to let her get it out.

After Susan settled down, her father appeared in the hallway and told them that Susan had calmed down and she would see them now.

"I'm really sorry you had to see the television report, Susan. The media seem to feel news is more important than human feelings anymore." Malone said, not trying to hide his disgust.

"I'm so relieved, and yet so angry, I just can't think straight right now! First my husband and father of my unborn child disappears, and then I have to endure that damned blonde bitch reporter speculating if the dead person is James! I just don't know how much I can take!"

Susan's mother excused herself saying she was going to the kitchen to make some coffee, and asked if they would like some.

"Sure." Worthy said. "In fact, let me help you."

Good boy, Malone thought. *Now that we're back to square one, get the old lady alone and drill her a bit. Maybe find out something the daughter isn't telling us.* Susan's father still sat with his arm around her. He asked Malone, "So what do you think happened to James? Was he kidnapped, er...well, abducted, or something like that?"

"We really don't know," Malone said. "We have a missing persons report out to all of the area law enforcement agencies, and so far nothing has turned up. I was hoping we would at least find his car. That's the real puzzler. You know, there is still the possibility that something totally unexpected came up and he just hasn't been able to call Susan."

"Do you really think so?"

"To be honest, no. But you can never tell. I hate to admit it, but we don't have a clue. We're hoping James will access an ATM or use his credit card. That would at least give us someplace to start looking. We talked to the bank and they will notify us the minute he makes a transaction."

Susan jumped into the conversation. "I thought I told you I wasn't giving you access to our bank records." *Yep, the old Susan is back.*

"It won't give us access to your records, Susan; it will only tell us the date, location, and time of the transaction. But I wish you would reconsider access to the records. It could give us a break in the case." Malone changed the subject. "Does James have a home computer?"

"Yes," Susan replied, "why?"

"If we had access to his computer, it might give us a clue as to what's going on."

"I don't think that's going to happen."

"Look, Susan. We respect your and James's privacy. But so far this case is a complete mystery. Phone records and emails sometimes give us a clue for places to look that you or we haven't considered. Please give it some thought."

Mr. Lamb—Malone had forgotten to write down his first name—interjected, "Well, Susan, if these records will help find James, perhaps you should consider giving the police access to them."

"I have considered it and the answer is still no. Our bank records are personal, and I don't know how the police finding out I wrote a fifty dollar check to the beauty shop is going to help find James."

"All right. I just thought..." Mr. Lamb's voice trailed off. *Yep, Susan is still in charge.*

Worthy and Mrs. Lamb came back into the room with steaming cups of coffee for everyone. She and Mr. Lamb seemed so gracious. *Too bad it didn't rub off on Susan. Maybe she is gracious, too, and it's the situation making her defiant. Or is it something she knows and isn't telling us?*

A few more questions, mostly general in nature, and Malone finished his coffee. He thanked Susan and her parents and headed for the door. Max stood and followed. Malone paused to ask Susan once again to reconsider giving them permission to check bank records and James's computer, emphasizing that technology sometimes plays a big role in providing clues.

"I'll think about it." Susan said.

"Visit with your attorney if you'd like. We just don't want to leave any stones unturned," Malone said, loudly enough for her parents to hear.

When they got in the car, Malone asked Worthy what the mother knew. "Nada. She didn't seem to know anything of value. Seems the marriage is fine. She just found out this morning Susan is pregnant. Her folks seem to be sensible people. Maybe we can use them to soften Susan up?"

"I'm thinking exactly the same thing." Malone nodded. "Let's grab some lunch and go back to visit with Fred Hawthorne."

Fred was still busy, but said he would take a few minutes to visit with them. Fred confirmed that he and James had purchased his father's pharmacy three years ago.

"Why you and James?" Malone queried. "Why didn't you buy it yourself?"

"Two reasons. First, I didn't have the money and my dad knew I had no business knowledge. You see, pharmacy school is mostly about clinical pharmacy. They teach you a hell of a lot about medications, but very little about business. Second, I just wanted to be a community pharmacist like my father, and not a businessman, *per se*. I just feel I am helping everyday people. James, on the other hand, spent two years taking business classes before going into pharmacy school. We felt we would be a good team and joined forces. So far it's worked out well." Fred smiled as if he had a punch line. "To add to the story, I was dating Susan, and things weren't working out, so I introduced her to James our sophomore year. Anyway, they hit it off and you know the rest of the story."

"Do you still have feelings for her?"

"Sure, but not that kind of feelings. She was interested in becoming an urban housewife, and was way too demanding for me. I'm still single and like my lifestyle. She tries to line me up with her divorced friends, but I'm not interested in them. Or her, for that matter."

Silence from Malone and Worthy. *Let him ramble.*

"Where's this going? You think I had something to do with this?"

"Just asking questions. Did you?" Max quipped. Sometimes Max's lack of tact amused Malone.

"Hell, no! I didn't even realize he was missing until Susan called all hysterical."

"What was your reaction?" Worthy asked.

"I told her to calm down. Told her he was probably out with the guys."

Malone asked, "Did you know she was pregnant?"

"How would I know that? James never said anything."

"Just a question."

"Well, I'm getting a little tired of your questions."

"Calm down," Malone said. "We're just trying to put all the pieces together."

"The hell you are! You think I had something to do with this."

"Do you know where James got the money for his donation to St. John's?"

"No. I don't know anything about it."

"What if I told you it was a substantial sum?"

"Exactly what does a 'substantial sum' mean?"

"I can't tell you exactly how much, but it wasn't pocket change."

"Are you implying that James was stealing from the business?"

"No. We're just trying to gather information."

"If you want records, I'll be happy to let you take a look at the books. If he was stealing, I want to know it too. But I think you're wasting your time. James wasn't stealing."

"Okay," Malone said. "We're going to send a private auditor by to look at the books. We don't have the expertise in our department. He is bonded and will have department identification. This will be kept completely confidential."

"Fine by me. I'll cooperate in any way I can. Especially if it will help find James. We're friends as well as partners."

Malone and Worthy thanked him and left their business cards. The rest of the day was spent checking out the list of James's friends. The answers all turned out the same. He was a nice guy, had no enemies, and everyone was shocked to hear he was missing. One big dead end.

"What now?" Max asked.

"I'm telling you, I still think we need to follow the money. Let's see if Susan gives us access to those accounts."

"Coming at it from another angle, you know we've been concentrating on James all along. How about Susan?"

"What about Susan?"

"Well, she's a nurse, works at the hospital, probably has access to drugs. Maybe James isn't the problem?".

"That's a long shot, Max. But we're at a dead end unless something else comes up, so why don't you check Susan out and we can talk later. In fact, let's do a background check on her last job also."

Tuesday, May 26
Council Bluffs, Iowa
8:30 A.M.

Dr. Cantelli saw the uniformed officer sitting outside room 313 as he stepped off the elevator.

"What the hell's going on?" he asked a nurse, nodding in the direction of the officer.

"They think someone may have tried to murder the patient in 313 last night."

"What?! You've got to be kidding me!".

The nurse told him the story of an orderly entering the room and finding another orderly there, and what he had said. It was only when the intruder left the room that the aide noticed the monitor wasn't lit. He checked the patient and saw he wasn't breathing and called the nurse. They resuscitated him immediately, but the intruder was long gone. "Since the monitor was unplugged, and there was petechial hemorrhaging in the patient's eyes, they were quick to assume that whoever that man was had attempted to smother him with a pillow. They called the police and now 313 has a guard."

"What about the other orderly?" Cantelli asked.

"Our guy, Dirk Medley, said he had never seen him before. He was average height, glasses, medium length hair, mustache and possibly Hispanic. Not much to go on. The police figure he had probably stolen a hospital ID, and used it to avoid suspicion."

"What is this guy? Some mobster from Chicago?" Cantelli asked with incredulity. He approached the officer and asked him the same question. The officer didn't know. All he knew was that he was assigned to allow only hospital personnel into the room.

Cantelli opened his cell and made a call. "Melvin, what the hell is going on with my patient?"

Melvin Marlowe, the Chief of Police, told him they didn't know who the patient was, "but apparently the mugging was more than just a robbery. Somebody wants this guy dead. We got no hits on his prints or his picture, so we just have to wait until he wakes up or something else happens. Until then, we're taking all precautions."

Cantelli said good-bye to the chief and shook his head as he continued on his rounds, wondering who the hell this guy was. *Never a dull moment around here.*

Nathan was on his phone. "What do you mean he's still alive? You said it was done!"

"It was. He wasn't breathing when I left the room. Apparently the orderly who came in called the nurse and they resuscitated him."

"So you screwed up?"

"No. It was done when the orderly came in. I don't think he suspects anything. Anyway, I will find out today."

"Can he identify you?"

"No. I wore a disguise. Even you wouldn't have known me."

"Okay. Do *not* call me back." Nathan's voice was filled with disgust. "I'll call you with a new number tonight." Nathan slapped his phone closed. "Damn, damn, DAMN !" he shouted as he banged his fist on the steering wheel.

"Oh, SHIT !" Brakes squealed and Nathan's seat belt jerked against his shoulder. He managed to stop just inches from the car in front of him waiting for a red light. He took a deep breath to relax, and turned on the radio.

"Greasy cheeseburgers and cheap cigarettes...ain't got me yet...living in fast forward..." Kenny Chesney blared over the radio. Nathan drummed the steering wheel in time with the music. He had always been a country music fan. His friends in high school used to tease him about his cowboy boots as well as his taste in music. Now important people respected his choice of dress, expensive jeans and even more expensive boots.

Nathan was worried. He had to get this thing under control or his whole world could come crumbling down. It was time to get creative. He dialed a number. "Meet me in the parking lot of the south Walmart tomorrow morning at nine. I'll be driving a white Ford pickup, and will park along the north side of the lot...never mind. I'll fill you in tomorrow." Nathan hung up, feeling he was on top of the situation at last.

Same Evening
Council Bluffs, Iowa

Sam was tired. He had worked serving a Memorial Day dinner at the shelter the day before. They had served over 300 meals. He was pleased it had gone so well, but thoughts of the patient in room 313 kept bugging him. After helping clean up and taking all the tables down this morning and afternoon, he had taken a quick nap, as he planned to go by the hospital and see if the man in Room 313 was recovering. He awoke to a crash of thunder and a downpour and decided to postpone his visit for a couple of days. He didn't understand why he was obsessed with the guy and wondered if he was going crazy. He put him out of his mind, instead concentrating on his plans for the next day. Sam hoped the storm would blow over, as it could ruin his planned trip to Omaha. This was his last chance before fall, as it was the last day of the spring semester in Omaha.

On Wednesday morning Sam awoke to a glorious day. He decided to attend the mass Father Shanks was offering at the shelter. Sam had been raised Catholic, but seldom went to church. It would disappoint his mother if she knew, but she was already disappointed in him for other reasons.

After lunch, Sam headed with Father Shanks to his Ford Explorer. Father Shanks had told Sam he was going to Omaha to visit with a potential donor for the shelter, and Sam had begged for a ride. Father Shanks was glad to oblige. He didn't have to ask Sam where or why he was going; he already knew. In fact, Father Shanks knew a lot more about Sam than Sam ever imagined.

Father Shanks dropped Sam off at the corner of Dodge and 33rd Street at 1:30. He told him he would pick him up at 4:45 that afternoon at the Walgreens on 30th and Dodge, and drove off. This fit into Sam's timeframe. The man he had to visit occupied an office just two blocks away. It turned out to be a short meeting, and afterward he headed north toward Myrtle Street. He checked his watch. It was two o'clock, and that would give him more than enough time to walk the ten blocks to his destination. Sam walked along 33rd Street until he found the right block. It was important he found a place that she would walk past.

He had seen the girl in the Old Market area earlier that month, and noticed her St. Cecelia's School sweatshirt. He knew she would walk down 33rd to Myrtle Street, but didn't know if she would take Burt Street or cut through Bemis Park. This block would cover both routes. He looked at the run-down homes, and selected one with a "For Sale" sign in the yard. It was a two-story frame house, once wearing a coat of yellow paint. The coat had worn until it became threadbare, showing only graying wood.

He ambled up the walk, stepping over weeds growing from the cracks. He stumbled when he attempted to step over a piece of sidewalk that had been pushed up by tree roots. Sam walked through the unkempt lawn, and debated if he should enter the house through one of the broken windows. He decided it might not be wise to be seen inside the house, so he walked around to the garage. The garage door faced the alley, but there was a walk-in door facing the street. Perfect. He could watch without being observed.

He readied the camera he had found about a month ago. Sam had replaced the batteries and checked the smart card. It was working fine. Now he just had to wait. The time dragged by, minute by agonizing minute. He got up and paced, then sat back down. He checked his watch: 2:10. He paced some more, and forced himself to wait a long time before checking his watch again…2:20. When Sam looked up, panic set in. A police cruiser had pulled up in front of the house, and an officer was getting out. Sam wondered if a neighbor had seen him and reported it to the police. He gulped as he struggled to stay calm.

The officer walked around the house looking it over. Before Sam could hide, the officer spotted him in the garage. He walked toward the garage, and said, "Do you own this house?"

Think fast. He remembered passing a mom and pop grocery on the way, and said, "No. I was walking to the grocery store and felt a little woozy, so decided to sit down for a few minutes."

"Are you okay now?"

"Not yet. I have diabetes and think my blood sugar is low. I sat down and ate a couple of pieces of candy. I always carry the candy just in case. The sugar should be working soon and I'll be on my way."

"Are you sure you don't want me to call someone?"

"Thank you, Officer, but this happens every so often and I know how to take care of it." Sam said with a convincing voice.

"Okay. I better check the address I was given." The officer grabbed his shoulder mike, and asked for dispatch for the address again.

"Got it, I'm a block away. 10-4." He looked at Sam one last time, then walked to his cruiser.

Sam watched him get in his cruiser and drive to the next block. Sam was afraid the officer would come back to check on him, so he left the garage and walked down to the corner, making sure the officer saw him.

Sam waved at him and continued on until he reached the alley. He doubled back and entered the garage from the alley side. He checked his watch. It was 2:50. Not much longer and St. Cecelia's School would be out.

At 3:10, the first group of kids walked by. They were too young. Sam was only interested in teenage girls, and one in particular. It wasn't long before he was rewarded. A group of five girls walked his way, all laughing and talking.

He picked out his target and started to shoot pictures of her. He watched her walk. He tried to memorize her face, took notes of her clothing and her actions. Soon the girls were almost past. He resisted the urge to approach her, knowing the time wasn't right. His time would come. He just had to be patient and smart. The time would come when he would be able to get her alone.

Sam looked at his watch; it was almost half past three. If he hurried he could make it to the Walgreens in time to get his pictures developed before Father Shanks arrived to pick him up.

Sam was waiting by the front door of Walgreens when Father Shanks arrived to pick him up, just five minutes late. His pictures were safely in his inside coat pocket.

CHAPTER 10

Grand Island, Nebraska
That Morning

NATHAN WATCHED THE GOLDEN RAYS of the sun rising in his rearview mirror as he headed west on I-80 that morning. He had left Omaha at six to make sure he would be in Grand Island by nine.

He exited I-80 at Aurora, about twenty miles east of Grand Island, and drove to the truck stop nearby. He used the restroom, and nonchalantly walked out the back door of the convenience store, where a pickup was parked. He pulled a screwdriver out of his pocket and removed the license plates.

Nathan assumed it belonged to the clerk on duty, and figured he had plenty of time to replace them before the clerk got off work. Nathan transferred the plates to his pickup, putting his own license plates under the front seat. It was important the truck had Hall County plates to avoid drawing suspicion. He then drove to Grand Island, went to the south Walmart, and parked along the north edge of the lot.

His man, a young Hispanic, wearing long gym shorts that hung to his knees and a numbered football jersey, showed up a few minutes before nine o'clock. Nathan sneered at his dress, handed him a light blue shirt, dark blue pants, and a hat. He also handed him a Walmart bag containing a tool box, work gloves, and a shoebox. The shoebox contained cash and a plastic bag filled with a yellow-brown powder.

"Is this what I think it is?" the man asked, pointing at the bag of methamphetamine.

"The less you know, the better," Nathan curtly replied, as he handed him a card with an address written on it.

"Change your clothes in the truck," Nathan said, and proceeded to give the man detailed instructions. He concluded, "Give me the keys to your car. I'm going to Tommy's Restaurant on South Locust Street and will wait for you there. Do not acknowledge me when you walk in. Leave the keys in the pickup, and I'll leave the keys in your car. Order yourself something and wait at least ten minutes before you leave."

Nathan ordered breakfast while he waited at Tommy's. He wasn't hungry but it kept his mind occupied while he picked at his food. It was out of his hands now.

A mile across town, Detective Worthy took the phone call.

"Is Detective Malone there?"

"No, he's not in the office right now. This is his partner, Detective Worthy. May I help you?"

"Yes. This is Susan Wilson. I visited with our attorney this morning and he suggested I give you access to whatever you need."

"That's a good decision, Susan. I just hope between James's computer and your bank records, we can shed some light on his case. I'll let Detective Malone know right away. Thank you for calling." Max disconnected without hanging up the handset, gave a fist pump, and dialed a number.

Larry, this is Max. Well, Mr. Lamb must have talked her into using some common sense. Susan called and said we had access to their bank records and James's computer."

"Great. Did you check with the hospital?"

"Good nurse. Punctual, professional, a little pushy at times, but overall a good report."

"What about access to drugs?"

"Only if she took them for herself. They use a robot to dispense them, and she doesn't have access to more than one or two pills at a time. Neither the pharmacist or her supervisor think that's an issue."

"What about her former job?"

"Still waiting to hear," Max said, "haven't gotten a call back yet."

"Okay. I've got a call waiting; hold on a sec."..."Yes, this is Detective Malone...I see...Well, it's not against the law to look out one's window with binoculars...Did he do anything else?...I'll send someone by...Yes, keep your door locked and your shades drawn." Malone switched back to his partner.

"Max, let's meet up after lunch and pay Dave Person a visit."

"I imagine you're looking forward to that."

"Yes, I am. But first, can you run by the Sunshine Apartments and check on Sarah Hardin. It's apartment 43. She says her neighbor is bothering her again."

"Is it urgent?" Max asked.

"I don't think so. She gets a little paranoid sometimes, and just needs reassurance."

"Okay. I'll head that way now."

Nathan was still nervous when his man walked into Tommy's restaurant. He had changed back into his own clothes. Nathan watched him sit down at the counter and order a cup of coffee and a donut. Nathan waited a few minutes and asked the waitress for his check. He got in his pickup and drove south on Locust Street toward the interstate.

He exited at a gravel road bearing a sign announcing Camp Augustine, and went about a half mile up the road. When he pulled back onto Locust Street, his own plates were on his pickup. He stopped at the rest stop in Aurora, replaced the stolen plates, and in a little over two hours was back in Omaha.

Max met Larry after lunch. "Thanks, old buddy."

"For what?"

"For sending me to see Sarah Hardin. She is one good looking babe."

"See, I knew you could handle her," Larry said, grinning.

"Yeah. Good looking, but crazy as a loon," Max retorted.

"I prefer paranoid!"

"You forgot to mention that."

"Sorry. My bad. Did you get her settled down?"

"Yes. I finally convinced her that she had to keep her window shades closed when she undressed or he could look all he wanted. I'm not so sure she isn't teasing this guy, and now she's afraid she may have started something she doesn't want to finish."

"Could be. Let's go see Davie boy."

Nathan waited until he was driving through Lincoln, less than an hour from home, before he called his man back in Grand Island. "Did everything go okay?"

"Piece of cake."

"So they fell for the gas leak in the neighborhood story?"

"Nope. Didn't need it. Knocked on the front door and there was no answer, so I went around to the back. Same deal, only the back door was unlocked. I went up to the spare bedroom, put the box with the money and bag on the shelf in the closet, and set some shoes in front of it. I was in the house no more than five minutes, then gone."

"And none of the neighbors saw you?" Nathan inquired to calm his own nerves.

"Nope. They have a stockade fence around the back yard, so there's no way anyone could have seen me."

"Good job. Open the glove box and you'll find an envelope. No need to count it now. It's all there." Nathan closed the phone. He pulled his truck into the next rest area, used the facilities, and dropped his phone in the trash bin as he walked out. He needed to make one more phone call to complete his plan, but that could wait until he had acquired a new clean cell phone. There was no hurry for the call that would seal the deal.

Same Day
Grand Island, Nebraska

"Detectives Malone and Worthy. We need to see Dave Person," Larry told the receptionist.

"One moment, Detective. I'll tell him you are here."

Dave was once again dressed impeccably, but this time he asked them into his office with a smile, adding, "Susan Wilson called this morning and authorized you access to their bank records. I took the liberty to print a list of their accounts, and all transactions for the last ninety days. Will that suffice, or will you need a longer history?"

Malone was impressed, but still unhappy about Dave's condescending attitude from their former visit, so insisted, "We really need to go back at least six months to find the transactions we are looking for."

"No problem. If you will have a seat, I will print it out for you in just a moment," Dave said as he started tapping his computer keyboard. He stretched behind him to reach the papers coming out of his printer on the credenza behind him and handed them across his desk. "Here you go gentlemen."

"Thank you," Larry said. "Do they by any chance have a safety deposit box?"

"Let me see." He typed on his keyboard, scanned what he saw and said, "No, there is no record of one."

"We'll take these records for now, and if we need more we'll let you know," Malone said as he and Max stood to leave.

"Good luck, Detectives. Let me know if I can be of any more help." Dave rose and shook their hands before they left his office.

"Max, was that a 180-degree turnaround or am I imagining things?" Larry said as he walked out of the bank.

"I thought the same thing, Larry. He was almost too willing to help."

"Yeah I know. When we get James's computer, I'll have IT see if they can access his accounts on line and make sure both sets of records match up."

"You really don't trust him, or just don't like him?" Max asked.

"Both. Hey, this is a mystery wrapped in an enigma, Max. I'm to the point that I don't trust anyone."

Nathan took the call just as he got back to Omaha.

"What now?"

"Well, I have news about our friend in Room 313."

"Get to the point."

"He is awake and can talk. But he has amnesia. He doesn't even remember his own name. The doctors have some fancy name for his condition, but they don't know if, or when, his memory might return. Apparently it can be weeks, months, or maybe never. What do you want me to do?"

"Nothing. I took care of things my own way. In fact, I don't think he's a threat anymore. But keep me informed anyway." Nathan hung up and wheeled the pickup into the lot of the dealership, whistling to himself.

Malone parked under the same trees, walked up the sidewalk, and knocked on the door.

"Hello, Detective, please come in." For once, Susan Wilson looked pleasant.

"Hi, Susan," Malone said as he entered the house and followed Susan into the living room.

"Susan," Malone began, "we checked your bank records, and thanks to having James's computer, found that they match his online records."

"Why wouldn't they?"

"Just a precaution, Susan. It wouldn't be the first time a bank officer altered records."

"You have got to be kidding me."

"Actually, it seldom ever happens. But it's our job to make sure we don't overlook anything. Which brings me to the reason for my visit. We found a $60,000 transfer from Hampton National Bank in Grand Rapids, Michigan to James's account at Community. That transaction was followed by a check written to St. John's for the same amount."

"Well, that only confirms that James made a donation to the school. What's the big deal about it?"

"Do you know the account balance in Hampton Bank?"

"No. That account belongs to James. We've never discussed it."

"He never told you that his current holdings, including that account plus other investments, amount to over one million dollars?"

"One million dollars!" Susan gasped, as she sat down.

"You weren't aware of this?"

"No. I knew James's uncle had left him a nice sum of money that paid for his college education and he said there was some left, but he didn't want to touch it unless an emergency arose. We did discuss the donation and he said he was taking it out of his account, so it wouldn't affect our personal budget. I had no idea it was that much money!"

"Would anyone else know about it?"

"I don't think so. After all, even I didn't know the amount."

"The bank in Michigan has agreed to contact us should James or anyone else attempt to access the account."

"How could they do that?"

"They couldn't, but James could."

"Why would he?"

"This adds another dimension to the case, Susan. We now have to consider kidnapping, blackmail, or both."

"Oh God, you don't think…"

"Our job is to find James, and we will consider anything that may be relevant. I have to get back to the Safety Center, but I'll keep you informed."

"Thank you, Larry." Susan spoke with a sincerity he had not seen before.

Larry headed back to the Safety Center, and found Max pouring over James Wilson's financial records.

"What have you found?" Larry asked

"Looks like the uncle left him about $650,000, and the original deposit occurred about six months after his uncle's death. The bank verified this and they are sending a history of his records, including investments. Fortunately he did everything at this bank. Apparently the bank president, Greg Messing, and his uncle were friends, so James just let him continue to handle the account. Mr. Messing advises James on a regular basis, and they're cooperating fully."

"Back to square one?"

"Yep, looks that way. Hey, it's time to call it a day. Are you going out with what's-her-name tonight?"

"No, and she has a name. It's Mary."

"Excuse *me!*" Max said, raising his eyebrows.

"Is your wife still out of town?" Larry asked.

"Yes. And she has a name, too." Max added with indignation.

"I know, and her name is Natalie."

"Now that we've established that, I was thinking that you owe me a burger and a couple of beers," Max said.

"Why's that?"

"For sending me out to see that wacko, Sarah Hardin, that's why."

"Yeah, sorry about that. C'mon. We both could use a night out." Larry smiled and slapped Max on the back as they walked out to their cars.

Council Bluffs, Iowa
That Evening

Sam lay in bed that night looking at his pictures until he finally fell asleep. When he awoke the next morning, he looked at them again for a while before he put them back in his backpack. He then gathered his other belongings and packed them. It was time to get out of the shelter for a while; he was beginning to feel cooped up.

The weather was getting warm and he felt free on the streets. He thanked Father Shanks for his hospitality and headed for the door. He stepped out and looked at the sky. It was warm, the humidity was high, and the sky was black. The rain was light but there was not a hint of wind. Sam remembered the tornado that had ripped down Dodge Street in Omaha in the 1980s, destroying everything in its path. The sky looked the same: dark, menacing clouds rolling over one another.

Sam decided to go back into the shelter to wait out the storm. He anxiously watched the weather channel on television, and saw that the rain wasn't going to let up until late that night. Another day in the shelter. At least it was dry. He took his pictures and retired to his bunk for the rest of the day, not bothering to unpack.

Dr. Cantelli kept in touch with patient 313's progress through Whitney Westin, who ensured that Social Services continued to help provide him care.

"Hey, Larry, I thought I should call you on this one." Larry recognized the voice on the line as Captain Rosen of the Nebraska State Patrol and head of the Drug Division.

"What's up, Mark?"

"One of our informants needed cash, and met with Officer Hamilton last night. Said he had some information about that missing guy, James Wilson."

"So why didn't you send him to me?"

"He would only meet with Terry. Probably because Terry has never jammed him up before. Anyway, he claims he heard on the street that Wilson was involved in drugs in a big way. Mostly meth, but other stuff too."

"I knew there had to be more to this story. I kept telling Max we had to follow the money, but everything kept checking out."

"You know how creative these scumbags can get, Larry."

"Yeah. What about the wife?" Malone asked.

"Her name never came up. We're getting a search warrant for their house and the pharmacy. We should have it in an hour or so, if Judge Busch finishes court on time."

"When are you going to serve the warrant?"

"Susan Wilson finishes her shift at the hospital at six tonight, and the pharmacy closes at the same time. I've assembled two teams and we want to hit the pharmacy at closing, and be at Wilson's house when she gets home."

Larry had begun to bond a little with Susan Wilson and still felt sorry for her. He really didn't think she was involved in any way, and asked, "Can I join you at the Wilson house?"

"Don't see why not."

Larry called Max and told him the situation.

"I just feel sorry for her. But you know it won't get in the way of my job," Malone assured Max.

"I know, but just be an observer, okay?" Max was emphatic. Larry couldn't see the eye roll.

"Okay. I just wanted you to know."

"Thanks." Larry was sitting in his car in front of her house when Susan Wilson returned from work. She had no more than unlocked the door when three more cars pulled up in front of her home. It wasn't Larry's jurisdiction, so all he could do was watch them serve the warrant. He witnessed the anger and defiance expressed by Susan Wilson when the warrant was served. Larry couldn't hold himself back any longer. He went up the steps and asked Captain Rosen if he could speak with the subject. Captain Rosen said he would allow it, but she couldn't enter the house.

Larry said, "Susan, let's go to my car and we can talk about this situation." Susan realized she had no choice and accompanied Larry to his car. Larry explained that this was a tip from an unreliable informant probably just looking for a quick buck. He advised Susan to wait with him until they satisfied themselves that there was no truth to the allegation. She finally agreed, began sobbing, and between sobs put her head on his shoulder. It made him uncomfortable, but he knew she needed to vent, so he let her cry on his shoulder.

Thirty minutes later, Larry found himself helping her out of his car and turning her over to Captain Rosen and his team. Larry advised her that she should accompany the officers to the station, and call her lawyer immediately.

As soon as the officers left with Susan, Larry called Max. "Max, you're not going to believe this. They found money and drugs in the house."

"Wow!" came Max's reply. "Do you think she knew?"

"Right now I don't know what to think!"

Max advised his senior partner, "Larry, go home. Get some sleep. We can discuss this tomorrow. You aren't thinking straight right now."

For once, Larry took Max's advice and went home.

PART TWO

THREE MONTHS LATER

CHAPTER 11

Council Bluffs, Iowa

J AMES PUSHED THE WHEELCHAIR ALONG the sidewalk. Sweat ran down his face and soaked his shirt in the humid August heat. He winced and grabbed his side as the exertion triggered the pain from his healing ribs. The pain ebbed, and he paused to look at the painters as they set up scaffolding along the front of the one-story, flat-roof stucco building. He noted their white overalls stained and dotted with dozens of colors of paint.

The buzz at the supper table the previous night was that the building was about to get a new coat of paint, and James hoped it would not be stark white again. The building was his rehabilitation center, and he thought another color would make it look less sterile and more like a home.

James heard a grunt from the man in the wheelchair. It was kind of an "arrrrgh" sound. James reached in the bag attached to the side of the wheelchair, pulled out a pack of Marlboros and groped around to find a book of matches. He placed a cigarette in the wheelchair man's mouth and lit it with a match. A deep inhalation followed by an exhalation of a copious amount of smoke led to another "arrrrgh." He knew by now that this was a "Thank you." James nodded and sat on the green grass beside the sidewalk while the cigarette turned from a white stick into a long gray ash.

This was James Wilson's life for now. He would awaken for breakfast, eat with twenty or so other patients, and report for physical therapy. Physical therapy was a grueling regimen, and tested his resolve. James liked his therapist. Her name was Grace. She was young, probably in her twenties, had long dark hair, and gorgeous brown eyes. She was also all business, and he worked hard to please her, as well as improve his own condition. By lunch he was exhausted, but he could feel the improvement every day.

The afternoon brought his psychotherapy session. His first therapist was a male, and he found him condescending and demeaning. He drilled James, grilled him, and tried to force him to remember information stored somewhere in his head. James rebelled, and now he had a new therapist. Her name was Kim, and she was more understanding, less demanding, and told James she would work with him as long as necessary to help him regain his memory.

Kim had seen the x-rays, read the diagnosis of amnesia, and heard the opinions of both the psychiatrist and neurologist that his memory might never return. She was determined to prove the doctors wrong. James's frustration would often interfere with any progress, but that was to be expected. When his mind reached its melting point, rather than pushing him, Kim suggested he work it off by helping the other patients. That was why he was behind the wheelchair. He pushed it around to the side door and back to the dining room.

After supper, he would help other patients recovering from accidents or strokes while they regained use of arms and legs. He would hold their playing cards, move their checker pieces, or just sit and talk. It was good therapy, made him forget—forget that he couldn't remember. He found it kind of ironic.

He tried to stretch the days out in an attempt to delay the night. When he was alone in his bed, the nightmares would return, along with the headaches, and he would often awaken other residents with a scream. It seemed that the harder he tried to remember in his sessions, the greater the headaches and more frequent the nightmares. At times, he just wished he had died.

Dr. Cantelli kept in touch with patient 313 through his occasional contact with Whitney Weston. She kept him informed of his current status, and had no good news over the past two months.

Sam had visited the hospital only to find out there was a new patient in Room 313. He asked where the former patient had gone, and the only reply from the nurse was that he was transferred to another hospital for rehabilitation therapy. Sam was satisfied that he had no more responsibility and shuffled out of the hospital to return to the streets.

Grand Island, Nebraska

She held her baby bump. Her pregnancy was extraordinary, exhilarating...sad. She wanted James there to share her joy. She had no idea where he was or if he was dead or alive. The baby kept her going, kept her hopes up, kept her from dropping into a depression.

Her mother had stayed on for a month after the drug incident, but had left to go back home to Minnesota. Now it was just her and the baby.

Susan's attorney had gotten her released on her own recognizance the night of her arrest, pending charges from the county attorney's office. Malone and Worthy had both supported her innocence, as the phone call about the drugs had only referred to her husband, and if involved, she was a savvy enough woman to have gotten any evidence out of the house. The justice system moves slowly, however, and since the hospital had put her on administrative leave pending charges, it left her with more spare time to think about James, her future, and continue to wonder if the baby would grow up without a father. Her friends were supportive, but their visits became less frequent as time went on. She didn't know if it was because they had to get back to their own lives, or were shunning her because of the possible drug charges.

A warrant had been issued for James' arrest on possession of controlled substances. Susan tried to convince herself that this was a good thing, hoping that it would add incentive for the police to expand their search for James.

How could my world get turned upside down in just a few short days? One minute I tell my husband we are having a baby...the next minute he disappears...and now I may be charged with possession of illegal drugs. It can't possibly get any worse. I'll take a nap, get out of my pajamas, and go shop for some baby clothes. Clear my mind. Susan curled up, cradled her belly in her arms, and fell asleep.

Two miles across town, Detectives Malone and Worthy were in the office catching up on paperwork.

"Hey, Lar, have you called Susan Wilson this week?" Worthy asked.

"No. What would I tell her? 'Your scumbag husband left town in a hurry,' or 'your scumbag husband got himself whacked'? 'All over some drug deal gone bad'?" Larry shrugged.

"You don't really believe that," Max said.

"No, I don't. In fact, I think it's probably a setup. But why? And who?" Larry put his head in his hands, and just sat for a couple of minutes. He raised his head, rubbed his eyes, sliding his fingertips over his cheeks, and just shook his head. "The guy's too clean. Susan Wilson is too clean. Then this phone call comes out of nowhere. When I talked to Officer Hamilton, he told me the informant is a meth addict. They met, exchanged money for information, and he felt he should follow up on it. That's the way it works. An addict, who is also a known informant, needs money for drugs. Cops pay money for information, and that helps get drug dealers off the street. Certainly not a perfect situation. Hamilton thinks it was a setup too, but he can't find the informant to question him further. He's gone off the grid."

Malone continued. "You know the pharmacy records checked out; no large quantities of ephedrine or pseudoephedrine, just average inventory. Granted, Wilson has access to the chemicals and certainly the background to manufacture meth. It just adds to probable cause, and muddies up the water. Anyway," Malone shrugged, "Hamilton's going to continue checking and keep us in the loop."

"I agree," Max said, "My grandmother could find a better hiding place than a shoebox, for Christ's sake. Maybe it's just to throw us off the track or to cover the real reason he's missing."

Larry said, "Yeah, and that means he was abducted and is probably still alive."

"And when we do find him, he's going away for a long time," Max said. "So Wilson is screwed either way. Whoever is responsible for this is really covering his bases. My grandfather used to joke about wearing a belt and a pair of suspenders just in case. Guess this guy has the same philosophy, or is really smart."

"Or really desperate," Larry suggested. "We need to re-think this one Max. There's more to this than meets the eye. Maybe Susan's constant interference caused us to overlook something obvious. I say we go back to day one, walk our way through it slowly and see what we may have missed the first time. But not today, we'll start tomorrow. Let's call it a day and get a beer. It's 4:45 and we're off in fifteen minutes anyway."

"Aye, aye captain. Me throat is beginning to feel parched, and me butt is beginning to get calluses. Let's go."

Larry was beginning to like having Max for a partner.

Ted Bingham was back at St. John's and coaching football. He finally had reconciled himself to the fact there would be Harlan Jensens wherever he taught, so he decided to live with the situation. Over the summer he had enrolled at the University of Nebraska at

Kearney to earn credits toward his master's degree. He had driven the forty-five miles west to Kearney three days a week for summer session. The other two days he helped a painting contractor to earn extra money. He had returned to the school with a new attitude.

Omaha, Nebraska

One hundred and thirty miles away, Nathan was back to his cocky old self. Jason and Tom resumed their weekly lunches with him at the Good Times Brewery and Jason had finally put closure on the incident. Tom, of course, knew nothing about it.

Nathan kept his eyes on James Wilson, however, keeping his sources close. It had been four months since his unsuccessful murder attempt on James, but he felt his tracks were covered. Even if James's memory returned, there was probably a warrant out for his arrest, and the planted evidence would assure him of a prison sentence. Nathan moved on with his two lives, the auto dealership and his drug dealing, both providing him with a substantial income.

Nathan's cell pinged one day while he was at lunch with his friends. He looked at the screen, recognized the number, opened his phone and said curtly, "Why are you calling me on my personal phone?... I don't give a rat's ass...I'll call you back in a while!"

"Problem, Nathan?" Jason asked with a smirk on his face. "Somebody piss in your cereal this morning?"

"Watch your mouth, Jason, or I'll be pissing in yours!"

"Hey, chill man. I'm just messing with you," Jason said as he grinned and hit Nathan in the arm.

"No sweat. Gotta go. Business calls." Nathan got up to leave. He threw some cash on the table. "Next week, same time."

"Whoa. I haven't seen him like that in a while," Tom said, watching Nathan's brisk stride out the door. "What the hell's going on with him?"

"Probably just lost a car sale," Jason said, feigning a laugh. Inside, his gut was churning. Nathan had assured him everything was all right, but Jason had never gotten past the incident.

Tom raised his hand, slapped Jason a high five. "See you next week," he said, as he got up and left. Jason sat alone for a few minutes, considered ordering a strong drink, then thought better of it. His gut told him that this thing was going to come back and bite him in the ass, despite Nathan's assurances that it was under control. Hell, he really never knew the whole story and doubted that Nathan would tell him even if he asked. To make matters worse, things weren't going well at home. He and Amy seemed to be fighting more than usual. He had to find a way to put this matter to bed and be rid of it. It was like a cancer that had invaded his life, and its carnage had spread to his marriage, his job, and his life in general. Filled with despair, he walked to his car, oblivious to the sleek black Ford Expedition parked across the street from the bar.

The occupant in the Expedition watched Jason walk to his car, shoulders slumped, head down, a hang dog look on his face. Nathan pursed his lips into a sneer and let out a sigh. What to do now? *As if I don't have enough problems without Jason losing it again! Dumb son of a bitch. Why doesn't he just go home and screw that good looking wife of his and forget about Wilson!?*

Nathan waited for Jason to drive off before he started his car and pulled away from the curb, heading east across the river. He had gotten about a mile from the bar, was getting pissed off at the noon traffic, when his throwaway phone chirped. He pulled it off the console, flipped it open, and answered brusquely, "What?" He listened for a minute, tried to control his anger, and finally said, "Okay, what's the big deal? If you hadn't fucked up the first time, there wouldn't be any problem. Now the state wants to cut him loose. We need to keep tabs on him. You run a shelter; make sure that's where Social Services place Wilson...Look, I don't care what you have to do to get it done: bribe somebody—threaten them—I really don't give a shit how you do it, just do it!...Yeah, yeah, call me when you know." Nathan snapped the phone shut and flung it back at the console, watching it bounce onto the floorboard of the passenger side.

Jesus, where do I find these idiots?

Nathan continued on. He crossed the bridge into Iowa, and wasn't far from the downtown area of Council Bluffs. He was looking for a couple of low rent properties close to a middle class area of town. His meth business was going well in Omaha and Grand Island, and Council Bluffs seemed to present an opportunity. Besides, it was close to home, and easy to keep his eye on. He had marked five properties for rent on an internet site. After driving past all of them, he thought about the first one. It wasn't too shabby. The owner had let it run down so that it matched the other dilapidated homes in the area, and yet it stood out as an ideal location, right next to a fairly well kept neighborhood, and needing just a little repair. Something to negotiate about with the realty company to lower the rent. Besides, rental home owners loved tenants who were willing to fix their place up a bit, as it did the neighbors. It had the added advantage of two weedy vacant lots between it and the next house. That would allow the cat urine odor to dissipate. From Nathan's perspective, it was the ideal place for a meth lab, because it would draw absolutely no suspicion from the neighbors or the police.

Nathan went back to the dealership and opened his file cabinet. He had a man in Grand Island who was the obvious choice to get his lab started. Tomas had been at one of his Grand Island labs for almost two years, had a clean record, and would fit well into the neighborhood. He was also a welder by trade, and Nathan had recently seen an ad in the *Daily Nonpareil* newspaper help wanted section looking for welders. He contacted Tomas and told him to meet him in Omaha the following morning at the dealership, under the pretense of searching for a new car. There was one other consideration that was in Nathan's favor. Council Bluffs had three casinos, and Tomas was totally opposed to gambling, another plus in his corner.

CHAPTER 12

DR. CANTELLI LOOKED UP AND saw Whitney Weston standing in the doorway to his office. "Hey. Are you just going to stand there, or are you coming in?" he asked with a smile.

"Just came to give you the news. The state is terminating physical therapy for patient 313. They'll continue psychotherapy but only on an outpatient basis."

"So what happens now?" Cantelli asked.

"Now," Whitney said, "I have until the end of the month to find him a place to stay and a lot of paperwork to get done. Just thought you would like to know."

"Thanks, Whitney. I appreciate your updating me on his progress."

Whitney left, and Cantelli sat at his desk thoughtfully, his mind lost in thought. *No memory. No progress mentally. Poor guy. Will he ever be right again? Unbelievable. He must have a family somewhere wondering where he is. He was just in the wrong place at the wrong time. Or was he?*

Whitney went back to her desk and started on 313's case; she had a volume of paperwork to get started on him. He was using the name John Doan for the time being, a version of John Doe. In addition to medical treatment, she would now need housing for him, a possible job, and something more permanent in the form of identification. She would also have to explore other avenues such as state-assisted wage employer incentives. She was glad it was close to the end of the day. She would wait until tomorrow to dig into it.

Detective Malone was already at his desk when Detective Worthy arrived at work.

"Wow, Larry! You're here pretty early." Max said.

"Yeah, I told you we needed to start at square one on the Wilson case. I thought about it all night and decided if I was going to be awake, I might as well be working."

"Okay, so what have you got?"

"Not much. I'm just going over the notes from our initial interviews, trying to find something we may have missed or overlooked."

"And?" Max asked, as he pulled a donut out of the sack in his hand. He noticed the exasperated look on Larry's face and said, "You want one? I bought two."

"Wouldn't think of interfering with your healthy breakfast," Malone said, with a roll of his eyes.

"So what have you got?" Max asked through a mouthful of donut, the powdered sugar clinging to his lips and chin.

"So far, not much. I did notice we never talked to that teacher Wilson called the Monsignor about."

"We ruled him out." Max said.

"No, the principal, Harlan Jensen, ruled him out." Larry said. "Remember...Jensen said the teacher wasn't aware of the phone call until the day after Wilson disappeared. We never talked to the teacher."

"Think it will help?" Max asked.

"I don't know, but I'm going to follow up on it. Why don't you start going over your notes. Maybe something will jump out at you."

"Yeah...maybe Susan Wilson in a bikini?" Max said as he mimicked someone jumping out of a cake with his arms raised.

"Hey, watch the Susan Wilson comments."

"I'm not the dumb shit who sat in his car holding her hand while the narcs searched her house."

"Max...go fuck yourself!" Malone said as he turned an about face and stomped out of the office.

Whitney Weston went to the rehab center to talk to James. She explained to him that he would have to leave the rehabilitation center at the end of the month, as the state would no longer pay for his physical rehabilitation. The state was going to allow him to continue his psychotherapy and Kim would remain his therapist, but he would have to live elsewhere at the beginning of October.

Whitney left the rehab center and returned to her office. To her surprise, Father Shanks was waiting for her. He said he'd been in the area with a little time and thought he'd stop in and make a social call. He smiled warmly at her, and Whitney gladly poured them each a cup of coffee so they could visit a bit. They discussed the difficulty of her current caseload, and during the conversation, the subject of 313 came up. She expressed concern about his predicament, and Father Shanks volunteered the services of his shelter until more suitable arrangements could be made. Whitney was pleased to have the issue of housing solved so readily, and agreed to the plan; Father Shanks said he would contact 313 and make arrangements to transport him to the shelter near the end of September.

Father Shanks showed up at the rehab center two days later. He introduced himself to 313, told him that Whitney had asked for him to move to his shelter as soon as his physician released him from physical therapy.

James was upset about having to move again, but he was learning to accept change, and knew he was not mentally capable of living on his own.

"What name should I call you?" Father Shanks asked.

"Well, when I moved in, Whitney suggested I pick a name. After some thought, I decided on John. No particular reason, it just struck me as a name I liked."

"John it is, then." Father Shanks said, adding, "John was one of the twelve apostles, so you have a noble name."

Two weeks later, James, aka John, was riding to the shelter in Father Shanks's Ford Explorer. Father Shanks showed him to his room, and introduced him to some of the habitual residents, and left him to get acquainted, telling him supper was in the dining room at 5:30. "John" adjusted to the routine in a few days, but was happy to see Kim, his therapist, when she came to the shelter for therapy.

"My nightmares are getting worse," he said. "I dream about snakes, and wake up screaming almost every night. I don't know if the other people will tolerate it much longer."

"I'll talk to Father Shanks," Kim said. "Maybe he can get you in a room further away from the others." That afternoon, he was moved to the far end of the hall away from the other homeless people.

The dog days of summer had cooled off in September and now the unpredictable cool and rainy days of October approached. The cool nights told Sam it was time to start frequenting the shelter again.

He walked in the door, saw a few of the habituals, the same people he had left at the beginning of summer, and noticed that they were still living in the relative comfort of the facility. When it was time for supper, Sam went into the dining hall and was stunned to see patient 313 sitting alone at a table.

What the hell is he doing here? Christ. How does this guy keep showing up? Feeling his detachment beginning to wane, Sam got his food tray and made a point to join 313. Sam asked if he could sit with him, and when James said, "Please do," Sam sat down and asked his name.

"John."

"Nice to meet you, John," Sam said, extending his hand.

One hundred thirty miles away, Susan Wilson decided to paint the room for the baby. She called the painter who had painted her house that summer to do the room for her. He told her he was busy, but would have one of the men he worked with stop by.

The next day, Ted Bingham stopped by to see Susan Wilson. He was acquainted with her because he had worked on her house during the summer. She told him what she wanted, and he said he could do the job the following weekend, as there was no football game for St. John's.

"Oh, do you work for St. John's?" Susan asked.

"Yeah, I teach and coach basketball. This fall I'm helping with the football team."

"I attend St. John's Church," Susan said. "My husband and I made a contribution to your new gymnasium," she added.

"Oh yeah, I remember now. You were both at the dedication. The team is looking forward for basketball practice to start this year so we can use the new facility." Suddenly catching himself, Ted added, "Wasn't your husband the one who disappeared?"

Susan held back the tears. "Yes," she said, "I still don't know what happened to him."

"I'm really sorry," Ted said. "I didn't realize who you were when we painted the outside of your house last summer."

"It's okay," Susan said. "I just have to accept it, but I still hope that he will return home safely." She shuffled her feet uncomfortably, looked down, then said, "I'd rather not talk about it right now; I'll see you next weekend."

"Yep, Saturday morning. I have the paint color and number, so I will pick it up and be ready to go. Must be a boy, huh?"

"Wow," Susan said, "you figure things out pretty quickly for a schoolteacher!"

"Well, you know, blue and all." Ted replied, his eyes twinkling as the topic got onto safer ground.

"Yes, and his name will be James, just like his father."

Ted smiled and headed out the door, the uncomfortableness of the situation still churning in his stomach. *If only he knew...*

Back in Council Bluffs, John was asking Sam a million questions. He had spent the day meeting some of the other residents of the shelter, and recognized that Sam was different than most of the other homeless people. Out of place in the shelter, Sam appeared to be educated and self-assured, and he somehow just didn't belong here.

It took Sam all of five minutes to tell John that he just wanted to finish his supper and didn't care for any more questions. John complied. There was something about Sam that asserted authority without dominance. John felt he had known someone similar to Sam in the past, but his memory remained blocked and he just let it go. He started to head for his new room as soon as the meal was over, but noticed that some of the other residents were clearing plates, wiping tables, and straightening chairs. John jumped in to help, eager to prove he was thankful to have a roof over his head.

Charlotte, a tough looking girl of perhaps twenty, with half of her black hair dyed purple, wearing a short black skirt and a tight gaudy teal shirt that showed enough cleavage to float a small watercraft, took John aside. John remembered her name was Charlotte, but everyone called her Char. He wondered if she was a hooker or just an unfortunate human being.

"Look," Char said, "whatever your name is, if you're still here in a week, you'll be assigned some duties in the shelter. You may be cleaning, cooking, waiting tables, or doing housework. Father Shanks makes a schedule every week, and posts it on the bulletin board." She pointed to a large corkboard on the wall at the end of the dining room. The corkboard was covered with typed papers and dozens of post-it notes.

"Thank you," John said, adding, "I'm just trying to get off on the right track."

"If you really want to start off on the right track, shut up your fucking yelling during the night. It keeps me awake and I'm getting tired of it, so knock it off!"

Stunned, John watched the defiance in Char's stride as she left the room.

John's headaches had been escalating, and it frightened him. He was terrified of what he might discover if his memory did return. Sometimes not knowing was a blessing compared to what he imagined about the truth. When he allowed his mind to wander, the fabricated versions of his prior life dominated his thoughts. *What am I? I could be a schoolteacher, a lawyer, a laborer, even a criminal. What if I killed someone? Could they still send me to jail even though I don't remember a thing? Do I have a family? Probably not. They would be looking for me—unless they don't want to see me again.*

Dejected, John walked down the hall to his new room. He sat on the side of his bed with his head in his hands. When the tears stopped, he took off his clothes and crawled into bed. He pulled the covers up tight under his chin, as if this would ward off the evil dreams the night would bring.

John awakened with a start, bolting upright in his bed. The thunderstorm raged outside, sending booms of thunder and flashes of deadly lightning illuminating his room through the closed curtains.

He was startled by a figure sitting beside his bed. The lightning subsided for a few minutes, and he cowered in fear, expecting to be harmed. As his eyes adjusted to the dark, the lightning flashed again, showing the figure to be Sam, the man he had met at dinner.

His voice was gentle. "No need to be afraid. I'm not here to harm you."

"Was I screaming again?" John asked.

"Yes. Something about snakes, bites, boats, or something. My room is two down and I heard you yelling. When I came in the room you were covering your head and face with your arms, like you were trying to fend off a blow. It's okay now. You can relax and go back to sleep. If you don't mind, I'll just sit here and wake you if the dreams start again."

"But you don't even know me."

"Sure I do. I met you at supper, remember?"

John gave a long look to Sam before nodding in appreciation. Sam smiled, and John laid his head back down. He slept the rest of the night, at least what was left of it. When he awoke, Sam was gone. John walked down to the restroom and showered, dressed, and walked into the dining room for breakfast. He saw that Sam was already there, sitting at a table by himself. John filled his tray, walked over to Sam's table, and said, "May I join you?"

"Please do," came the response. Before John could speak, Sam said, "Let's not talk about last night. This is a new day."

John told Sam that he had a meeting with his social worker later that morning. He explained his situation to Sam. "The doctors in the hospital told me I was mugged and beaten. My physical injuries have healed, but I've got amnesia, and can't remember anything about my past. I don't even know if my name is really John; I just picked it so people could call me something."

Sam nodded in understanding.

John went on. "My psychologist feels I'm making progress with my memory, and says the nightmares are my subconscious trying to jar my conscious thoughts back to reality." John slapped his palm on his forehead in frustration and shook his head. "I don't know. Sometimes I think it's hopeless. My brain still gets things I should know all mixed up."

Sam didn't say anything.

John began to feel uneasy and apologized, "I'm sorry, Sam; I shouldn't have dumped all my troubles on you."

Sam sat there in silence while John's discomfort grew, then said, "I think you may be in the wrong room. Why don't you get ready for your meeting with your social worker, and I'll see you later."

John stared in astonishment as Sam stood up and walked away from the table. *What in the world did he mean, wrong room?* John checked his watch and realized he had better get going or he would be late for his appointment with Whitney.

Ted Bingham stood on the sidelines talking to one of his players. Malone waited patiently while he was explaining a pass pattern to the player. Ted slapped him on the helmet, and said, "Now get in there and do it right this time."

"Ted Bingham?" Malone asked.

"Yeah. Sorry, but I'm coaching right now."

Malone said, "I can see that. After all, I am a detective," he added with a smile as he raised his badge.

"Can't this wait 'til after practice?"

"Tell you what, Ted. You give me five minutes and you can finish your practice, okay? Or…we can go to the Safety Center and you can come back tomorrow. Your choice, Ted."

Ted stood for a minute, then turned and yelled, "Pat, take the ends for a little bit."

"Let's sit," suggested Malone as he headed for the bleachers.

"What's this all about?" Ted asked.

"Tell me about the gym dedication, Ted."

Ted got a confused look on his face. "You mean the dedication last spring?"

"Was there more than one?" Malone asked.

"No," Ted said, adding, "but I don't know what you want to talk to me about the dedication for."

"Harlan Jensen said you had an altercation with a student afterward. Is that correct?"

"Yeah, but that's past history. Harlan was pretty pissed off, but I thought that was the end of it."

"Did you know James Wilson?"

"I met him briefly after the dedication. I thanked him for the donation, started to leave, and that's when this student opened his big mouth. I admit, I should have let it go, but we exchanged some words, and a lot of people heard us, including James Wilson."

"Did you confront Wilson after the incident?"

"No. I didn't even know he had called Monsignor Kelly until the day after the dedication when Harlan Jensen reamed me out for it."

"Are you aware that James Wilson went missing after the dedication?"

"Yeah, the whole school knew. Probably the whole town," Ted said.

"What did you do after the dedication?" Malone asked.

"I went home to change clothes. I had invited some college buddies to come and one of them, Nathan, was staying over. We were going out on the town."

"And did you go out on the town?"

"Well, yeah. But not with him."

"So why not with him?"

"I waited at my apartment, but he didn't show up. I called him about twenty minutes after I got home, but he said he had to go back to Omaha. Apparently something came up at his car dealership and he had to head back..." Ted's voice trailed off as horror crossed his face. "You don't think...?"

"I don't think anything, Ted. I'm just trying to get the facts straight. So let's get the timeline for your whereabouts, okay? Start with the time you left the dedication and end when you came home that evening."

"I don't have exact times. It took me maybe fifteen minutes to get out of the gym, ten minutes to get home, ten minutes to change, and then I waited about twenty minutes for Nathan to show up, and that's when I called him. I got mad when I found out he had left without calling me, and headed to Ed and Nettie's to join some of the other teachers. I stayed late, and then went home to bed."

"Fair enough. What time did the dedication end?"

"I don't know. Maybe 4:45 or 5:00."

"Okay, so you left at say...five o'clock, twenty minutes to get your car and get home, ten minutes to get dressed, and waited twenty minutes for your friend to show up. That would put the time at about six o'clock or maybe ten minutes earlier. Then you went straight to the bar. Does that sound right?"

"Yeah, that's about right. I was hungry by the time I got there, so it must have been close to six. So why are you talking to me? Rumor is he got tired of his marriage and just took off."

"We don't know, but it's my job to find out. You played football in college, right?" Malone asked.

"Yeah, so?" Ted said indignantly.

"So maybe you decided to take your anger out on Wilson."

"I already told you that I didn't even know Wilson called the Monsignor until the next morning!" Ted said with a glare.

"And maybe someone else heard him call and told you right after the dedication," Malone asserted.

"Well, you're the detective, so why don't you ask around and find out?"

Malone had planted the seed; now it was time to get things back on track.

"What are the names of your three friends from Omaha?"

"Nathan Landry, Tom Meyer, and Jason Hughes."

"Okay. I doubt if you know their phone numbers or addresses off the top of your head, and you want to get back to practice, so let's do this. Here's my card. Either drop off the information I need at the Safety Center, or email it to me. My email address is on the card. In addition, I want the name of everyone who was with you at the bar, and anyone who may not have been with you but saw you there."

Ted toyed with telling the detective that he would be painting a room for Mrs. Wilson, but decided to let sleeping dogs lie. After all, he didn't have a clue what had happened to Wilson, and whether or not he painted a room for Mrs. Wilson was really none of Malone's business. Instead he just said, "I'll get it for you tonight after practice."

Time to be the nice cop. Malone thanked Ted, then nodded at the field and added, "Your end seems to have plenty of speed and quickness, but he needs a new set of hands."

"Yeah, he's only a sophomore. Got to learn to catch the ball before he starts to run with it. He'll figure it out soon; he's a smart kid." Ted shook Malone's hand and loped back onto the field.

Malone left with mixed feelings. This didn't seem like the Ted Bingham Harlan Jensen had talked about.

Malone was tired and decided to take his notes home with him and go over them with a much-needed beer in his hand. On his way home, Mary, whom he still dated occasionally, called his cell.

"What's up, Mary?" His usual phone greeting was, "Malone," but she had earned a slot on his phone contact list.

"What are you doing for supper?" she asked.

"Just heading home to check the fridge and see what's in there that's still edible."

"I just fixed a pot of soup and was looking for someone to share it with. Thought you might be interested."

"What kind of soup?"

"You'll have to stop over if you want to find out."

"All right, what time?"

"Anytime in the next hour. Oh, and if you want a beer, you'll have to bring your own." Malone could hear the smile in her voice as she said, "See you in a bit."

Malone smiled as he stopped off at a liquor store, thinking. *The notes can wait. The beer, I need now. Some days just get better as they go on.*

Malone got home about eleven. To his surprise, he had an email from Ted Bingham. The addresses and phone numbers of

Bingham's three friends were listed, as well as the names of the teachers he joined, and the name of the bartender and other people he had seen in the bar. Malone printed two copies, and hit the hay.

The next morning Malone was waiting for Max. "Okay, partner, we have work to do. Bingham was very cooperative. He gave me a list of the names of three guys who came to the dedication from Omaha. Apparently college buddies of his. Two of them were headed back, and one was going to stay over with Bingham. As it turned out, all of them headed back afterwards. Bingham claims he went to Ed and Netties bar with some other teachers and spent the evening there."

"I still think we need to check it out. I'll call his buddies in Omaha. You talk to the teachers on the list and anyone else who might have seen him at the bar. Let's pay particular attention to the timeline, he didn't account for the time he left the bar until he went to school the next morning. That leaves plenty of time to do a lot of things."

"Yeah, but he didn't know about the call until the next day."

"That's what Harlan Jensen said. Who's to say someone else didn't hear the call and tell Bingham about it that evening?"

"I see where you're headed," Max nodded. "Maybe we screwed up when we assumed Jensen was correct."

"Yeah, maybe," Larry said. "But at the time we really didn't suspect foul play. In fact, I didn't expect foul play until those damned drugs and money showed up. Why plant them...unless Wilson is still alive and a threat to someone." It wasn't a question , but a statement of what he'd been suspecting for a long time.

"Or...maybe to get Susan Wilson out of the way," Max said, deep in thought. "She only has her parents who might stand to get her money. No other relatives. There's that pompous banker, Dave Person, who now knows about it, and the bank president in Grand Rapids, Michigan. What was his name—Messing, or something like that? I think we need to talk to Susan's attorney again, follow up with the guy in Michigan and see if he knows an attorney Wilson may have used in Grand Rapids."

"Let's not get the cart before the horse, Max. Those are all possibilities, but let's get Bingham wrapped up first. Like my doctor used to say, 'When you hear hoof beats, think horses. When you can't find any horses, *then* think zebras.'"

CHAPTER 13

T HE SHELTER WAS DESERTED WHEN John returned from his meeting with Whitney. He went to his room, but it was empty. He began to panic. *Did they kick me out because of my nightmares? Was that bitch Char responsible for this?* Confused, he went and knocked on Father Shanks's door. There was no answer. He called out. No one was here. Not knowing what else to do, he went outside and started to walk.

Whitney had told him that he could stay at the shelter until she could find suitable housing for him. She also told him that the state would pay some money for his housing, food, clothing, and medical bills. He didn't remember the amounts. Her good news, or so she thought, was that she had found him a part time job. It was at a McDonald's, but it would give him something to do with all his spare time. Whitney knew that the job was below John's capabilities, as he exhibited superior intelligence and speech, but it was a start for now.

In the next month, the state employment people would administer some tests to determine his level of ability and interests, and try and find something more suitable. His lack of social security number and actual name were an obstacle to full time employment. In fact, the McDonald's would actually pay the State Department of Social Services for his work time. It was all very confusing to John. The more he walked, however, the calmer he felt as the brisk fall air seemed to clear his mind. He noticed the leaves beginning to turn. The oaks and maples gleamed with orange, yellow, and red.

Some of the other tree's leaves just turned a dull shade of brown. He imagined himself a tree; he would be the tree with no name. People would ask what that dull brown tree was, and no one would know. He found it irritating that he could remember the names of trees, but not his own.

He checked his watch. It was four o'clock. Time for supper at five. That is, if he still had a home. He had been walking a long time, not paying much attention to where he was going. Could he even find the shelter? He headed in the direction from which he thought he had come, looking for a recognizable landmark. Nothing looked familiar, and he started to panic. It was getting dark sooner these days, but as he turned the corner, he saw the skylines of Omaha and could figure out which way to go.

As he hurried in that direction, he noticed three young long-haired guys standing on the sidewalk ahead of him. They were all wearing black t-shirts and baggy jeans with chains and buttons on them that barely covered their skinny asses. They were leaning against a crumbling brick building smoking cigarettes. At least he assumed they were cigarettes.

John's first impulse was to cross the street to avoid them, but he was in a hurry to get back, so he kept going. As he began to walk past them, one of them stepped in his path. His face was so close to John he could smell his foul breath. John politely said, "Excuse me," and began to step around him. The punk side-stepped and blocked his path again, while the other two started to chuckle.

"I don't want any trouble," John said. "I just want to get home in time for supper." They all laughed.

"You'll go home when we tell you it's time to go, man. Where you live, anyways?"

"I live at a shelter," John replied, hoping his homelessness would take away the kids' incentive to pick on him.

The punk shoved him backward and said, "Give me your cigs, homeless man."

At first John didn't understand. He asked, "Cigs?"

Another shove. "Yeah, and your money too, if you got any, that is!"

This shove threw John off balance and he fell to the sidewalk catching himself with one hand. The punk was standing over him yelling, "Get your sorry ass up, motherfucker." John got to his knees, and felt the pain burning in his side. He was afraid he had broken his ribs again.

The punk reached down and grabbed John by his shirt collar and started to haul him back up.

John heard a voice behind him say, "I think you better let my friend go."

John tried to see who had spoken, but was off balance and fell to the sidewalk again.

The punk let go and said, "This ain't none of your fucking business, so move on, old man!"

"Well, actually," the voice spoke slowly and confidently, "this man is my friend, and it became my business when you shoved him down."

"Oh yeah, what are you going to do about it?" the punk asked in a confrontational tone, as his friends moved to either side of him.

John was able to look up and see Sam's huge hulk standing behind him. Sam stared at the punk, his eyes almost as black as his skin.

Sam was calm. "I'm going to make you wish you had never gotten out of bed this morning."

"Bring it on, motherfucker, there's three of us," the punk said, raising his fists.

Sam looked at them and said, "I can count; glad to see that you can, too. Now I'm going to tell you one more time. All three of you get moving or get hurt...and I'm going to start with you." Sam pointed his index finger at the mouthy punk.

Sam stood his ground, staring at the three young men, and after what seemed an eternity to John, the punk said, "We was just havin' a little fun," and turned, waving for his buddies to follow him. It was obvious they didn't want to mess with Sam.

"What are you doing here?" John inquired as he regained his composure.

"I was just on my way back to the shelter, and saw that you were facing slightly unfavorable odds, so I decided to even the playing field."

John was at a loss for words, and finally managed to say, "Thank you."

"No problem," Sam said. "Glad I happened to be able to help."

"What are you?" John asked, "some sort of guardian angel?"

Sam laughed. "John, I am about as far from being an angel as you can get. Let's get back to the shelter so we can eat. I'm starved."

John hesitated. "I'm not sure I'm welcome there. I went back earlier and my room had been cleared out. They may not want me."

"Oh yeah," Sam said, smiling. "That was my idea. Couple of the guys helped move your stuff into my room. We're going to be roommates. Sorry I didn't ask you, but I figured you would say no."

"Why would you do that?" John asked with incredulity.

"Damned if I know," Sam said. "Guess I need some company. C'mon, let's get back. I'm hungry."

John replayed his conversation with Whitney for Sam on the way back to the shelter. Sam didn't say much, just listened. They ate at a table with several other residents, so there was little time for a two-way conversation. After dinner, Sam said he was going to bed. John asked if he would wake him up if he stayed up a little later. Sam said, "Don't care how late you stay up, just be quiet when you come to bed. And don't turn the light on. Oh yeah, shut the door in case you have one of those nightmares again." And he was gone.

John complied. He stayed up a while talking to a couple of the other residents, then went into the room, quietly so as not to disturb Sam, undressed, shut the door, and crawled into bed. In the middle of the night, the nightmares returned, and John woke up terrified, but Sam was there, reassuring him that they couldn't hurt him, and he went back to sleep.

The next morning, John started to say something to Sam. Sam looked him in the eye and said, "New day. No sense talking about yesterday. Let's get some breakfast."

After breakfast, Sam got up and was gone. No words, no advice, no indication where he was going. Sam was the strangest man John had ever met. At least he thought he was. He didn't really have anyone to compare him to given his lack of memory.

A mile away, Nathan was meeting Tomas at the rental he'd chosen. He explained his situation, and told Tomas he was going to be the man in charge. He took great pains to impress the importance of anonymity on Tomas's part. He also stressed the need to be a leader and be in charge of the operation. "You answer only to me. You are my number one man in Council Bluffs and I have the utmost confidence in you. You will select one employee to begin with, and train him to be obedient, efficient, and discrete. At the first indication he is using, selling on his own, or in any way jeopardizing the operation, I want to know. Is that understood?"

"Yes, of course," said Tomas.

"Good," said Nathan. "I believe you have seen how I handle disobedience."

"You are a fair man," Tomas said, using bravado to mask his fear of Nathan.

"So we have an understanding, then? Good. Now here is your new identification and the name of the realtor for this rental house. I have given a verbal commitment to rent and all the paperwork is ready to sign. The truck I drove is registered in your new name. I will take your old truck when we leave. Give the realtor this envelope with $6000 inside, and tell him you will pay the rent every six months in advance." He handed Tomas a new cell phone, saying, "Use this to call me only if there is a problem. If I don't get a call, I will expect that within two weeks, you will have moved in, will have someone recruited to help you, and will have the lab up and running in another two weeks after that. Any questions?"

"I assume you will provide the equipment and necessary chemicals," Tomas said.

"It will be delivered next Tuesday along with furniture for the house. Unless you call me with a problem, that is." Nathan handed Tomas an envelope, and said, "This should cover motels until next Tuesday and your first month's salary." They shook hands, and Nathan added, "And I will never see you at this location again." Tomas nodded his agreement and left. Nathan took a final look back at the house, got in Tomas's truck, and drove off.

Neither Tomas nor Nathan had noticed the black homeless man standing in the shadows across the street. He had been walking by when he recognized Nathan and decided to watch the two men. He saw the envelope exchange hands, but it didn't look like a drug deal. Not at ten o'clock in the morning. It was something else. The cell phone was the clincher. It was a throw-away in case of trouble. Landry was making meth and Sam was looking at his new lab. He had been through prosecution, humiliation, despair, and hatred, and now it was time for revenge. He was finally going to get even with that son-of-a-bitch Landry!

CHAPTER 14

"SO HOW DID YOUR DAY go?" Malone asked Max, who looked exasperated.

"Not very productive. I talked to all the teachers on the list, the bartender, and most of the other people Bingham said saw him at the bar. His story checks out. He got there at 6 or 6:15 by most accounts, and stayed until the last of the teachers left around midnight. One of the teachers said they were going to play golf the next day, but it rained and the round was cancelled. So, he can account for his time between six o'clock and midnight."

"Did you ask any of them about the argument with the student?" Malone pressed.

"Didn't have to. Two of them volunteered the information, but they knew nothing about a phone call from Wilson. Apparently Harlan Jensen takes confidentiality seriously. At any rate, one of the teachers, a Miss Ashley, said the kid had it coming. He was a jerk."

"What about the other teacher?" Malone asked.

"He said it was in poor taste, but didn't dwell on it. Oh, and I asked most of them if Bingham seemed different in any way that night. Nervous, up-tight, pre-occupied, whatever. They all said he was normal. Funny, crazy, having a good time. It didn't sound like he was dealing with any moral issues or had just committed a crime. So what about you?"

Malone said, "Be right back." He went to the soft drink dispenser, watched the machine suck in his dollar bill, heard the clunk of the can drop, popped the top on a can of Diet Coke. Then he walked over and plopped his butt on Max's desk. Max looked at him a minute and said, "Okay, I get it. You found out something, but I'm going to have to wait for you to spring it in a 'Malonesque' fashion. Right?"

Malone took a long swig, let out a small belch, paused for a little more effect, then said, "I called all three of Bingham's buddies. First was Nathan Landry, owns Landry Ford in Omaha. He had planned to stay over in Grand Island and go out with Bingham. Claimed he got a call during the dedication, and was needed back at the dealership the next morning, so he left right after it was over. He said there was an issue with a large client of his, and he wanted to handle it personally. I asked him about Bingham's argument with the student and he had seen it. He also added that Bingham had a quick temper, but he was surprised Ted lashed out at a student in front of all those people."

"Then I asked him if he had heard about James Wilson."

"What did he say?" Max asked.

"'Who?' was his reply. He didn't seem to remember Wilson's name or know that he had disappeared. I asked him if he had seen Bingham since the dedication and he said he had. Ted had come to Omaha and spent the evening telling him how pissed he was about the principal chewing him out. I asked him for the date that Ted was there, and he said he thought it was the night after the dedication. They got trashed and Ted slept at his house because his wife was out of town. He claimed that was the last time they talked.

"So...I called the next guy on the list, Tom Meyer. I thought that name was familiar. Turns out he was a deputy sheriff in Hall County for a couple of years, and now is a deputy at the Douglas County Sheriff's Office in Omaha."

"Oh, yeah. I remember him," Max interjected. "Nice guy, good officer. In fact I worked a drug bust with him along with the F.B.I. and the Drug Enforcement Agency a couple of years back," Max said. "So what did he say?"

"Not much," Larry said. "He saw the argument, but he had driven, so he hustled outside to get his car. He said he had to park about four blocks away from the school, on 11ᵗʰ Street. He worked his way back to the school in the traffic to pick up Jason Hughes, the third guy. There were so many people he double-parked and ran into the gymnasium to get Hughes. He didn't see him, so had to do the four block circle a couple of times. Finally he saw him coming down the walk, picked him up, and headed for Omaha. They stopped in Aurora at an Arby's, got some food to go, and were back in Omaha around 8:30 P.M. He knew nothing about Wilson's disappearance either, and hadn't seen or talked to Bingham since the dedication."

"Okay," Max said, "I get it. We're back to square one, unless Bingham did something after he left the bar. But, according to the people at the bar, Bingham had a little too much to drink. I doubt he was in any condition to pull off some pre-planned act of revenge."

"Not quite square one," said Malone, a sly smile crossing his lips. "My next call was to Jason Hughes. He's a big shot financial planner in Omaha. Hughes said Tom Meyer had picked him up after the dedication and they rode back to Omaha together. I asked him about the student-teacher confrontation and he got all up-tight. Said he had seen it, but so did a lot of other people. Then he got real defensive. Asked me why I was calling him. He emphasized that all he had done was attend a school dedication at the request of a friend, and didn't know why the police would be calling him four months later. I explained that James Wilson, the main donor for the gymnasium had disappeared, and we were just following up with everyone who was there, to see if anyone saw anything irregular after the dedication. I said, you know, anyone talking to Wilson, or Wilson leaving with someone. He got very insistent that he had left right afterwards and didn't know anything. Maybe a little too emphatic, if you know what I mean. Gut feeling. I pushed. I said, 'So let me get this straight. You walked out of the gym, got in the car with Tom, and left town.' He said, 'Yes, that's correct.'

Then I asked him why Tom said he had to circle the block a couple of times, double park his car and look for him, before he came out. He said he may have had to go back into the school to use the bathroom or something. He didn't remember. I thanked him for his time and gave him my number in case he remembered anything."

"I think I know where this is headed," Max said. "Where was Jason that five or ten minutes? But Larry, what could this guy from Omaha have to do with Wilson's disappearance? I think you are so bent on proving foul play, you are the one seeing zebras when we're looking for horses. Is this because of your detective instincts or your infatuation with Susan Wilson?"

Malone started to react, then thought better of it. "Okay, I kind of like the lady. But if I wanted to follow up on it, I would want her husband to be an asshole. I would want him to have left her. I wouldn't be bent on proving that something had happened to him, would I?"

They both sat in silence for a minute. Max spoke first. "That's probably right. I just want to be clear that there isn't some hidden agenda here."

Larry started to counter Max, but decided against it. His actions the last couple of months had probably raised some questions in Max's mind. He let the silence hang in the air, then said, "Is it perfectly clear that I have no ulterior motive in this case? If not, I'm taking myself off of it."

Max gazed at Larry for a long moment. With an abrupt shrug, he said, "So did this Nathan Landry ride to Grand Island with Meyer and Hughes?"

"Yes," Larry said, relieved the tension between him and Max had subsided.

"If he was staying the night, how was he supposed to get back to Omaha?" Max asked.

"Good question," Larry said. "I asked Tom Meyer the same thing. He said Landry was going to pick up a car while he was in Grand Island, and drive it back to Omaha. Apparently they had repossessed it because the owner wasn't making his payments. The last Meyer knew, Nathan was going to spend the night with Ted, and drive the car back to Omaha the next day."

"We should be able to trace that," Max said. "I also wonder how he was going to get to where the car was parked, since he never hooked up with Ted Bingham."

Larry said, "Maybe you need to follow up on it? See what Landry's story is on Monday. I'd like you to call Jason Hughes and put a little more pressure on him, too. I think he's worried about something. This just might be our first break!"

Saturday morning at eight o'clock Susan Wilson answered the door. Ted Bingham was at her home with the paint and his equipment just as he had promised. She told him to go on up to the room and get started. She had a class which started at 8:30.

To be polite, Ted asked her what kind of class. She got a funny look on her face and said, "A conceal and carry class," raising her eyebrows while tilting her head.

It was Ted's turn to get the funny look on his face. "You mean like a class to carry a concealed handgun?"

"Yes," and she reached into her purse and pulled out a semi-automatic handgun. "I'm here alone in the house now, and someone already broke into my house a couple of months ago. I just decided to take some measures to protect myself."

Still a little stunned, and worried she didn't know how to handle a firearm, he said, "Do you know how to use that thing?"

"Yes I do. I dated a guy in high school who was a real gun nut. I've shot rifles, shotguns, and handguns. This is a Kimber 9mm, Model 1911, and I'll be shooting hollow-point bullets, so you had better do a nice job on my baby's room, okay?" She was laughing.

Ted laughed also and said, "I'll take extra care on this job."

Susan left and Ted headed upstairs to get started. About an hour into the project, Ted began to wonder what he had gotten into. This was an old house, with plaster walls. It had been painted, patched, wallpapered, and painted and patched again and again over the years. The woodwork was original and had been recently sanded and stained. Keeping paint off them presented a challenge for Ted. He was used to painting siding and soffits, where mistakes were easily covered up. No way was Susan Wilson going to be happy if her newly stained woodwork had blue paint spatters on it. He took great care around them all day, and looked over his work as he began to clean up. He was pleased. The question was, would Susan Wilson be satisfied?

Ted got a call about 4:30 from Susan. "Is the room done yet?"

"Yep, just finished the second coat and am cleaning up now. Do you want me to lock the door behind me?"

"That depends. Do you like Chinese food?" Susan asked.

"Well, yeah."

"I'm done with the class and was going to stop by Hunans for carryout. If you don't have any plans, I could pick something up for you."

Ted thought for a minute, and said, "I'm not sure that's a good idea."

"Why?" Susan replied. "Because I'm married or because I have a gun?"

Ted laughed, and said, "Both."

"Sometimes it gets lonely eating alone, especially on the weekends, but that's okay, I understand."

Ted could sense the despair in her voice and said, "Oh, what the heck. I like Cashew Chicken and Hot and Sour Soup. You can give your approval on the room—but leave the gun locked up!"

Susan said she would be there in a half hour.

The freshly painted room passed inspection. In fact, Susan was thrilled. As they ate, Susan talked mostly about her conceal and carry class. Ted was surprised there were so many rules to carry a gun, and very impressed that she had to put twenty-four rounds in the target from twenty-two feet away to pass the test. Mostly, Ted was glad she didn't pour out all her problems about her husband.

Feeling a little self-conscious about staying for supper, he gave Susan his bill and made an excuse to leave about 7:30.

Sam and John were surviving the roommate situation. Sam was patient and helpful when John had nightmares. Sam had noticed that they seemed worse the nights after his therapy sessions with Kim, so he asked Kim if they could visit after the next session. She agreed that it might be a good idea, and said she would get permission from John to visit about their sessions.

Kim sought Sam out after John's next session, and told him that John had given written permission for them to visit, but she was still unwilling to discuss some details. That was fine with Sam. He told her that he only wanted suggestions that would help John. He wasn't interested in lurid details about John or his past or current condition.

"So just why are you so interested?" Kim asked.

Sam said, "I don't know. And I don't want John to know this, but I'm the person who found him in the alley. I asked someone to call for help, then I left. Ever since I found out he survived, there has been some bond between us. I don't know if it's real or imagined, but I have this compulsion to help him with his recovery."

"It's natural to bond sometimes when people share a frightening experience," Kim said. "Occasionally the bond lasts, more often it fades with time. You know, if John gets his memory back, he may not be the person you imagine him to be. He may have a family far away, move home, and that bond will be broken. I just want to be frank with you about this, Sam. I know you have good intentions, but don't get too involved emotionally. You could end up becoming my next patient."

Sam assured her that he was prepared for that outcome, and had an understanding of psychology in similar instances, and wouldn't end up needing her counseling.

"So just what do you do, Sam?" Kim asked.

"I'm just a homeless man wandering through life the best I can," Sam said.

"No, Sam," Kim said, looking him in the eye, "you're much more than that. You're smart, educated, and don't belong here. In fact, I would like to try and help you."

"You can't help me," Sam said. "You can only help me if I choose. And right now I choose to remain as I am."

Kim raised her eyebrows in surprise and acknowledgment. "If you ever change your mind, Sam," she said with a serious look, "I will always be available." She paused for a moment for a mental change of gears. "So let's talk about John, and how you can help him."

Kim explained John's amnesia, and how it was taking time to find the right trigger to begin some memory recall. Sam asked about the nightmares.

"Part of the healing process," Kim explained. "Whatever events led up to his loss of memory is buried in his subconscious. He didn't choose to bury them. It is just too horrifying in his mind, and his subconscious must reflect on these memories while he is sleeping. When you're awake, it's easier to keep the door closed on memories and have the ability to control your thoughts. When you sleep, you give up some of that ability."

"I understand all that," Sam said. "He keeps mumbling about snakes biting or hitting him, and when I hear the screams, I find him all curled up in the fetal position, as if he's trying to fend off a blow."

"He was beaten badly," Kim said, "but I don't know where the snakes come in. You wanted suggestions on how to help? Just keep being a friend, Sam. Listen. Don't try to understand it or make sense of it for now. Hopefully, his words will become clearer or take on more meaning with time."

Sam thanked her for her time. His background included psychology, and he knew she was right. The bond between him and John existed now, and as long as it existed, he was determined to see this thing through. Some of the other residents were still complaining about John's screams, but Sam defended him, and it was difficult to argue with Sam. Finally, Father Shanks had come to Sam and voiced the complaints on behalf of some of the other residents. Father Shanks was afraid if residents began to move out, his census would become too low, and his shelter would fall short of funds. Sam understood...and yet...hell. The truth was, he had never really felt completely comfortable with Father Shanks. No matter how often Sam reminded himself the man was a priest, and a man of God, somewhere underneath it all, Sam didn't feel Father Shanks could be trusted. It was imperative he find a way to help John so that his nightmares went away.

After a couple of more nights of nightmares, Sam decided to take matters into his own hands.

CHAPTER 15

"**T**HIS IS DETECTIVE MAX WORTHY from Grand Island, Mr. Hughes. I believe you spoke to my partner, Detective Malone, on Friday. I have some follow-up questions for you. Please return my call at your earliest convenience—" The message concluded with his number and a thanks.

Jason's wife, Amy, was puzzled, but when she listened to the message again, she became concerned. *Why would a detective from Grand Island be calling Jason? Well…maybe it's something to do with a client he has there. But why didn't he mention the first detective's call to me? We were home all weekend and he didn't say a word.* She listened a third time, wrote the number down and called Jason's cell.

"Jason, there was a message on the phone from the police in Grand Island, a Detective Max Worthy. He said you had talked to his partner on—"

Jason felt as if he'd been slugged in the solar plexus, but interrupted, trying to stay calm and stem the flow of panic coming from Amy. "You don't need—"

"Jason, just shut up and listen to me! What is going on? You've been withdrawn and moody the last few months. It's like the kids and I don't even exist. We don't have a marriage anymore; we just live under the same roof. God, Jason, have you done something wrong?"

Now that he had an opportunity to talk, he had little to say.

"No, no, I haven't done anything wrong."

Jason's gut had been churning ever since the call on Friday. He'd thought everything was okay until then. Nathan had assured him that Wilson was okay, and there was no problem. He had tried to reach Nathan all weekend, but he wasn't answering.

He was deep in thought, staring at the mahogany bookshelves in his office, when he heard, "Jason, talk to me!" from his frantic wife.

"I'm sorry." His mind raced to dream up an excuse for the call that would satisfy his wife.

"Jason, what the hell is going on?" His wife was getting hysterical.

"Uh, nothing that concerns us. It was about Ted Bingham."

"What did Ted do?" came the anxious reply.

"Well, he got into an argument with a student while I was at that dedication he invited us to attend. Remember, it was just before school got out for the summer." Jason was calming down a little now, and words were coming more easily.

"So how are you involved? Do they think you have something to do with it?" his wife pressed.

"I don't know," Jason was scrambling for words. He could feel the perspiration soaking his shirt under his armpits. He needed Nathan. *Where is that son of a bitch? God damn him. He said everything was taken care of. He said Wilson was all right.* "I mean, no, they don't think I had anything to do with it. They were just asking what was said between them. I couldn't remember exactly what Ted said. Maybe the kid's parents are suing or something. Anyway, it's nothing to worry about."

"Well, you better call this detective back. It must be something for them to call you twice. He said he had more questions for you. This is his number." She waited while he grabbed a pen and a piece of paper, then read it off to him. "And call me back after you talk to him. I want to know exactly what's going on!" She closed her phone and collapsed onto the sofa. She told herself it was nothing, remembering that Ted always had a temper, and Jason was probably right about a lawsuit or something. She looked around the room, stopped to reflect on the family picture on the wall opposite the sofa. They were a model family. Jason was a model husband and father. *Stop worrying. Jason will call back in a little while and it will have been some silly question.* She got up and went into the kitchen to warm her coffee and put away the groceries. And wait for his call.

Jason tried Nathan again. No answer. They were meeting for lunch at noon, and Jason checked his watch. It wasn't even quite ten o'clcock. Two more hours to go. He didn't want to call the detective back until he had talked to Nathan. Instead, he called Amy back.

"Hey, I just talked to that detective. Yeah, it was nothing. He just wanted to confirm that I couldn't remember more of what was said between Ted and the student. I asked him if Ted was being sued or something and he said that he couldn't discuss that with me. Anyway, he thanked me for calling back and that should be the end of it." His shirt was soaked now, and he waited for her reply.

"That's a relief. It scared me when the police had called. And why didn't you tell me about this before?" The anger was evident in her voice.

"It wasn't a big deal. I forgot about it after we left."

"Well, remember it, because I want to know exactly what happened!"

"Okay," Jason said meekly. "We'll talk about it tonight. Love you, bye." He shut his phone and tried Nathan again. No answer. *That SOB better be at lunch!*

Across the river in Council Bluffs a different conversation was taking place.

"I know you don't feel ready for this, John," Whitney Weston said, "but I think it would be good for you. You spend all day at that shelter with nothing to do, are still having nightmares about snakes, and I understand that the other residents are complaining to Father Shanks."

"But I've moved rooms. Sam has taken me in as his roommate. He says I'm a little better."

"Yes, well Sam isn't a psychiatrist. I've just read Kim's report and she indicates very little progress. I asked her about this job, and she agrees it would be good therapy for you. You will meet new people, get a feeling of self-worth, and it will take your mind off of your problems, at least for part of the day."

"Do I have a choice?"

"Sure you do. You can turn it down, but that puts me in a predicament. I'm working my fanny off trying to keep your medical funding, and now I'm asking something from you, and you don't want to do it." Whitney tried to hide her exasperation. "I'm really only involved because you were a patient here at the hospital. I don't work for the Department of Health and Human Services. They are talking about cutting your benefits, and I don't want to see that happen. Take this job, John. If you can show that you are attempting to earn an income, it will help your case with DHHS."

"I just don't think I'm ready, Whitney."

"It's your choice, John. You can choose to live on the streets like Sam, or become a productive citizen. You see what his choice has gotten him."

"No. Tell me about Sam. What did he do that forced him onto the streets?"

"Sam wasn't forced to do anything. He had choices, but in my estimation, he made the wrong one. You can ask him about it yourself. It's really very sad, and mostly of his own doing. I know you like and respect Sam, John. Actually, I do, too. And that's exactly why you need to take this job."

John thought about it. "Can I give you an answer tomorrow?"

"No, John," Whitney said, "I need an answer today."

John nodded his head, indicating yes.

"Great," Whitney said. She handed John a card with the address of the McDonald's and the name of the manager. "Be there at ten A.M. tomorrow."

"Yes, ma'am." John said, taking the card. His shoulders drooped as he got up and left the office.

Whitney leaned back in her chair and let out a sigh. *Oh God, I hope I know what I'm doing. Am I really helping John, or am I trying to help Sam? Just please don't screw this up, John. You have no idea how much depends on it!*

CHAPTER 16

MALONE WAS JUST RETURNING FROM lunch, and saw Max's car pull into the parking lot of the Safety Center. He waited on the grassy courtyard for Max to catch up with him.

"Well, did you hear back from Jason Hughes?" Malone asked.

"No, not yet. I left a message on his home phone. I imagine I will hear from him soon."

"What if his wife gets the message before he does?" Larry asked.

"Gee, I never thought of that!" Max said, slapping Larry on the back and giving him a shit-eating grin.

Larry laughed, and followed Max into the Safety Center, slipping through the door on Max's ID card. *This kid gets better every day.*

Jason was at the restaurant a half hour early. He had tried Nathan a dozen times since Amy's call. *Where the hell is he? Goddammit, the SOB better show up!*

He forced himself to sit and wait. Tom showed up ten minutes before noon and joined Jason at the table. Jason made some small talk with him, and finally asked, "Where do you suppose Nathan is?"

"Vegas, man," Tom replied. "Don't you remember, he said he had a meeting in Vegas this week. I really feel sorry for him. Missing lunch with us while he sits through some boring meeting." The sarcasm was seeping through Tom's voice. He knew Nathan probably never attended any sessions, but just registered so he could deduct the trip and head for the tables.

Jason realized now why Nathan wasn't returning his calls. *Damn! What if that cop calls the house again? Amy will know I lied to her. Shit, shit, shit!*

Jason managed to get through the lunch without puking. Tom was in rare form, talking non-stop about his latest bicycle ride. Jason didn't register a word of it. He wondered if it was obvious his mind was elsewhere. He tried to appear interested and make some small talk. *Don't act weird, Jason. Tom needs to stay in the dark about this.*

On the way out of the restaurant, Jason asked Tom when Nathan was supposed to be back.

"Don't know. He never said. Probably see him next Monday. See you then," Tom said as he walked off, leaving Jason standing alone on the sidewalk.

Sam was in his room when John returned to the shelter. "Hi, John, how did your meeting go?"

"Okay, I guess," John replied. He sat on his bed staring into space.

"I take that as a not so good," Sam stated. It was more of a question.

John looked at Sam, and asked him right out, "So why do you live on the streets, Sam?"

Sam looked at John for a long time. Then he got up and walked out of the room. John decided not to follow. He knew he had touched a nerve, and didn't know if it had cost him the only friend he had. He lay down on his bed and felt the tears welling up in his eyes.

When John went to supper, he saw that Sam was absent. He expected him to return that evening, but he still wasn't back when John went to bed.

John was up early the next morning. The first thing he noticed was that Sam's bed hadn't been slept in. He busied himself after breakfast with getting ready to head for his job, feeling he had lost his only friend.

About that time, Sam walked into the room.

"I'm sorry, I didn't mean..." John began. Sam raised his hand. "I'll talk about it if and when I'm ready. Now you better get going or you'll be late your first day."

John met the manager, and he took him through the operation. John was amazed. He had been in a McDonald's before, but he had no idea of the complexity of the equipment and procedures necessary to fix his Big Mac. His first day was spent mostly observing and convincing himself that he would never be able to learn everything.

But he adapted to the equipment and routine with ease, much to his and his trainer's surprise. After two days, he was actually making that Big Mac he always ordered.

The days settled into a routine faster than John expected. He moved from the cooking line to the front counter, and found he didn't mind taking orders as much as he'd thought he would. He found himself wiped out after a day's work, having lived a life of no exercise for so long. He would go to bed right after supper, sometimes too tired even to have nightmares. When he did have one, Sam was there for him. He continued to have his sessions with Kim, and she was aware his nightmares were less frequent. She was beginning to worry that, when his mind finally broke down the wall it had built, a dragon would be released. She had no idea what effect that could have on John.

John noticed that Sam wasn't around the shelter as much as usual. He was worried that he had done something to irritate Sam. But Sam was always there at night when the nightmares happened, so John just decided not to dwell on it.

Sam had his own issues going. He was concentrating on the house where he had seen Nathan Landry. The *For Rent* sign was gone, and the Hispanic man had moved in. Sam watched while a truck from a used furniture store unloaded some basic furnishings. He also watched while a panel truck unloaded several cases of unmarked boxes. This confirmed Sam's suspicions. Tomas was setting up a meth lab for Landry. To the rest of the neighborhood, working couples and retired folks, this was just another tenant moving into the rental. They were too busy with their own lives to care about the new neighbor. Hell, they had probably watched a dozen tenants come and go over the years. A meth lab in their neighborhood? C'mon, he seemed like an average guy. Waved, smiled, went about his business, never bothered anyone. Sam had seen it on the news a thousand times. The only difference was, Sam could write a book about the serial killer next door. Jimmy Buffett had even written a song about it, and Sam figured Jimmy Buffett knew a lot less about serial killers than he did.

Sam had been spending each day hanging out around the neighborhood, knowing he was invisible to almost everyone. A homeless man walking along the street is just a part of the landscape. Most people turn their eyes away either in guilt or denial—just another statistic they choose to deny.

Sam's anger, frustration, and hatred had been building, but needed to remain under control. He had the goods on Landry and, after five years, he was not going to let this opportunity slip away. Landry was wealthy, smart, crafty, and one of the most ruthless men Sam had ever encountered. If he were going to win this one, he had to be patient, as well as smarter and craftier. He also had to be just as ruthless, which was normally not in his nature, but five years of hatred had evened the playing field.

Sam noted it would be dark soon, and headed back to the shelter. He didn't want a change in his daily habits to create suspicion. Besides, he needed to be there for John.

The truck pulled into the driveway as Sam turned the corner. Sam glanced back over his shoulder at the pickup, and said softly,

"See you tomorrow, Mr. Sanchez." Yes, Sam knew his name. And his other name from before. He had done his homework

Ted arrived at school on Monday in a great mood. The team had beaten the local rival school on their own field on Friday night, the first time in three years, and he was still riding on an adrenalin high.

He opened his mailbox and found a note inside. It read: "Msgr. Kelly would like to see you in his office."

Oh, shit! I suppose that God-damned detective was talking to him. I don't need this crap right now! Ted crumpled the note and threw it forcefully into the trash. He forced himself to calm down and went to his first class. Late that morning, at his free period, he decided to get it over with. He walked to the rectory, dreading the meeting that was about to take place.

He was greeted by the housekeeper, who smiled and led him down the hall to Monsignor Kelly's office. Ted was more than a little shocked when the monsignor stood, walked around his desk, shook his hand, and thanked him for coming. He asked Ted to sit. Ted could feel the sweat on his forehead, and his underarms beginning to feel wet. He was braced for the worst.

"Ted," Monsignor Kelly began, "I was visiting with Harlan the other day, and—" *Here it comes!* "—he recommended you as a delegate to the Catholic Stewardship Conference at Creighton University this month. Doris Whalen was supposed to go, but she's had a family emergency, and had to cancel."

Ted's body almost wilted with relief. He managed a weak, "Thank you, Monsignor. I would be honored to represent the school." The sweat still wouldn't stop.

"Good. There will be four delegates, two teachers and two lay members of the parish. We are meeting here in my office at 3:30 this Thursday. Will that work for you?"

"Sure," Ted replied, "we always have an easy practice the day before a game, so I won't be missed."

"Good. See you then. Oh...and that was a great game the boys played last Friday. It's always good to beat the local rivals on their home field."

Ted, still a little bewildered, walked back to the school and into the teachers' lounge. Ted headed for the coffee pot, nodding to the other teachers in the room. Nancy Ursted walked in right behind him.

"Hey, Ted," Nancy said, "are you coming to Omaha with us?"

Bashfully, Ted said, "Uh, yeah...I didn't know you were going, too." His spirits started to escalate.

"Afraid you're stuck with me," Nancy said, as she flashed him a smile.

Ted smiled back. "Or worse yet, you're stuck with me."

Wow. Two days with Nancy Ursted. The Gods of fate have smiled on me.

Ted literally floated out of the teachers' lounge.

Three days later, Ted headed to the rectory for his meeting with Monsignor Kelly about the church conference. He saw Nancy Ursted leave the building about twenty feet ahead of him, and would have liked to just walk behind her and enjoy the view, but resisted the urge, and hurried to catch up with her.

The housekeeper must have been standing just inside the door, because it opened before either of them could knock.

"Come right in," she beamed, "the Monsignor is waiting in his office for you." They shared a look, then began to chuckle.

When they entered the office, Ted stopped so abruptly, Nancy ran into him. Sitting in the room was a man Ted knew to be the father of one of his basketball players, and...Susan Wilson!

Monsignor Kelly introduced everyone, and Susan exclaimed, "I already know Ted. He was kind enough to paint the nursery for me." She beamed brightly at him.

Ted smiled, feeling his cheeks burn and hoping it wasn't too obvious.

Monsignor Kelly got right down to business, and in fifteen minutes, arrangements were made, and everyone was on their way.

Ted and Nancy walked back to the school. Ted was shocked when Nancy reached out and put her arm around his forearm.

"That was really sweet of you, Ted. Poor woman. God only knows what she must be going through, losing her husband and having to endure her pregnancy all alone. Does anyone know whatever happened to her husband?"

Ted told her he didn't know, and that Susan never mentioned it to him. Ted was savvy enough to know that Nancy's linking her arm around his was a matronly gesture, but all he could think about was spending two days with her, even if she was married. It was good to be on her nice list.

"Hey, here comes the retard. Can you believe that guy? Jesus, I'm getting tired of fixing his mistakes. He screws up two orders for every one he gets right!"

John overheard the high school kid talking about him as he walked into McDonald's for his shift. *Am I really that bad? I've made some mistakes, but so has everyone else. Maybe the kid is right. I'm never going to learn this.*

Dejected, he took off his shirt which sported the McDonald's logo and dropped it on the counter. He turned, his head hanging, and started back out the door. One of the other kids, a nice girl he worked with, ran after him. She called his name as she reached him and grabbed his hand, saying, "Never mind Trevor; he complains about everybody. You're doing just fine, John. It just takes time to learn it all."

John thanked her for her kind words, but walked out anyway. He just walked aimlessly until he came to a lake. He sat on the shore, not sure what he would do next. He wished he had been killed. It would be better than this.

There was a gentle breeze blowing, and he watched the sun's reflection dancing off the ripples in the water. A small sailboat glided noiselessly by, a man and a small child on board. The boy smiled and waved at him, but John couldn't muster the will to wave back.

There were homes across the lake. John could see small figures running and playing in the fenced yards. John imagined what their families must be like. Mom, dad, and a couple of kids. Brothers and sisters playing together. *Do I have a home somewhere? Do I have kids? I must have had parents. Brothers? Sisters?* John banged his fist on a rock. His frustration, anger and loneliness exploded, and he hit the rock again and again, each time crying, "I need to remember, I need to remember!" He finally put his head in his throbbing bloody hands and sobbed uncontrollably.

He sat for a long time after getting his emotions under control. He decided he had better get back to the shelter since it would be getting dark soon. He got up, stretched, and changed his mind—he didn't want to go there. There was a grove of trees nearby. John walked into the nearby woods, sat on the prickly pine needles under the canopy of a tree. He wrapped his arms around himself. It was getting cold and all he was wearing was a t-shirt. He had left his jacket in the restaurant with his McDonald's shirt. He finally lay down, exhausted, and drifted off to sleep.

Sam awoke to a scream in the middle of the night. He jumped up and stepped over to John's bed. No one was there. *What the hell? Where was John? And who had screamed?* Sam tried to clear his head. He turned on the light. John's bed was still made. Sam had come back after supper and gone straight to bed. It never occurred to him to check and see if John was in the building. Besides, he could have been working. McDonald's was open late and re-opened early for breakfast. Sam had gone to bed around eight, and John could have come back late and left again early. Oh well, strange, but not alarming. Sam went back to bed.

Las Vegas, Nevada

The phone jarred Nathan out of his drunken sleep. "What the hell?" he said to nobody in particular. He squinted at the hotel clock. Midnight. He untangled himself from the sheets, stretched and reached across the body lying next to him for the phone, almost dropping the receiver when the body stirred.

"Hello?" He didn't even try to cover the irritation in his voice.

"Nathan, what the hell is going on?" It was Audrey's voice on the other end of the line.

"What time is it in Omaha? It must be 2:00 A.M.!"

The body under him with the tangled blonde hair turned from her stomach to her back and reached out for him. Nathan put his hand over her mouth, and gave her a look that said, "Shut up or else!"

"Nathan, I just got off the phone with Jason Hughes. Now I want to know what is going on!"

"Jason called you at 2 A.M.?"

"Isn't that what I just said?" the pitch of her voice rising with the increase in her irritation.

"What did he say?" Jason asked, his senses starting to come back.

"He said he had to talk to you right away. I told him you were out of town, it was two A.M., and asked what was so damned important!"

"He said it was personal. Now just what in the hell does 'personal' mean , Jason?"

"I have no idea. Except that he was hot on some new stock just before I left town. You know Jason. He carries his job to extremes. You didn't tell him where I was staying, did you?"

"I should have! I told him I would call you in the morning and have you call him then."

"Thanks, hon."

"Don't thank me, Jason. I'm still pissed about him calling at this hour of the morning!"

Trying to defuse the situation, Nathan added, "Hey, babe, what're you wearing right now? Something sexy?"

"No! And don't try and sweet talk me. I'm going to try and get back to sleep. This isn't over, Nathan. I intend on talking about it when you get back!" The phone went dead. Audrey was tiring of Nathan's indiscretions. She knew about his affairs and his involvement with drugs. The call from Jason had fueled her anger.

Nathan told the girl to get up, get dressed, and get out. She tried to coerce him back into bed, placing her arms around his neck and rubbing her breasts against him. He removed her arms, pushing her down until she was sitting on the bed, and told her she had to go. "I have to get an early flight out in the morning," he explained as he pulled on his jockey shorts. Nathan picked up the phone and asked for the concierge.

"I need to get an early flight out of Vegas back to Omaha in the morning. You have my information on file. Let me know as soon as you have a flight confirmed. Yes, I mean *this* morning."

The girl was dressed and getting ready to leave. Jason got his wallet and gave her a hefty tip, saying, "Sorry about that, but I've got to try and get some sleep." Jason sat on the edge of his bed for a moment, rubbing his eyes with the palms of his hands. *Jason! Dumb fucking Jason! What a loser! Shit, shit, shit!* He lay down and waited for the flight confirmation call.

CHAPTER 17

S AM GOT UP AT HIS usual time, showered, and went to breakfast. Still no sign of John. If he was working, he should be back around eleven. Sam decided to stick around and wait for him.

One-hundred miles away, the Suburban cruised along I-80 at a steady eighty-two miles per hour. Monsignor Kelly was adamant that St. Christopher would protect them, even at seven miles over the speed limit. Ted just thought he drove too damn fast. Frank rode shotgun, and Ted volunteered to take the third row seat, giving the captain chairs to Nancy and Susan.

It was a beautiful October afternoon and the temperatures were predicted to stay warm over the weekend. The cornfields had turned from green to gold, lining the landscape flanking the interstate. Conversation ranged from the price of corn to the projected bushels per acre. It soon changed to the schedule of events for the weekend, held at Creighton University. The theme of the conference was "Helping the Poor," and caring for the poor was Monsignor Kelly's passion. Frank read over the schedule while Monsignor Kelly drove. The conference included several speakers on Friday, a visit to a homeless shelter on Saturday morning, then free time the rest of the day.

Nancy Ursted was excited to have Saturday afternoon off as she wanted to visit the Old Market area in Omaha. Susan was eager to go also, although she was worried she couldn't keep up, as the baby limited her endurance. Ted and Frank were more interested in when the cocktail hour began at the Embassy Suites. The monsignor was going to stay with an old friend and teacher, Fr. Anton Murphy. Father Murphy was a professor at Creighton, and was instrumental in convincing the young Mike Kelly into becoming a priest. They had remained friends throughout the years.

Monsignor Kelly drove to Father Murphy's residence, and handed the keys to the car to Frank. "It's all yours," Monsignor Kelly said. "See you at the conference in the morning." They headed for the Embassy Suites, unloaded the luggage, and Frank opted for valet parking. Ted helped Nancy and Susan get their bags to their rooms. Susan had booked her own room, as she didn't sleep well and was often up half the night. She let them think it was because of her pregnancy, but it was just as much thinking about James. It was a nightmare that manifested itself day and night, and was still as painful now as when he first disappeared in May.

Sam had to wait as another shelter resident was currently on the resident line. The resident phone was located in an outer office, and had a doorway leading into Father Shanks's office. Sam could see Father Shanks using the phone in his office as he waited his turn.

The other resident concluded his call, and Sam sat down and thumbed the telephone directory. He placed his call to City Hospital, and asked the operator to connect him to Whitney Weston.

As Father Shanks hung up his own call, he glanced up and saw Sam. He had never seen Sam use the telephone. Curious, he decided to check in on the call.

Sam was watching Father Shanks, and noticed him push a button on the phone. Sam heard a slight click on the line, and although Father Shanks appeared to be talking, he was a little too animated. Sam had lost his trust in Father Shanks some time ago. Something just wasn't right about him.

"Social Services Office, may I help you?"

"Yes. This is Sam Washington. I would like to speak to Whitney Weston."

The robotic voice on the line said, "She is on another call. May I take your number and have her call you back?"

Sam envisioned the secretary as she spoke in her condescending manner. A little overweight, dressed in her proper secretarial attire; white collared shirt, brightly colored jacket and slacks, with a scarf to match, her designer glasses perched on her nose, held in place by a bucket of makeup. She was overwhelmed by her importance, and had absolutely no empathy for the poor class of people she was hired to serve.

"I'm afraid not," Sam stated. "This is a matter of extreme importance, and if you will tell her who is calling, I'm sure she will take the call."

"As I said, she is currently on the line. You will just have to wait for her to return your call."

"No, you will step in and tell her who is on the line, or I will hold until she hangs up."

"I can't do that."

"Sure you can. I've seen you do it while waiting in your office." The line went silent for a couple of minutes. Sam was expecting the dial tone any second. "Sam, this is Whitney, what's so important that my secretary has her panties in a wad?"

"I have to see you as soon as possible." Sam said with urgency.

"May I ask what this is about?" Whitney asked.

"I don't want to talk on the phone; I need to see you in person." Sam noticed that Father Shanks still had the phone to his ear, but was no longer pretending to talk.

"Okay. What time?"

"I can be there in twenty minutes if I hurry." Sam figured he would thwart any attempt Father Shanks could make to talk to him or Whitney by making it right away.

"I'll see you in twenty minutes," Whitney said, hanging up.

Sam had to hustle. He put on his coat and hurried out the door. He walked as fast as he could toward the McDonald's on Broadway Street. It was out of his way but he needed to make sure John wasn't at work. A quick look inside told him John wasn't there. He made good time until he turned east onto Broadway. There was a strong northeast wind, and it almost stopped him in his tracks. He pulled his stocking cap down over his forehead, and pulled his coat together with his right hand at the collar, keeping the other warm in his pocket. He put his head down like a runner crossing the finish line and propelled himself against the wind. He was so intense he didn't spare a glance for the crossed mustard- and ketchup-colored lances forming an honor guard above him as he crossed the bridge, a feature of its design he admired. He was freezing. Finally, he made it to Kanesville Boulevard, and had to turn northeast. The wind was directly in his face, but Sam just put his head down and pushed on.

Sam checked his watch. Ten minutes had passed. He was still a mile away, but could see the top of the hospital building looming ahead. He wasn't going to make it. He let go of his collar, pulled his warm hand from his pocket, and began to run. By now he had worked up a sweat and the cold no longer was a factor. He was on a mission and was not going to be late. His legs tired, but he pushed on. *Thought I was in better shape than this. Jesus, that cold air burns my lungs. Got to keep going.* Sam's breath formed billows of steam from his mouth and nose in the frigid air. He could feel the sweat forming under his coat and his armpits; in fact, he imagined he was soaked. His hands felt like clubs and he could feel the tears freezing as they tried to run down his cheeks. Finally he reached the hospital and got to the front door.

Sam stepped inside, and bent double, placing his hands on his knees for support. He stood there, gasping for breath, chest heaving, and head rising and falling in rhythm.

Sam didn't wait until fully oxygenated. He hurried down the hall, ran past the elevator, and took the stairs down. Whitney's office was in the basement close to the stairwell. Sam slowed as he neared the office, and walked through the door as casually as he could.

"Good morning," Sam said to the obnoxious secretary, "I'm—"

"I know who you are!" the secretary said, giving him her best glare.

Much to Sam's relief, before he could exchange barbs with the secretary, Whitney appeared in the doorway. "Hi, Sam, come on in."

Sam entered her office, and hesitated before he sat. "Do you mind if I close the door?"

"I'll get it," Whitney said, walking around him. "You're sweating, Sam. What did you do, run all the way? Why don't you take off some of those clothes and cool down."

Sam took off his overcoat, scarf, his sport coat, and decided to remove his sweater also. He carefully placed them on the chair next to his own. Whitney smiled and said, "Might help if you took your hat off too, Sam."

Sam, flustered, apologized. "I'm sorry, not much of a gentleman, I'm afraid," as he removed his stocking cap and placed it atop the pile of coats and sweaters. His shirt was soaked clear through.

Whitney asked, "So what is this emergency, Sam?"

"It's John," Sam replied. "He never came home from work yesterday and didn't sleep in his bed last night. I haven't seen him since yesterday morning."

"I got a call from his manager yesterday about noon," Whitney replied. "He left work early. In fact, according to one of his co-workers, he actually quit his job. Apparently one of the other employees was making fun of his mistakes and John heard him call him a retard. John couldn't handle it, and threw in the towel, so to speak. That was the last time anyone at the restaurant saw John. I had an appointment with him yesterday after he got off work. When he didn't show for his appointment, I called Father Shanks to see if he was at the shelter. Father Shanks said he hadn't seen him. I'm surprised he didn't call me this morning to let me know he hadn't come back. I'm glad you called me, Sam; we need to find him."

"Father Shanks disturbs me," Sam said. "I didn't want to talk on the phone earlier as I'm sure he was listening to our conversation. I know he's a priest and all, but lately there's something I can't put my finger on. I just don't trust him anymore."

A smile touched Whitney's lips. She cocked her head and looked at Sam. "Well, apparently you trust me."

"Yes I do," Sam said. "I know I have been a disappointment to you in the past, but I know you are always there for me."

"That means a lot to me, Sam. Now let's get going and see what we can do about John." She picked up her phone and dialed an extension. "Steve, this is Whitney. Remember your former patient in 313?...Yes, well he walked off his job yesterday, and no one has seen him since...Yeah. Well, I know you are a friend of Melvin Marlowe and would like to ask you a favor...That's right. I know this is not in his job description, but he might take an active interest in finding John if you were to personally ask...Okay, I'll expect your call...And thank you ever so much." She placed the receiver down, sat up straight in her chair, crossed her hands, and looked at Sam.

"Here's the deal, Sam. Dr. Cantelli, John's former doctor, is a personal friend of the chief of police. He's agreed to call him and ask him to get everyone on board looking for John. I'm sure they will find him soon. I just hope he's okay when they do."

"Thank you Whitney. God bless you." Sam said.

"Wait here a minute, Sam." Whitney said as she stood and left her office. She was back in about five minutes and handed Sam a scrub top. "Take off your wet shirt and put this on, Sam. You'll get pneumonia in those wet clothes. I'll step out while you change, and see that you are informed as soon as we located John."

Sam turned to thank her, but she was already closing the door.

The plane jarred Nathan awake as it bounced rather than glided onto the runway. It was 11:50 A.M. Nebraska time, and Nathan, who found it impossible to sleep on a plane, was cruising on about four hours of sleep. The concierge had managed to book an early flight out of Vegas, and Nathan was glad for that, but he wasn't ready to be home. He had spent most of his time gambling, drinking, and whoring. He believed completely in the saying, "What happens in Vegas, stays in Vegas." The girls had been awesome. Nathan always used the same escort service. They were reliable, discreet, and provided him with everything he needed. The price was outrageous, but hell, he had the money.

Audrey didn't expect him back until Saturday, and that was going to involve a little maneuvering. He purposely hadn't checked out of his room, so that any calls she made to the hotel would go to the room's voice mail. Nathan was confident Audrey didn't know what he was up to, the Vegas behavior, the drug business, or that he had an apartment for his mistress in Omaha. He assumed that if she ever found out, she would choose her high society lifestyle over his escapades.

In Nathan's mind the whole arrangement gave him the best of all worlds, the freedom to carry on his drug business as well as his extramarital affairs, all while being married to a lovely woman. His mission now was to find Jason and clear the air with the Grand Island Police Department. After that, he was going to take care of matters to get this mess behind him once and for all! Dead men tell no tales.

He walked stiffly down the long hallway to the baggage claim area, his body still loosening up from the cramped airline seat. On the way, he called Jason.

"Nathan! Thank God you called!"

"All right Jason, calm the fuck down, now! Do you understand?" Jason started to talk, but Nathan interrupted. "Meet me at the Crescent Moon on Farnam in forty-five minutes." He didn't wait for an answer, he just hung up. Nathan was still so pissed when he reached the baggage area he almost knocked over the lady standing behind him as he yanked his bag off the conveyor belt. *Gonna be a bitch of a day!*

"Hey, Max, did you ever hear back from that Hughes guy in Omaha?" Larry asked.

"Yeah. He called back and left a message. I decided to just let him stew awhile, or maybe relax a little. I'll call him Friday and set up a meet for Saturday morning. That work for you and Mary?"

"Sure. She knows we may want to do a little work along with play, but she doesn't mind."

"Okay, then let's leave work early on Friday, maybe get checked in, and catch some dinner. Saturday morning the gals can sleep in, or do a little shopping. You and I can meet this Hughes guy around mid-morning, and we can be with the girls by lunchtime. Oh, by the way, Natalie is looking forward to spending some time with Mary. They seemed to hit it off pretty well last week at dinner."

"Yeah, Mary mentioned that to me, too," Larry smiled to himself.

Max playfully slugged his arm. "How does it feel to be back in the saddle again, Lar?"

"None of your damned business, Max. Let's go over things on this Wilson timeline again.

Nathan wasn't surprised when Jason was already at the Crescent Moon when he arrived. He was wearing his usual conservative suit and tie, but looked like hell. He clearly hadn't slept in a couple of days judging by the dark rings under his eyes, and his perfectly coiffed hair looked like it had gotten caught in a blender. A beer sat half empty in front of him on the table.

Nathan picked up the beer and set it on the table beside them before sitting down across from Jason.

"Hey, what the hell !..."

"Alcohol is the last thing you need, Jason. No more booze until this thing is settled, got it? Booze shuts off your mind and lets your mouth run away. You need to know it's time to control your mouth before you get both of us in the shithole." He gave Jason an appraising look. "So what's the problem with this detective? What does he want with you?"

"He suspects that I know something about this Wilson guy. He almost sounds like he knows what we did." Jason said, the fear reflected in his hollow sunken eyes.

"Jason. Think about it. It's been what, four months? He told me they were talking to everyone that was at the dedication for the gym. He talked to Tom, me, and probably a hundred other people."

"Yeah, but he didn't call you back."

"No, because I told him I left right afterwards, and you and Tom headed back to Omaha. What did you tell him?"

"The same thing." Jason's tone was defiant. "But Tom told him that he had to drive twice around the block, and wait five or ten minutes before he picked me up at the school. He wants to know where I was during that time."

"Oh, for Christ's sake, Jason," Nathan said with disgust. "Tell him you had to take a shit or something. Haven't you ever had to make up a story for Amy?"

"I told him I didn't remember. Maybe I went to the bathroom or something. He asked me why I wasn't sure what I did. Like he didn't believe me."

"Okay. That's all we need." Nathan grabbed a napkin, reached over and took the pen out of Jason's shirt pocket, and proceeded to draw a diagram. He pushed it across the table in front of Jason. "Okay, this is the school, and this is the gymnasium, just as they sit on the property. Here is where Tom parked, a couple of blocks away. The gym has three entrances. One from the school, one on the side, and one in front with the horseshoe drive. We parked, walked around the long block and entered at the horseshoe entrance," Nathan said as he put an "X" on the paper. "We sat here," Nathan added, placing another "X" on the paper. "The restrooms are in this hallway off the entrance from the school. All you need to do is tell this police officer that you remember that after we left the gym, you decided to stop and use the restroom. Tom said he would get the car. You used the restroom, then got turned around in the crowd of people when you left, and ended up back in the gym. You tried to find your way back into the school, but ended up going out the wrong door, here." Another "X" on the paper. "The door locked behind you. You banged on the door to get someone's attention. No one came for a few minutes, but when you started to walk around the outside, the door opened. You ran back and grabbed it so you could go back in and get your bearings. You went back into the gym, the crowd had cleared out, and you remembered you had entered at the end opposite the scoreboard. When you got to the other end, you saw the concession stands, and knew you were in the school near the front entrance. You went out; Tom was waiting for you in the street outside the horseshoe. He *was* parked in the street, wasn't he?"

"Yes," Jason said.

"Okay. Joke with him a bit. Tell him Tom asked you where the hell you had been and you told him you were shooting hoops." Nathan glared at Jason as he lowered his voice to an ominous rumble that meant business. "And *stop there*. Do not add *anything* else. If he asks about time, you don't know. Just stick to that story and you will be fine. Remember, *do not volunteer any information, and do not vary from your story*." Jason was staring hard at Nathan, trying to find courage in the angry confidence he saw there. "Take this drawing and memorize it along with the story. And no more booze until you talk to him!"

"But won't he be suspicious since I didn't tell him this before?"

"Tell him you really hadn't thought about it. We went to the dedication, we left, and it was no big deal. We saw Ted arguing with a student, and I suggested we walk on by, as it was none of our business. We went outside to go to the car, and you decided to use the restroom, so went back in. I went my way, and Tom said he would bring the car around."

"You make it sound easy."

"It *is* easy, dammit. You take your kids to games, other places, every day. Do you remember if you used the john? Hell no. You just do it. You don't make notes so you can remember it four months later."

Nathan's phone interrupted the conversation. He answered the phone, sleep deprivation and anger evident in his voice. "Yeah, what do you want?"…"Look, I'm in the middle of an important meeting. I'll call you back." He slapped his phone shut, and muttered, "Jesus Christ!"

"Everything okay?" Jason asked.

"No. Now let's go over this one more time," Nathan said. They went over it again, then Jason asked Nathan, "So why are they still looking into this? You said this guy was okay."

"He is okay. He's got a job and working in the area. It was probably a good thing for him. He has amnesia and doesn't even remember the incident. But he hasn't chosen to go back home either, so maybe things weren't so good between him and the wife. Maybe we did him a favor. At any rate, he couldn't identify us if he saw us, because he just doesn't God-damned remember any of it. So get your shit together. Go over this story until you can recite it in your sleep. Call me later this afternoon, we'll go over it, and then you call the cop back."

"Okay, but it scares the hell out of me."

"Jason," Nathan said, "you're beginning to scare the hell out of *me*!

They left the bar and Nathan dialed his caller back. "Now what's so damned important you had to call me in the middle of a meeting?"

"Well, I'm worried. John…er…Wilson didn't show up for supper last night. And he also didn't sleep at the shelter last night."

"That's the only reason you called? What makes you think I give a shit?"

"Well, Washington was all worked up about it, and called that social worker, Whitney. I think they went to the police."

"Of course they went to the police, stupid. That's what people do when someone is missing," Nathan said, rolling his eyes as if the caller could see him.

"What if he remembers what happened?" the caller asked.

"Then he will go to jail for a long time. I told you I had my bases covered. Now just settle down and let me know how this plays out, okay?" *Christ, who's going to lose it next?* Nathan ran through all the possible scenarios in his head. He was satisfied that they were all covered, and headed for an out-of-the-way motel in West Omaha to get some much needed sleep.

Susan assured the others she'd be happiest if she took a short nap, so Ted, Frank, and Nancy went to the free cocktail hour. Ted was a little uncomfortable to be drinking with Nancy. She was always so professional and reserved at school, but both she and Frank turned out to be witty and funny. Ted noticed Frank, like himself, had trouble keeping his eyes off of her tight fitting top, along with several other males in the room. He finally loosened up and began to enjoy himself. They were laughing and having a great time when Susan showed up in time to go to supper. They headed for their rooms after eating. It was going to be a long day tomorrow. A long, boring day as far as Ted was concerned.

Council Bluffs, Iowa

Sam's feet dragged as he headed back to the shelter with slumped shoulders. A police cruiser pulled up alongside him, and an officer got out of the car. Sam just kept moving. The officer caught up with him and said, "Sam Washington?"

Sam stood still, took a deep breath, raised his head, then lowered his shoulders as he exhaled. After what seemed like an eternity, he turned to face the officer.

"I'm Sam Washington."

"We would like you to come with us, Mr. Washington; we found your friend."

The first words out of Sam's mouth were laced with concern. "Is he okay?"

"Yes, he's okay," the officer said. "He's being treated at the hospital, but we need to make a stop along the way."

Sam didn't like the sound of the situation. "I think I would rather just go to the hospital. Is it City?"

"Yes," the officer replied, "But first we have orders to take you to the station to meet with the chief of police."

"You don't have probable cause to arrest me," Sam said with resentful force.

Sam saw the cords tighten in the officer's neck. "This isn't an arrest, Mr. Washington; it's a request from Chief Marlowe. He wants to speak with you personally, and I would appreciate your cooperation."

Sam just stood still for a minute, his indecision showing in his eyes.

"Look," the officer said, "I know who you are. And for what it's worth, I think you were set up. There are a lot of other officers who think that too, including Chief Marlowe." Pausing, and getting no reply from Sam but a suspicious look, he finally said, "It's your choice, Mr. Washington. Personally, if I were you, I would honor the Chief's request. You have nothing to lose, and maybe a lot to gain."

Sam hung his head, appeared to be staring at his shoes. When he raised his head, the officer noticed the wetness in his eyes. Sam didn't speak; he just walked toward the patrol car. The officer hustled ahead of him, and opened the passenger door, shutting it after Sam got inside.

When they reached the station, the officer pulled into a secure lot behind the building. They entered through a secure door, accessible only to staff. Sam was grateful he didn't have to parade through the entire office, among desks manned by secretaries and police officers. The officer offered Sam a seat and asked if he would like some coffee. Sam declined, sat and waited, but not for long.

Sam saw Chief Marlowe come out of his office. He walked up to Sam, holding out his hand. "Sam, it's been a long time. Thank you for coming."

Sam stood and hesitated before shaking the chief's hand, nodding at his words.

"Let's go into my office," extending his hand and leading the way. The chief closed the door behind them.

He offered Sam a chair, moved around his desk, and sat in his own chair. "First things first, Sam," the chief said. "Your friend John is in the hospital, but should be released in a day or so. Our officers responded to a call about a body in the woods beside the Missouri River. He was seen by a bicyclist who called 911. The cyclist went into the woods to see if he was alive, but he was combative and seemed out of his head. We dispatched a unit and an ambulance, and he is now hospitalized at City, recovering from exposure."

"Thank the Lord," Sam said, the relief coursing through him.

"What do you know about this man, Sam?"

"Well, first, thank you for finding him, and for notifying me. I'm grateful. I'm also a little uncomfortable being in your station."

"Understandable, Sam. But let's put that aside for now. What do you know about this guy?"

"Nothing. You know, I'm the one who found him, went to the Thrift Store and asked the clerk to call it in."

"I wasn't aware of that, but it's a good thing you did. He probably wouldn't have lived if you hadn't found him," the chief said. "But we don't know a thing about him. Whitney Weston tells me you have become close. I was hoping you could tell me something about him. Something he had told you in confidence."

Sam laughed, "You really don't understand. John knows nothing about himself. All he seems to know is when he sleeps he has nightmares, so he tried to avoid sleeping, until I moved him into my room. He still has nightmares, but he seems to take comfort that someone understands. I honestly believe he knows nothing of his prior life, just like the doctors said. I've spoken with Kim, his therapist, and she feels our friendship is good for John."

"You know there were two attempts on his life, Sam. First, in the alley, or wherever. My people think he was beaten somewhere else and dumped in the alley. Then someone tried to smother him in the hospital. We set up police protection for the duration of his stay. Once he went to the rehab center, protection became difficult, so we discontinued it."

"I wasn't aware of any of this." Sam said, surprised.

"We ran his picture through the agencies, fingerprints through all the databases, and came up with nothing. That eliminates PTSD, as he wasn't in the military, wasn't a police officer, has no criminal record, and so probably isn't involved with organized crime. So why does someone want to kill him so badly? And to make it more confusing, why the hell didn't they finish the job before they dumped him in the alley?"

"Maybe they thought they had."

"No, you and I both know better. When someone orders a hit, the job gets done. Bullet in the head, slashed throat, strangulation, but not just a beating. Somebody knows who he is, Sam, and they want him dead."

"So why are you telling me all of this?"

"Well, since you have been back, you have been a loner. No friends, no family, no contacts. Suddenly, you find a friend. Not just another bum from the shelter or the street, but some stranger you claim to have found in an alley. From my perspective, that's not much of a connection to form a friendship."

Sam narrowed his eyes. The anger was beginning to boil inside. "Sounds like you think I'm involved in this somehow. Maybe even think I'm the guy who beat him up. I don't like the way this conversation is going, Chief...and if I'm not under arrest, perhaps it's time for me to go see my *mysterious* friend," his emphasis filled with resentment. He stood to go.

"Wait a minute, Sam," the Chief said. "I'm not implying anything, just explaining why I'm perplexed. I'm asking for your help. Dr. Cantelli, John's physician, along with Whitney Weston, asked me to personally look into this guy. I'm doing it as a favor to them, and if you can shed any light on his prior life, I would appreciate it. That's all."

Sam stayed standing and thought. *He sounds sincere, but is there an ulterior motive? Can I trust him? Perhaps, but he was still a cop.* Sam didn't care much for cops. He decided to go along for the time being. "Guess there's no harm in keeping you informed if I find out something. As for the connection we seem to share, I can't explain it. When I found him in that alley, we bonded somehow. I visited him in the hospital after hours a couple of times. Just stood there, wanted him to know someone was there, but never spoke. He was in a coma. Always made sure no one saw me, 'cause I never wanted to be involved. Anyway, one day I went back, and he was gone. Then I had a real shock hit me when he showed up at the shelter. That was when I figured the Lord had a job for me. Sending me a message I had to look out for him. So maybe we can both work on this dilemma. If I find out anything, I will let you know."

Sam turned and left.

Chief Marlowe sat deep in thought. *Sam visited the victim in the hospital after hours. Christ, he wouldn't have been the guy with the pillow...or would he?* The chief picked up his phone. "Get me the case file on that John Doe beating victim from last spring. And I want it now!"

PART THREE

CHAPTER 18

T ED, FRANK, AND NANCY WERE at happy hour as the white Nissan Altima merged onto Interstate 80 just outside of Grand Island. Its four occupants were excited about a weekend in Omaha. Malone, ever the alpha male, insisted on driving. Max didn't care. He sat in the back seat with Natalie eating red licorice and being his usual funny self. Mary thought Max was cute, which irritated the hell out of Malone, but he knew enough to keep his mouth shut. Malone set the cruise just a little over the seventy-five miles per hour speed limit, not wanting to use his badge as a bartering tool to avoid a speeding ticket.

Mary and Natalie were planning an itinerary of malls for shopping on Saturday and Sunday as they sped along. Larry and Max would find some sporting goods stores nearby to look at handguns while the girls tried on clothes. By the time they reached Lincoln, Max was hungry. Larry ignored his whining and drove on to Omaha. He headed for the Old Market area and found a parking space in front of the Upstream Brewery.

Mary wasn't too excited about eating in a brewery, until she walked in and saw the delicious plates of food being carried past by the waiters. Max headed directly for the bar, ordered a beer and a dish of pretzels. Mary walked over to the open kitchen and was amazed as she watched the chefs cooking, and others presenting the food on the plates.

They soon had a table and Max and Larry wanted to try some of the beers brewed in the huge vats behind the glass wall. Mary was astonished when Max cleaned up a huge plate of meat loaf, then dug into a huge slice of chocolate cake. It was more than enough for the four of them, but Max didn't offer to share. After Max's feeding frenzy was over, they headed for the Embassy Suites a couple of blocks away. Mary had never been in the Old Market area, and was charmed by the old warehouse buildings outlined in white lights.

They checked in, and Larry and Mary headed up to their room. Max and Natalie decided to stay in the atrium and have an after dinner drink. It wasn't often they got away without the children, and they were going to make the most of it.

Ted Bingham walked through the atrium, unnoticed by Max.

Malone and Worthy were up early on Saturday. They went into the atrium for breakfast and to go over Max's interrogation of Jason Hughes. They reviewed the timeline from the day of the dedication over omelets made to order. Malone was appalled. Max had ordered two omelets, both for himself. *Jesus, how does he do it? If I ate that much, I'd weigh three hundred pounds! Maybe he has a thyroid problem?* He ordered himself to get his mind back on the case.

Malone tried to ignore Max's attempt to explain his line of questioning between bites of his omelets. At least he wasn't talking with his mouth full of food. They finished breakfast and headed for the bank of elevators. It was time to wake the girls so they could eat and start shopping as soon as the stores opened. As the doors closed and their elevator started skyward, the doors to the adjacent elevator opened, and Ted Bingham and company stepped out to have breakfast and head to the conference.

Max was sitting in the atrium waiting for Jason Hughes. Malone had walked with the girls to a nearby art gallery, somewhat against his will. Mary had talked him into going because she absolutely loved Thomas Mangelsen's wildlife and nature photos, and his studio was within walking distance of the Embassy. She had informed everyone at breakfast—where Malone was astonished to see Max eat again, a cinnamon roll this time—that Thomas Mangelsen was a Grand Island native.

Max glanced at his watch. 11:10. Hughes was late. Max was getting angry just as a well-coiffed young man walked into the atrium. His dark suit and perfectly matched shirt and tie practically screamed "financial advisor." Nathan had advised Jason to "dress to the nines" so to speak, as superior dress dictates the alpha role in a conversation.

Max stood, in his baggy khakis and blue sweatshirt with the Grand Island Safety Center logo prominently displayed, to get Hughes's attention.

Jason stiffened when he saw Max. Not that Max frightened him, but he knew he was going to lie to a police officer.

The interview went just as planned by Jason and Nathan. Max asked the expected questions, and Jason had the right answers. When the conversation ended, Max stood, shook Jason's hand, and thanked him for his time.

"Do you think this will clear up your case, Detective Worthy?" Jason asked, hopefulness in his voice.

"Well, it certainly clarifies your whereabouts after the dedication," Max said. "We still have some digging to do, but I think you and I are done for the time being."

Jason was taken aback. "For the time being? I thought this would clear things up. I've told you everything I know, for God's sake."

Max sensed his anxiety. "Mr. Hughes, we take one day at a time on our cases. We don't assume innocence or guilt, we just deal with the facts."

"And the facts, as of today, are?" Jason asked. He knew he was pushing, but stood, waiting for an answer, shooting his cuffs to ease his tension.

"My notes state that you were in the gymnasium and know nothing about the incident."

Jason let out a sigh of relief. "Well, thank you Detective Worthy. I'm always ready to cooperate with the police." He extended his hand to Max before turning to leave.

Ten minutes later the girls came in with Larry in tow. Larry was carrying a tube about two feet long.

"Hey guys, what's up?" Max asked. "What's in the tube, Lar?"

"Oh, Max," Mary said with a smirk on her face. "You won't believe this, but Larry purchased a poster from the art gallery."

"Probably a nude," Max said, widening his grin.

"No," Mary said, laughing. "It's a bear about to catch a salmon in its mouth. Show him Larry," the excitement notching up the pitch of her voice.

Larry rolled his eyes, opened the tube, and pulled the poster out to show Max. Then he proceeded to tell Max about the photographer and all his other works. Mangelsen had captured another fan.

Max listened, or at least pretended to, and finally said, "That's great Larry. Nice to see you're getting some culture. Want to know about my interview?"

"Tell you what, Max," Larry said. "I'm going to take this poster up to the room. Why don't you get the car and meet us out front. The girls want to go to a mall in West Omaha. They just happen to have a Scheels Sporting Goods store there and we can look at guns or whatever." He tossed the keys to Max and headed for the elevator.

Natalie and Mary went toward the entrance and Mary stopped to look at the small stream running through the atrium. "Oh, look at the beautiful fish!" she said to Natalie, pointing. A voice behind her said, "They're Koi." Mary and Natalie turned to see a petite blonde woman. "I love to watch them," the lady said. Mary, noticing that she was pregnant, asked when her baby was due. "Eight weeks," came the proud reply. "It's a boy."

"Oh, I'm so excited for you," Natalie said, adding, "we have two of our own."

Just then another woman walked up and said, "We'd better hurry, Susan; I think everyone else is already in the car." Susan Wilson and Nancy Ursted walked out the door and climbed in the Suburban as Max pulled the Nissan up behind it.

Monsignor Kelly had left the closing lecture of the conference and was already in the car. He was wearing a plaid shirt, jeans, and boots. "Okay," he said, "from now on I'm just Mike. Not Monsignor, not Father, just Mike. Got it?"

"I got it Father—oops, I mean, Mike," Frank said, "but I don't understand."

"Priests try and impress other priests," Mike said. "They also know that we can direct where our collections go. It said in our packet that the shelter we are going to visit is in Council Bluffs, across the river. It also said that the director is a Father Shanks. I'm betting this Father Shanks will schmooze every priest who shows up, in hopes to impress him and get donations. Hell, I would."

Frank gave him an astonished look. Ted just laughed.

"What's the matter, Frank?" Father Mike asked. "Haven't you ever heard a priest cuss before?"

"Actually Monsignor, no," Frank replied.

"Well, I'm Mike today, and I'll cuss if I damn well please," the Monsignor said with a laugh. "You know, Frank, we're people just like everyone else, and while we try and set a good example, we're not exactly saints." They were across the Missouri River and in Council Bluffs now, and he glanced at the GPS and made a left turn.

The shelter tour was interesting, but Susan had a tough time dealing with the odor that pervaded the entire place, a stench she would never forget. *Is this what homeless people smell like? This is worse than a nursing home.*

The rooms were small and sparse, with only a bed and table or sometimes a small dresser. The stucco walls had once been white, but time and cigarette smoke had turned them a brownish yellow. It was gloomy, to say the least. There were no suitcases, only plastic bags and backpacks strewn about. A man was in one of the rooms, the sickening smell of vodka penetrating everyone's sensory glands.

They were all surprised to learn that the average homeless person stayed in a shelter less than two days, and the chronic residents numbered less than ten percent. They had all thought the chronic population was much greater.

Father Shanks then took them to the mess hall. Father Shanks was a funny duck. He was short, thin, and looked like a shifty character to Susan. His beady eyes flicked from right to left, like a nervous hamster, or ferret, or some hunted animal. He was creepy. She mentioned this to Nancy, who agreed he was, indeed, creepy. Nancy leaned close to Susan and murmured, "Makes that shopping much more appealing. Can't wait to get this over with."

It was like high school all over again. They picked up their trays, silverware, napkins, and started through the line. The servers were homeless residents and needed haircuts, dental work, shaves, and a myriad of other things, but were pleasant. The food looked, well, palatable. Ted was grateful it was hamburgers, beans, and French fries, because it had been cooked, and salmonella wasn't an issue. *Of course, there is always E. coli. Don't think about it, Ted.* Nancy smiled at him and he forgot about all those horrid little organisms that could turn his intestinal tract into a bloody battlefield.

Ted collected the trays, and took them to the end of the line where the dishwasher was located. One of the residents, a black man, approached Ted and asked if he could talk to him a moment.

"Uh...sure," Ted said.

"Would you ask Father Mike to visit with me for a few minutes?" the man asked.

Ted started to ask how he knew Father Mike, but decided against it. "I'll tell him you want to see him."

Ted went back to the table and told the monsignor that the black gentlemen would like to have a word with him. To his surprise, Father Mike said, "Good; that saves me the trouble of asking him." Father Mike got up from the table and said, "You kids go on. I'll find my way back. I'll call you later to make arrangements to head back tomorrow." He stood and left the table, the four of them completely bewildered. After a moment's startled silence, Susan said, "Let's get out of this place. We're losing valuable shopping time, Nancy."

Monsignor Kelly walked up to Sam. "Hello, Sam. I understand you want to talk."

Sam said, "Hi, Father. Let's go to my room," waving his hand for Father Kelly to follow him down the hall.

Sam walked into his room and stepped aside for Monsignor Kelly to walk in. Sam closed the door. The Monsignor held out his hand. "It's been a long time, Sam."

"Yes, it has, Father. I was surprised when I saw you in the food line. Noticed you aren't wearing a collar."

"No, I know better. I'm here for the Catholic Conference, but it's still my time off. Besides, this way, the priest who runs this shelter will leave me alone."

Sam laughed. "Father Shanks has two or three of them trapped in his office trying to get funds right now."

"So tell me what's going on, Sam," Monsignor Kelly said.

"I'm sure you know the story, Father. Hell, everybody who ever lived in Greeley County plus the rest of the entire state knows the story. I paid my debt to society for a crime I didn't commit. I lost my family, my dignity, my life."

"Don't you want it back, Sam?" the Monsignor inquired.

"It's not that easy, Father. Once you're labeled a dirty cop, it never changes. You have no friends. Everyone talks about you behind your back. I can shout my innocence as loud as I want, but to every other police officer, it's like having a tattoo on my forehead that says "dirty cop."

"I spoke to your mother a while back. She is concerned about you, Sam. She says she hasn't heard from you in two years. She keeps in contact with your wife and girls, but they haven't heard from you either. It makes her very sad."

"I have my reasons."

"I'm sure you do, Sam. But are they the right reasons? I look around this place and I see people without families, without hope, without love. But you have a loving family, Sam, and they need you. They don't care if you are innocent or guilty. They love you for who you are."

"You've never been in my shoes, Father."

"No, I haven't, Sam. And I wouldn't presume to tell you that I understand your pain. I can sense your bitterness, Sam, and from your words and actions, I have a feeling you intend to continue until you can vindicate yourself."

Silence ensued. It hung like a dark cloud over Sam's head. Finally, Sam said, "Father, I asked you to see me for two reasons. First, I have found a friend who needs me." Sam related the story. "Second, I am very close to proving my innocence. Perhaps only two months."

"And what happens then, Sam?" Father Kelly asked.

"I continue to help John by being his friend until his memory returns," Sam replied. "And then I go to my family and ask them to take me back."

"Have you thought what you will do if your attempt at proving your innocence fails?"

"It won't fail. I promise you that."

"Be careful what you promise, Sam. Even if it fails, get back with your family. God didn't put you on this earth to extract revenge. He put you here to help people, and that's what you do best. Look at your record. You spent most of your adult life helping people in need. And now you are frustrated because you can't help yourself. Bottom line, Sam? Trust in the Lord. I can still see the good in you, and He can, too." Father Kelly looked at Sam's expressionless face. "Enough of a lecture, Sam. What can I do to help?"

"Guess you can pray for me and John. I'm not much good at it anymore."

"I'll do that, and something else, as well. Do you have a cell phone?"

"No. I have to use the phone here, but I don't like Father Shanks eavesdropping on my conversations."

"Okay. I'll get a cheap cell phone, and put my personal number in the phone. You can call me anytime if you need my assistance or just need to talk."

"I appreciate that, Father. And now I need to go, and so do you, before Father Shanks finds out we are talking and gets suspicious."

They made arrangements for Monsignor Kelly to leave the phone at the reception desk at City Hospital.

Father Kelly stood, put his arms around Sam, and told him to be careful. Sam didn't know how to respond, and after a moment's hesitation, left his arms at his side and said, "Thank you, Father."

Sam went back to the dining room to help clean up. Sure enough, Father Shanks popped up behind him as he was washing dishes.

"Who were you talking to, Sam?" his voice more accusing than curious.

"A fella from my mother's home town," Sam said matter-of-factly. "Guess he knew my mother, and recognized my name tag. If there's anything you want to know about Greeley, Nebraska, I can fill you in. Even the current price of corn!" He laughed.

"Uh, no thanks," Father Shanks said as he turned and walked away. Sam smiled to himself, pleased he'd diverted that one so readily.

Father Kelly left the shelter and dialed his phone. "Tony, this is Mike. Hey, can you pick me up in Council Bluffs?...Long story. Anyway, I'll be at the McDonald's on Broadway. You can't miss it.

It's just before you cross the bridge with the red and yellow lances on it...16th Street, I think...Okay, thanks."

Father Murphy was waiting at the McDonald's when Father Kelly arrived. Father Kelly climbed in and asked Tony if he had time to make a couple of stops. "Only if it doesn't make us late for my poker game," he replied, dead serious.

"I promise," Father Kelly said. "Wouldn't want God's work to interfere with a high stakes poker game."

"Sorry, Mike. I imagine even God has priorities. In fact, I'm hoping He has poker tournaments in heaven."

"Shut up and let's find a Radio Shack," Father Kelly said.

CHAPTER 19

J ASON CALLED NATHAN ON HIS way home. "Hey, Nathan, this is Jason."

"I know who it is," Nathan replied. "So how did it go?"

"Piece of cake. I went over it just like we discussed. Wore my best suit and tie. Didn't miss a beat. He asked the questions we talked about. Tried to trip me up a couple of times. But I stuck to my story, and he said he was satisfied with everything. He thanked me for coming and that was it. Wow! Thank you, man. I owe you big time."

"Yes, you do," Nathan said. "You woke Audrey up at two A.M., and she woke me up after that. I missed a whole day in Vegas to come back and save your sorry ass. Not to mention the night in the hotel I paid for and couldn't use. And it cost me $300 to change my flight!"

"God, Nathan, I'm really sorry. I'll pay you back. Anything you need, man."

"Anything, you say? Okay, to apologize to Audrey, who I might add is still suspicious as to why you called, and still more than a little miffed, you and Amy meet Audrey and me at M's Pub in the Old Market tonight. I'll make reservations for 6:30, order the most expensive wine the house has, and you're buying. In fact, to make it even more painful on your wallet, I'll ask Tom and Julie to join us."

"Yeah, I can do, Nathan—it'll be like old times, and will be fun!"

"Yeah, Jason," Nathan trying to mask his sarcasm, "Just like old times." *Jesus, I hope this is the end of this shit! I like Jason, but he still may end up collateral damage.*

Fifteen miles west, in the Village Pointe Shopping Center, Max let Natalie and Mary out at a dress shop they wanted to visit. Larry spotted a parking place close by and Max grabbed it.

As soon as they exited the car, Larry said, "Okay, let's hear it."

Max said, "I need something to drink first," and headed across the street to a coffee shop. Larry reluctantly followed, knowing if he was going to hear the story, it was going to be over coffee and probably a brownie.

Max got his latte and some kind of pastry Larry didn't recognize. Larry just got water.

"Well," Max said, his eyes bright with excitement, "he was able to account for all the time lapses we were concerned about. He had his story down pat. In fact, so pat he must have rehearsed it a hundred times. Never wavered a bit. Bottom line is he's lying through his teeth. He sat there in that expensive suit of his, smiling and being so very concerned and helpful, but he couldn't hide his clammy hands. When he shook my hand, I noticed how sweaty it was. Our boy Hughes knows more than he's telling us. Trouble is, I just don't know what he has to do with Wilson, or why."

"So what's our next step?" Larry asked.

"Our next step," Max said, "is to go across the street to Scheels and look at some impressive hardware with names like *Colt* or *Glock* stamped on it. I'm here for some fun, and not going to discuss it again until Monday." He got up to leave and Larry followed.

The tables were wiped clean, the dishes done, and the leftovers stored in the refrigerator, to be warmed again in a few hours for supper. Sam was tired, but desperately needed to go visit John in the hospital.

It was a balmy day, and the sunshine warmed Sam's heart as well as his body. He was beginning to feel alive again. He had pushed his own family out of his life, and he despised himself for that. Father Kelly was right. It was his foolish pride, fueled with hatred and a lust for revenge, that drove him on. It was almost over now. In fact, for the first time in years, he wished it were over. For five long years, he had bided his time, waiting for a break to vindicate himself. Now he was riddled with doubts. Was it really revenge that drove him on, or was it simply the adrenalin-fueled thrill of the hunt? Did that make him just as bad as Landry? Was it really time to end this now, and get back with his family? Would they even want him back? He was eager to get to the hospital, see John, and finally tell him the truth. Father Kelly had quelled the demon living within Sam's soul. It was a resurrection, an awakening that sent Sam on an emotional roller coaster. For the first time in five years, Sam was remembering what it was like to be a loving father, husband, and son. Tears welled in his eyes as he approached the hospital.

The receptionist turned Sam away when he couldn't remember John's last name. "Privacy regulations," she said with an air of authority. Sam rolled his eyes, thinking what she could do with her regulations. As he turned to leave, he remembered Whitney telling him that the man was using John Doan, a takeoff on the old John Doe, for his name. The receptionist gave her best plastic smile this time, and curtly informed Sam the patient was in Room 420. Thank heavens. Sam had enough of Room 313.

Sam approached Room 420 with trepidation. He was about to tell John a story he had been holding inside for a long, long time.

John was awake and watching football on television. John was pleased to see Sam, but looked depressed. "I was hoping you would come. Boy, I screwed up. It just got to me, Sam. I don't know who I am, what will happen tomorrow. I wish whoever had beaten me up had just killed me. I don't know if I can go on living like this. I really don't."

The compassion flowed out of Sam like a river running downhill. For five long years, he had been where John was. The only thing that kept him going during those years was hatred and the hope of revenge. How ironic. The things that he despised most in life were the things that he clung to. But it was also the very things he despised that pulled him out of the depressions, the despair, the hopelessness of going on. He was still hanging on to these emotions, but John had changed things. He had to let go and go on, for John's sake, as well as his own. *God, You put me on this merry-go-round; You have to help me get off.*

"Look John," Sam said, "it's going to get better. I know you are going through a bad time, but it isn't of your choosing. You think you can't go on, but you have to go on. If not for yourself, for me."

"What are you talking about?" John asked, screwing up his face.

"Let me tell you the answer to your question when you asked me what my story is." Sam's words were slow and deliberate. "I grew up in Chicago, John. My dad and mom met at Loyola University. My dad was from a poor black family in Chicago, grew up in a rough neighborhood, and his mother cleaned the Catholic Church, along with other places. College wasn't in the picture. There just wasn't enough money. He was smart, and his mother was determined he was going to have a better life. The pastor of the church she cleaned was sympathetic and pulled some strings to get him a scholarship to Loyola." John was quiet as he listened.

"My mother is Irish," Sam continued.

"Irish my ass," John interrupted, waving his hands in the air. "How can your mother be Irish?"

"It wasn't her fault, John," Sam said with a laugh. "Her name was Mary Catherine O'Conner. Red hair and freckles, the prettiest girl in Greeley County, Nebraska."

"You really expect me to believe this?" John said, narrowing his eyes and jutting out his jaw.

"Anyway, they fell in love and my mother took him home to Greeley to meet her folks. I only heard about it, but guess it caused quite a stir. Heck, a lot of people in Greeley had never seen a black man. And to see him with Mary Catherine, who every farm kid for miles around was secretly in love with, fueled the fire. Anyway, some of the locals decided they were going to give my dad a lesson when he left the bar with my mother.

"A kid overheard the conversation outside the bar, and ran all the way home to tell his folks what he had heard. They rounded up some neighbors, went to the bar, and gave my dad and mom a ride to her folks' farm, preventing an ugly racist assault.

"Things settled down, and a year later my folks were married. Some people in Greeley accepted it, some still didn't. I was born a couple of years later. We went to Greeley to visit my grandparents, but folks were accepting by then. I never knew the story until my grandparents told me."

John raised his hands to stop Sam. "Whoa, Sam. Where is all of this going?"

Sam squared his shoulders. "Please just indulge me, John." He collected his thoughts and continued.

"Anyway, my folks are both lawyers in Chicago, my dad for a private firm, and my mother does pro bono work for anyone who needs legal help. I admired them, and the good they did, and followed in their footsteps. Went to law school, but later decided that I needed a change. I left my practice and joined the FBI. Eventually got married, and have two daughters."

John listened intently. Occasionally he looked surprised, but most of the time, he nodded his head as if he'd expected the story he was hearing. He finally asked, "So where is your family now?"

"They live in Omaha. I haven't spoken to them in a couple of years."

A light came on in John's mind as his eyes opened wide. "The pictures of the girls you took—they're your daughters!"

"Yes," Sam replied, tears forming in his bloodshot eyes, and sliding down his cheeks.

"So why are you living on the streets?" John asked, not understanding, but no longer concerned about his own problems.

"There was a drug bust going down in Grand Island." Sam didn't notice the flicker of recognition in John's eyes as he continued on. "I was part of a joint task force with the DEA, FBI, and local law enforcement. We hit eleven meth labs in one day. Everything went down without incident. We filed our reports, and I came back to Omaha. The next day two deputies from the Douglas County Sheriff's department showed up at my door with a search warrant. They found $1200.00 in cash wadded up under the spare tire in the trunk of my car."

John didn't blink, but asked bluntly, "Did you take it?"

"No," Sam said, "I didn't."

"So what happened?" John asked.

"I spent two years in a minimum security facility after a Grand Jury investigation. Lost my badge, my dignity, my family, everything."

"Jesus!" John said. "And you never took the money?" Not really a question.

"No," Sam reiterated. "One of the perps told the local cops that he had a thousand dollars of his own money in the bedroom. He claimed he saw me take the money and pocket it."

"There must have been some way to vindicate yourself." John's voice was emphatic, with the confidence of one who's never been falsely accused.

"Yeah, there was," Sam said. "The cop who rode with me on the bust was willing to testify he and I counted the money together, and the money was put into an evidence bag. He also stated he had not seen me go into the bedroom alone. Unluckily for me, the cop wasn't able to testify before the Grand Jury. He was killed in a boating accident a week after the bust. Ran his boat into a dock at full throttle."

John's eyes grew wide with horror and he shook his head. "This is unbelievable! Do you have any idea who's responsible?"

Sam was bewildered that John wasn't questioning his story. Everyone else rolled their eyes when he proclaimed his innocence. "I got too close to the biggest drug dealer in the state," Sam said. "It was serendipity. I was assigned to an alleged money laundering operation in Omaha, and the more I followed the money, the closer I got to the source. It led to a prominent Omaha businessman who was running the biggest drug operation in the state. I pushed him a little, and he retaliated by having someone plant the money in my car. The son of a bitch portrays himself as a model citizen, but he's been responsible for murder, as well as his drug dealing. Not just the cop who got killed in the boating accident, but some 'accidental'"—Sam made quotation marks in the air with his fingers—"explosions in competing meth labs. Two people died in those explosions. Anyway, I've wanted to get the bastard from the moment the Grand Jury decided to press charges. I'm so full of hatred and revenge, getting him is all I can think about some days. It's cost me my family and my former life as I knew it. I'll always be a dirty cop until I put an end to it."

"Can't anyone help you?" John almost pleaded.

"You already have," Sam said.

"Me?" John said. "How could I have helped you?"

"By being my friend," Sam said, tears starting to flow again. "You have amnesia and virtually no knowledge of your past. Like I said before, you can't do anything about your situation until your brain heals, but I can. I can put the hate and the revenge behind me and go back to my family."

Sam paused and took a deep breath as he looked toward the ceiling. Emotions back in hand, he looked back at John and said, "Remember the kid I told you ran home to tell his folks that someone was going to beat up my dad? He visited me today. He's a priest in Grand Island and came to the shelter with a group of other people attending some Catholic conference. I recognized him from my grandmother's funeral service, and I asked him to see me. We had a long talk and he...he restored my faith in myself."

"So...where does this story end?" John asked, puzzled.

"I don't know," Sam replied, letting out a sigh as he shrugged his shoulders.

Across the river in Omaha, Max was trying out new holsters for his service weapon, a Glock 17, and blabbing with the salesman. The girls were still shopping, and Larry was impatient and ready to move on. When his phone rang, he grabbed it so fast he almost dropped it. "Hello...Oh yeah, we're having a great time. Lots of guns and neat stuff...Twenty minutes? Sure, we can do that." His voice was cheery but when he clicked off the phone, he shook his head. *Another twenty minutes? My God, how can they possibly still be shopping?* He walked over to Max and told him he would pick him up at the front door in fifteen minutes.

The shopping bags were setting on the walk when Larry pulled the Nissan up to the curb. He popped the trunk, got out, and helped the ladies load four or five bags each. The trunk was half full when he closed the lid. *We're going to have to ship our suitcases back if they keep up this pace.*

Larry put on his happy face as he climbed back into the car. He tried to ignore Max wetting his finger to wipe a food spot from his seat cover. "So where are we going now, ladies?"

"The Old Market," Natalie said. "Mary and I saw some neat stores last night when you drove through. Why don't you guys drop us off and then run across the river to Bass Pro Shop, and we can meet about six for supper. One of the clerks recommended an Italian restaurant in the Old Market. It's called Vincenzo's and is walking distance from the hotel. In fact, drop us off there, and we'll make a reservation before we start shopping."

"Sounds good," Larry said, keeping his happy face glued on.

There was a knock on John's door. Sam rose and went to the door as it was pushed open. It was Father Shanks. Sam said, "I was just leaving, so you can have John all to yourself." He looked back at John and said, "I'll be back tomorrow to get you when they cut you loose."

Sam left the hospital and headed to continue surveillance on the meth lab he had discovered. He had gone about two blocks when his old instincts took hold. He saw the movement out of the corner of his eye. He was being followed. Sam stepped up his pace. His first impulse was to lure him into a trap and find out who had sent him. That would tip Landry off, however, and Sam needed to keep under the radar. Landry would shut down the lab and Sam would be back to square one. Sam slowed his pace, and headed back to the shelter. Best to keep a low profile. The man followed but stayed in the shadows across the street. For the first time since Sam moved into the shelter, he locked his door before going to bed.

Father Shanks kept his visit with John short. An orderly came in the room and Father Shanks took the opportunity to leave. The orderly started to assess John, then abruptly stopped. John saw the stunned look on the orderly's face and asked, fear in his voice, "Is something wrong?"

"No, no...everything is fine. I just remembered something I need to do. I'll be back later."

The orderly left the room and went to the nurses' station. He pulled up the hospital phone directory on the computer and dialed Whitney Weston's home number.

Whitney recognized the hospital number and answered, "This is Whitney."

"Whitney, this is Dirk Medley. You don't know me, but I'm a med student and work part time at City as an orderly."

"What can I do for you?"

"I'm the orderly that found the patient who had the attempt on his life. That patient is back in the hospital, and he had a visitor. Remember I told the police that the attacker was Hispanic, had a mustache and long hair?"

"I remember."

"Well, something has been bugging me and I just found out what it was. When I described him, I kept telling the sketch artist to make his eyes closer together. He had these beady, squinty eyes that bore right through you. Well, I just saw those eyes—this same guy was visiting John Doan a few minutes ago. And it suddenly dawned on me what's been bugging me all this time. His eyes were green. Hispanics don't have green eyes. And today, this guy was dressed up as a priest!"

"I'm sorry, did you say your name was Dirk?"

"Yes, Dirk Medley."

"Okay, Dirk, are you sure about this? Short, balding, beady green eyes?"

"It's the same guy. I'm sure of it. I was so obsessed with the mustache, long black hair, and dark skin, I forgot about the eyes."

"This is impossible. You just described Father Shanks!"

"I don't know his name, but he's the same guy; I'm sure of it."

"Okay, Dirk. Call the police and I will be there in twenty minutes!"

Dirk hung up the phone. He dialed the Council Bluffs police department, and asked the operator to send an officer to the fourth floor nurses' station of City Hospital right away. He told her his name, and said it was regarding a murder attempt at the hospital. He got up, pushed his chair back, and used his walkie to page the charge nurse. He explained the situation and asked her to find someone to cover for him while he talked to the police. He went into the restroom and was standing in front of the urinal when he felt a sharp stabbing pain in his lower back. He turned in time to see the priest plunge the knife again, this time into his gut.

The orderly watched the priest go to the sink and wash the blood... his blood... from the knife. That was the last image he saw.

Whitney pulled into the parking lot, shut off her car, and pulled the handle to open the door. She felt resistance, and the door was pushed back shut. Startled, she looked out the window to see Father Shanks with a gun pointed at her. He tapped the barrel on the window, motioning for her to roll it down. She complied. "Do not start the car, Whitney, or attempt to run. I will shoot you without another thought." He kept the gun trained on her. "Roll up the window, then get out of the car, hand me the keys, and walk beside me as if we are old friends." She kept her eyes on the gun as she followed his instructions and stepped from the car. He hit the remote to lock her car. "Can't be too careful," he laughed at the sound of the beep, knowing the window was still open. "Now let's get in my car." She opened the passenger door, and he struck her on the head with his gun. She fell half in and half out of the car. He picked up her legs and pushed the rest of her into his Explorer. He drove out of the hospital lot expecting to see a patrol car, but they hadn't arrived yet. He drove on, letting out a sigh of relief, as he had averted a potential disaster. But now he had another problem to deal with.

CHAPTER 20

THE ATMOSPHERE IN M's PUB was lively on Saturday night. Nathan, Jason, and Tom were making the most of it. Their wives were enjoying themselves too, as they didn't have a lot of chances for all of them to get together. True to his conversation with Jason, Nathan had ordered the best wine in the place, and it had brought out the tales from their college days. Tom had to work the weekend, so he and Julie left about eight. Nathan, Audrey, Jason, and Amy stayed for an after dinner drink, a Colorado Bulldog. It was a tradition with the guys to finish the night with one. Bottoms up, and both Nathan and Jason gave the car keys to their wives as they left the restaurant.

Ted, Frank, Nancy, and Susan had an equally good time at the Spaghetti Works, on the corner across from M's Pub. Ted wanted to hit a couple of bars on the way back to the hotel, but Susan said she was tired and needed to go back to the hotel. "Ted, would it be an imposition to see me back?" Susan asked. It wasn't in his plans, but he nodded, smiled, and said, "Sure."

Nancy asked Ted where he would like to meet her and Frank. "Let's go to that bar across from the Embassy. I'll be over after I see Susan to her room."

Ted and Susan were going down the concrete steps of the Spaghetti Works as Nathan and Jason were crossing the street.

A slightly drunk voice called out, "Ted Bingham, what the hell are you doing here?"

Ted looked up and saw Jason coming his way, hand extended. Ted shook it, and then Nathan shook his hand, smiling at the good fortune to see their old friend. Ted hugged Audrey and Amy, and then said. "Oh, I should introduce you," as he looked at Susan standing on the corner alone with an uncomfortable smile on her face. "Nathan, Audrey, Jason, Amy," Ted said as he nodded at each of them, "meet my friend Susan Wilson."

Jason turned white as a sheet. His knees started to give out. He grabbed Amy's arm. She thought he was just a little drunk. He thought he was going to hurl.

Nathan stepped forward. "We're old friends, went to college together. Nice to meet you Susan," as he reached to shake her hand. She gave him a limp handshake, still exhausted and a little bewildered.

"We're here for a church conference," Ted said.

"Want to join us for a drink?" Nathan boldly asked. Audrey gave him a look.

"Thanks," Ted replied, "but Susan is tired and I'm taking her back to the hotel. Really sorry guys. But it's great to see all of you. I'll make it a point to get back soon. We'll get together."

As Ted and Susan headed for the Embassy, she said, "I'm sorry, Ted. Looks like I'm spoiling your evening."

"Not at all, Susan. Besides, I think those guys have had enough to drink for the night already."

Susan took his arm. "You really are a sweetie, Ted."

Ted saw Susan to her room, then headed for the elevator to go down and meet Nancy and Frank. His elevator descended, and Malone and Worthy's ascended a few feet away.

The phone shocked Sam awake. At first, he was startled, but then realized it was the cell phone Father Kelly had given him. He groped in the dark, and finally got it out of his jacket pocket. "Hello?"

"Sam, this is Father Kelly. Hope I didn't wake you."

"Not at all Father," Sam said as he tried to see the clock in the dark.

"Anyway, Sam, I wanted to tell you that I asked around about Father Shanks. No one seems to know him, or anything about him. He isn't from this diocese."

Gathering his senses, Sam asked, "So how did he get on the list of shelters to visit?"

"Still the special agent, aren't you Sam," Father Kelly said. "Good question. I asked the same one. He heard about the conference and volunteered. Guess no one thought to question his credentials. A Roman collar opens a lot of doors."

"So he's not a priest?" Sam said with incredulity.

"I wouldn't say that," Father Kelly said, "but no one seems to know anything about him. I asked the local priests, the Jesuits at the school, and no one knows who he is."

"I don't know what to make of this," Sam said.

"I don't know either," Father Kelly said. "Let me do a little more research and I'll get back to you. In the meantime, maybe you can ask some questions."

"You can bet I will," Sam replied, his brain now in high gear, and his senses on high alert.

"I'll try and get back to you on Monday, Sam," Father Kelly said.

"Thanks, Father, I appreciate your help."

"Goodnight, and God bless, Sam."

Sam closed the phone. *What the hell is going on? Am I that gullible? Jeez, I've lost my instincts.* Sam lay awake for a long time before finally dozing off.

Audrey went upstairs to bed when she and Nathan arrived home. Nathan told her he would be up shortly.

Ten minutes later his phone vibrated. "Nathan, this is Jason. Jesus, man, what the hell was that all about? Ted with Wilson's wife! This is too fucked up, man. I can't handle any more of it!"

Nathan let him vent, pacing as he listened. Finally he couldn't take any more of it. "Jason, shut the fuck up! I'm getting sick and tired of your whining. Didn't you tell me this morning that the detective was satisfied with your story?...So what in the hell is the problem?...Okay, Ted was with Wilson's wife. Big deal. Maybe he's screwing her, maybe they were just at a church meeting like he said. I really don't give a damn. What I do give a damn about is your paranoia...Don't interrupt me! I am going to hang up this phone in a minute, and don't you dare call me back. Nobody knows what went on. Just you and me. Keep your big mouth shut and it's over. Now go to bed." Nathan closed his phone shut, then flung it across the room. He sat on the sofa, his head in his hands. *I had too much to drink. Not a good time to sort things out. Stupid, dumb Jason! The son of a bitch is a liability, and damned if I'm going to lose everything, friend or not. Better deal with it in the morning when I'm sober.*

Nathan took a deep breath and exhaled loudly as he rose from the sofa. He shook his head as he started up the stairs and then the phone rang. *If that's that fucking Jason, I really am going to kill him!* He searched for his phone, not sure where it had bounced when he threw it. On the fourth ring, he realized it was his throwaway phone ringing. He answered it brusquely.

"What?...Wait a minute; slow down...You did *what?*" Nathan listened as Father Shanks told him the sequence of events earlier in the day. Nathan felt his blood pressure rising as blood rushed to his head. He walked outside to clear his head, and where he was certain Audrey wouldn't overhear.

"Let's go over this again. You killed the orderly in the bathroom?"

"I had to," Father Shanks said. "He saw me the night I tried to kill Wilson, recognized me today, and called the police!" His voice was an urgent whisper.

"Did he tell them your name?"

"No, I overheard the conversation. First he called Whitney Weston, the social worker, and he told her. I heard him tell her he would see her in twenty minutes, and then he called the police. He just asked them to send an officer to the hospital. Just said he was witness to a murder. Never mentioned my name."

"Wait a minute. I thought you said you wore a disguise. How could he recognize you now?" Nathan was worked up, waving his arms in the air, waiting for an answer.

"It was my eyes. You know how they are so green and kind of close together—"

"Yeah, yeah I know. So what about this Weston woman? Where in the hell is she?"

"I took her to the shelter. She's in the storm cellar on the west side of the building. I tied her up and gagged her. Do you want me to kill her too?"

"No," Nathan said with exasperation, "I want to kill *you*." His tone was menacing. "You have fucked this up from day one. Do not even think about touching that woman. Now here's what you are going to do..."

CHAPTER 21

WHITNEY FLOATED IN AND OUT of consciousness. She could feel her skin pull from the caked blood stuck to her cheek. Her head throbbed with pain. She was finally conscious enough to gather her senses. She was bound, hands behind her back, ankles tied together, something stuffed in her mouth forcing her to breathe through her nose.

Panic set in. Her breathing increased and she was close to passing out. She forced herself to relax and breathe slowly and deeply. Thoughts raced through her mind. Her family. Would she ever see them again? Was he going to kill her? Why didn't he just do it already? It was complete blackness. She could tell she was on a cold cement floor. There was a musty smell in the air. *A basement? My God, Father Shanks? I never particularly liked him, but he was a priest, for God's sake. A man of God. And he's the son of a bitch who tried to kill 313, and now me? Dirk Medley. What did he do to him? Oh, please Lord, spare us from this monster. Please, please let me see my family again.* The stress had worn her out. Her breathing accelerated, and she passed out again from hypoxia.

Fifty feet away, Father Shanks was saying Sunday Mass. His sermon centered around hope. Unfortunately it fell on mostly deaf ears, ears that had abandoned all thoughts of hope. They lived day to day. The food and drink they could scrounge was their driving force. The shelter provided just that. Food and shelter. It did *not* give them hope. They thought Father Shanks was an idealist. A man who ran a shelter but didn't understand they no longer had a soul. Or if they did, they had tucked it away or walled it off from the rest of their body.

They sat in folding chairs, mostly inattentive. It was something to do. When you are homeless, you have all the time in the world. Nowhere to go, no one to talk to—at least anyone who cares—and no hope for the future. You just exist, fulfilling your bodily needs as they arise, not caring for others, the same as they don't care about you. Life in your own little vacuum.

Father Shanks concluded the Mass with his usual blessing. Some of them crossed themselves, the rest did not. He turned from the table, removing his vestments as he walked away. One of them turned on the television before he was out of the room, changing channels until he found a sports network.

Father Shanks dropped his vestments in his room, closed the door as he walked out, left the shelter, got in his Explorer and drove away.

Across the river, Frank picked up Monsignor Kelly in time to head for Sacred Heart Church. They had heard that the Mass there was a moving experience. The front of the church had a small group with drums, guitars, and piano playing music for the choir on the right side, and it rocked, just as Monsignor Kelly had been told. He wanted to see for himself. He led them to the choir loft as most seats were taken. They soon found themselves singing and clapping and smiling with the rest of the congregation. Monsignor Kelly would later tell them that he was impressed, but afraid the congregation at St. John's wasn't quite yet ready for the Renaissance.

Ted and Nancy exchanged glances. She managed a smile which he returned, then cast his eyes away. She had knocked on his door the night before, and asked to come in. Still smitten, he gladly obliged, never expecting the next series of events.

Nancy asked if Ted was attracted to her, or if he had a thing for Susan.

Ted was taken aback. "I painted Susan's nursery," Ted said. "She was needy, not in that way, but just wanting company. I stayed for supper and we talked. I felt sorry for her, and yes, I will be her friend and help her in any way I can. But that's it."

"You only answered half of my question." Nancy said.

"Nancy, let's be honest. Yes, I have always been attracted to you, in a physical sense. After this weekend, I also realize that you are more than just a hot body, you are a fun, witty, intelligent person. A person I like, not just a goddess to be ogled. But there's a problem. You're married, and I'm not the kind of guy who runs around with somebody else's wife behind his back." He paused. "If I'm misreading this Nancy, I'm going to be embarrassed as hell, and probably just lost a new friend."

"No, you're not misreading it Ted. You just don't know all the facts."

Ted tilted his head. "And those would be?"

"My husband and I are separated. We are getting a divorce. We won't actually start proceedings until after the first of the year. I need my job, and I don't imagine the school board will allow a divorced woman to remain a teacher in a Catholic school. I'm hoping they will let me finish the spring semester after they find out."

"Wow," was all Ted could muster to say, shaking his head.

"Yeah, wow," Nancy replied. "You're the only other person who knows, Ted, and I hope I can count on your confidentiality."

"Sure, of course," Ted managed to say.

"Well...I guess that's all I really wanted to say." Nancy rose and started for the door. Ted stood and reached out to give her a hug. He reflected later that it was a matter of opinion whether that had been the wrong move or the right move.

When Ted woke up, Nancy was gone, along with her clothing she had left scattered on the floor before they made mad passionate love.

Ted had avoided breakfast, not wanting to face Nancy or Susan. He was relieved when they met at the car and Nancy gave him a matter-of-fact greeting. "Missed you at breakfast, Ted," followed by a knowing smile.

Nathan hadn't slept all night. Six months had passed, and one moment of anger was about to destroy his life. He had decided that Jason wasn't the problem. It was his own stupid actions that had caused the situation. That, plus the ineptitude of his people.

Nathan told Audrey he had to go to the dealership to do some paperwork. She began to object, as it was Sunday, and she wanted him to attend church with the family. He left in a huff.

The Ford Explorer was sitting in the abandoned parking lot. Nathan drove in and parked directly behind it. He got out cautiously, and approached the car. This was the risky part, as he knew Father Shanks would be armed. "I want your hands on the steering wheel," Nathan said loudly. Father Shanks complied. "Keep them there," Nathan said as he got in the passenger side of the car.

"I need your registration slip. Is it in the glove compartment?"

"Yes, Father Shanks replied."

Nathan found it along with the insurance papers. He put them in his coat pocket.

"I'm really sorry, Nathan," Father Shanks said, looking at him for the first time, white-knuckled hands still clutching the steering wheel.

"Save your confession for God," Nathan said sarcastically. "He's more forgiving than I am." Nathan let his comment soak in, then said, "Take I-29 south to Mound City, Missouri. It's a little over an hour down the road. Take the exit. You'll see a McDonald's on the east side of the road. There's a Super 8 behind it. A white Ford pickup with In-Transit stickers will be in the parking lot. Put your luggage in the truck, leave the key in the Explorer, and I never want to see you again." Nathan got out of the Explorer and watched it drive away. He also saw the car parked across the street pull away from the curb and follow the Explorer.

Sam woke early. He attended Sunday Mass for the first time in a long while. *Did Father Kelly get to me? Apparently so.* Sam dwelled on Father Shanks's sermon on hope. It hit home—he had hope now. After mass, Sam went to the window to see if his shadow was still across the street. He didn't see him, but that didn't mean he wasn't lurking out there somewhere. Sam went to his room, made his bed, and grabbed his jacket. It was going to be a beautiful October day, but it was a little cloudy and cool. Sam decided to check for activity at the meth house. He had time to kill as John wouldn't be released from the hospital until lunch.

Sam walked past the house. Tomas's white pickup was in the drive, along with the other occupant's car. It was quiet and the curtains were closed. Sam casually walked by, not looking at the house. He was looking for the man tailing him. No sign of him. Good. One less thing to worry about. Sam went to the park to catch a quick nap before going to the hospital. He hadn't slept last night, and he didn't want lack of sleep to dull his senses.

Nathan went back to the dealership to wait for a call. He paced around the showroom, walked through the service bays, occasionally slamming his fist against a car. *Damn! How could I be so stupid?* He would hear from the man following Father Shanks in about an hour. He kept looking at his watch. The minutes dragged by. He tapped his watch to make sure it was working.

Nathan was thirsty. He put a dollar in the Coke machine, pressed the button. Nothing. He banged it with his fist before he remembered pop was a dollar twenty-five. He put another quarter in, pressed the Diet Coke button, and the can finally tumbled into the dispenser. He looked at his watch. Only twenty-five minutes had passed. Nothing to do but wait.

Nathan jumped when the phone rang an hour later. He answered, "Yes?"

"We've got a problem," the voice on the other end of the line said.

CHAPTER 22

S AM AWAKENED FROM HIS NAP on the bench, and headed for City Hospital. It was still cloudy, but the air had warmed considerably.

Sam's radar hit high alert when he saw the police officer seated outside of John's room. Sam walked up to the officer, who stood and blocked his path. The officer said sternly, "Only approved visitors."

"Is John okay?" Sam asked with concern.

"What's your name?" the officer asked.

"Sam Washington. I'm a friend..."

The officer held up his hand. "You're on the list. You can go in."

"But what happened?"

"I'm not at liberty to discuss that," the officer said. "Sgt. Valdez will be here soon, and you can talk to him."

"I'll go you one better," Sam said, reaching for the phone Father Kelly had given him. He pulled a card from his pocket, and dialed a number. "Sorry to bother you on a Sunday, Chief Marlowe. This is Sam Washington. I'm outside of John Doan's room and he has a police guard. May I ask what's going on?" Sam saw the dumbfounded look on the officer's face.

The chief had gone over all the reports from the beating and the attempt on John's life, and determined that Sam wasn't involved, and was happy to answer him. "Yes. The orderly who found John after the first attempt on his life saw the perpetrator in John's room last night. He called the police and we sent an officer. He arrived on the scene and found the orderly in the men's restroom. He had been stabbed."

"Good God! Is he going to be okay?"

"We don't know at this point. The doctor says it's touch and go," Chief Marlowe said.

"There's more, Sam," the Chief added. "Whitney Weston, the social worker for the hospital is missing."

"*Whitney?*"

"Yes. Her husband said she left home in response to a phone call from the hospital around 8:30 last night. She hadn't returned by ten, so he tried her cell. When she didn't answer, he called the hospital and no one had seen her. He drove to the hospital, and found her car in the parking lot. They searched the hospital and grounds, but there was no sign of her. We're doing all we can, Sam."

"Too much coincidence for the two to not be connected," Sam said, his FBI mind assessing the situation.

"I agree, Sam," Chief Marlowe said. "They're going to keep John in the hospital again tonight. The doctor thinks he had a reaction to some medication, but they will probably release him tomorrow. In the meantime, we'll keep an officer outside the door."

"What can I do to help?" Sam asked.

"Inquire about Whitney from your friends, Sam. But remember, you're not an FBI agent, and I don't want you taking any action on your own, understand?"

"Yes," said Sam dejectedly.

"Oh, and I would feel better if you were there when John is released tomorrow. Take him back to the shelter and keep an eye on him."

"You can count on me," Sam said.

Sam closed the phone. He asked the officer some questions, and got answers this time. He then walked past him and entered John's room.

John perked up immediately when he saw Sam. "Sam! I'm really glad to see you! Did you hear about all the excitement last night?"

"Yeah, I did," Sam replied, still trying to put everything together.

John said, "Some guy was stabbed and Whitney is missing! What's going on, Sam?"

"Wish I knew, John...Hey, what's that rash on your leg?"

"Oh, I had a reaction to a drug. I told them I was allergic to Penicillin and Macrolides. The doctor ordered Clarithromycin. As soon as I heard what they were giving me, I pulled the IV out, and called the nurse. By then my body had reacted to it, and I ended up with this rash. It should go away in a week or so. Itches like hell, though."

"I'm not following, John. How did you know all this drug stuff?"

"I don't know, I just do. Clarithromycin is a Macrolide antibiotic, and guess the doctor didn't see it on my chart or something. Got by the pharmacist and nurses, too. It happens," he added matter-of-factly.

Sam sat processing this information. He had heard John talk about his drugs for his brain trauma too, but figured his doctor or therapist had told him the information. Sam's thoughts were interrupted with John's exciting revelation.

"Sam," John said, the excitement in his voice evident, "the snakes weren't snakes!"

Sam's mind was a mile away. "What snakes, John?" He wondered if the medicine was making him hallucinate.

"My nightmares, Sam. The snakes biting me, remember? They weren't snakes biting me, they were snakeskin boots kicking me! I remember now, Sam."

"Snakeskin boots?" Sam stared at John with a puzzled look on his face. "What made you remember that?"

"One of the doctors came in and when he sat down, I noticed he had these unusual cowboy boots on. I asked him what kind of leather they were made from. He said Python. Then I remembered—I was being kicked by a guy wearing snakeskin boots!"

"Can you remember his face?" "No," John said. "All I remember is the boots. But Sam, that's great! It's a step and maybe my nightmares will be over!"

Sam knew it was progress, but wanted more. He wanted a face or a name. He sat lost in thought before a light went on in his head. *Landry! That SOB wears white snakeskin boots! What does John have to do with Landry? Oh, shit, don't tell me they were involved in something.*

Sam tried to get more information from John, but it proved futile. He even mentioned Nathan Landry's name, but there was no recognition in John's eyes. He finally gave up, and decided to go back to the shelter. He knew he had Landry linked to the meth lab, but would he bring John down at the same time?

On his way back to the shelter, Sam stopped and told several homeless people to keep on the watch for Whitney. They were shocked. No one had seen her, but if she was around he knew they would find her. She was their advocate and they would give their lives for her. Sam checked his six o'clock on the way back, and sure enough, he had a shadow. *That's okay. I'm safer knowing he's following me than not knowing it.*

He went to his room and tried to digest it all. He made notes. He placed them on his bed. Nathan Landry, John Doan, Whitney Weston, the stabbed orderly. *There has to be a common denominator somewhere. But how could Whitney be connected to Landry? She had a definite connection to John. Or better yet, how could John be connected to Landry? It has to be drugs. Did John work for Landry? Did he double-cross him? Did Landry order the hit? And where does the orderly play in the big picture? He was the one that discovered John the first time...hmmm...what did he see this time? He must have seen something. He must have called Whitney, and that spooked somebody.* Sam thought it through over and over again. *The orderly had to have told her something. Now he's in critical condition and Whitney is missing. There's a piece missing from this puzzle and I've got to find it.* Sam stood, placed his hand on the wall high above his head, and let his forehead rest on the wall. He stood that way for a long while, before backing away, still racking his brain to figure out where— or who—was the missing piece. He went for a walk to clear his head. No sign of his shadow. *Strange. Why would the guy leave his post?* He returned in time to get supper, not realizing Whitney was struggling for her life less than one hundred feet away.

CHAPTER 23

WHITNEY FINALLY REGAINED FULL CONSCIOUSNESS. She was bound, hands and feet, and gagged. *How long have I been here? Need to find a way out. There has to be a way.*

Her eyes had adjusted to the dark. She knew she was in a basement or somewhere musty, cold, and damp. Her breathing was becoming more difficult as the dampness caused her sinuses to swell. She couldn't seem to get enough air through her nostrils. She had to get that gag off so she could breathe through her mouth. Whitney tried to push it out with her tongue, but the rag around her head held it tight. Her tongue and jaws were sore from trying.

She lay on her side, and saw some sticks or poles standing in the corner—she couldn't quite tell what they were in the darkness. Other than that, the room was empty. Well, other than the creepy bugs that occasionally crawled on her. *At least they aren't mice. Or rats!* She decided she had to find a way to get to the corner. She tried digging her shoulders into the floor, while pushing with her knees. All she accomplished was rubbing her knees raw on the rough concrete floor.

Whitney finally just collapsed from lack of air and exhaustion. She lay there for awhile, then decided to try again. She was *not* going to die without a fight. She finally figured out she could *roll* towards the corner. It was difficult with her hands bound behind her back, but she basically threw herself from her back to her chest. Progress was slow. She stopped every roll or two to rest. As she got closer, she saw the sticks were tools, a shovel and a rake leaning in the corner. She pulled her head up as far as she could, in an attempt to catch her gag on the shovel. She hooked it on the third try, but as she pulled, the shovel tipped and fell on top of her. Frustrated, she purposefully knocked the rake over, hoping it would fall with the tines upward. It did. She hooked the gag on a tine, but the rake just slid on the floor as she tried to pull. She finally lay on the tines of the rake with her chest and shoulders to hold it in place, and hooked the gag on a tine at the other end. She kept hooking and tearing her lip before she realized it might be easier if she pushed the gag down under her chin. It worked after three or four tries. It took equally as many tries to spit the large saliva-soaked rag out of her mouth.

She gulped in the musty air. As bad as it smelled and tasted, it felt wonderful. *Okay Whitney, now you're going to get these plastic ties off and get out of here.* She pulled herself next to the shovel and began to twist so she could try and use it to cut her bonds. Her ankles and wrists were already raw, bleeding, and hurt like hell. When she rubbed them against the rusty, dull shovel blade, it just increased the pain. It kept sliding away from her wrists. She finally worked it between her and the wall to get some leverage. After what seemed like an hour, she could feel no progress. It was going to take a long time to cut through the plastic ties. She had to rest. She would wait and try again. While she rested, she thought about her husband, David. She could see him in his workshop filing the blade of a shovel to sharpen it when it became dull. He was meticulous with his tools. He would never have this piece of crap shovel in *his* garage. Tears came to her eyes. She wondered if she would ever see him again, or her children. She closed her eyes and the tears flowed down her cheeks.

Nathan was still pacing at the dealership when the car pulled into the parking lot. Nathan unlocked the door and let him in.

Nathan was in a rage. He threw up his arms and said, "How in the hell could you lose him? Jesus, all you had to do was stay behind him, and take him out when he went to change cars. But no, you lost him. Are you stupid, or what?"

"It wasn't my fault. I got pulled over by a state cop. I don't know if they had some sting going or what. Anyway, he pulled me over, and then I couldn't catch up with the Explorer. The cop pulled in behind me so I had to watch my speed until he took an exit. I punched it, but no sign of the priest. He may have taken an exit and gotten off of the Interstate."

Nathan growled and grabbed him by the shirt with both hands. He shoved him down on his back and raised his fist to hit him, but stopped short. Panting, he stood upright, and told the man to get off the floor.

"Stay right here," Nathan barked. The man didn't move. He knew Nathan was out of control, and it scared the hell out of him.

Nathan went to his desk, put his hands over his face, and let out a sigh. *Okay. Father Shanks is gone. Along with my Explorer. He knows everything, but he's running for his life. He knew he was dead when he drove away. Damn cop screwed it up for us. So eliminate him for now. I'll deal with him if he ever shows up again.*

That leaves the social worker. She has to go, but first things first. Wilson and Washington are my real threats, Wilson for his memory, and Washington if he ever gets his ambition back. They have to go.

Nathan yelled at the man still standing in the showroom. "Get your ass in here." The man hustled into the office. "Sit," Nathan said. "This is what you do to redeem yourself."

The homeless population of Council Bluffs consisted mostly of loners. They kept to themselves, sometimes forging a friendship with other unfortunates, but never with outsiders. Things were different this Sunday night. They were accustomed to finding one of their own freezing, sick, suffering, or even dead. But Whitney Weston was not one of their own. She had touched most of their lives at one time or another, and it was incomprehensible that she was missing, possibly the victim of foul play.

They hung together in small groups, approaching outsiders to ask if they had seen a tall, black woman. They were greeted with fear, apprehension, and sometimes anger. They didn't care, they were adamant to do all they could to help. The groups milled around, not knowing how to organize productive efforts without a leader.

The pedestrian and automobile traffic died down as Sunday night wore on. Normally listless individuals now had a purpose. They rallied together, and as the chill filled the night, they built a fire in a trash container. They milled around the container, discussing what might have happened to Whitney, while warming their chilly hands.

The police were on the scene to ensure that the crowd remained in control. This displeased some of the participants, but they soon realized the police were not there to disrupt their vigil, such as it was; they were only there to ensure things remained in control. This went on most of the night, people bringing fuel for the fire, and the crowd still expressing concern and hope for Whitney. By daylight, the few remaining were asleep, and the police no longer a presence. They would be back in the evening, however, unless Whitney was found.

Detectives Worthy and Malone had discussed strategy on the drive back to Grand Island. Max was convinced that Jason Hughes knew more about Wilson than he was admitting. In fact, Max was convinced that Jason had been coached so his statements would back up those of his friends.

"The question is," Max said, "are they involved as a group or individually? Or did they just see something they don't want to relate to us?"

"On the surface they're all solid citizens," Malone interjected.

"So was O.J. Simpson, until he killed his wife," Max countered.

"He was found not guilty," Malone said.

"Sure, and President Clinton never had sex with Monica Lewinsky, either," Max said with a chuckle. Malone just shook his head in reluctant amusement.

"Okay, let's get back to business," Max said, terminating the banter. "We were willing to accept that Wilson may have left his wife until two things happened. First, he never tapped his bank account. Second, it was obvious the drugs and money were planted. That means he's probably still alive, but just in case he comes back, they want him put away."

"So where do we go with this?" Malone asked.

"Well, someone has access to drugs and money. The deputy sheriff could be the one, although I don't think so. He had a good reputation when he was in Grand Island. Hughes doesn't have the balls to do anything. He's the weak link. I'm going to give him a call in the morning, shake him up a bit. Time to trip him up, if you know what I mean," and he gave Malone a cheerful wink. Malone knew Max was very good at this tactic, and was glad to have him go with his plan.

"What do you propose for me?" Malone asked.

"I don't know," Max said. "You're the senior detective, and all. Surely you can find something to do."

"Smart ass," Malone said. "Actually, I'm going to talk to Officer Hamilton with the drug unit again. Then I'm going to follow up on Landry. And...if we come up with a dead end, I say we put the case to rest. We've spent way too much time on it already."

"Okay, but you're the one who has to tell Susan Wilson," Max said with a grin.

Across town, Ted had helped Susan Wilson put her suitcase in her car. Then he and Nancy met at his apartment to continue where they had left off Saturday night.

They were grinning contentedly at each other when Nancy said, "I had better get home."

"I thought you and your husband were separated," Ted objected.

"We are," Nancy said, "but we still live in the same house. I don't want adultery allegations in the divorce. It would get messy, and might affect my settlement."

"So what does that mean?" Ted asked, as he pulled his shirt over his head.

"That means," Nancy said, as she put her arms around Ted's neck and gave him a long, passionate kiss, "that you and I have to be very careful we don't get caught."

Ted stood speechless as she opened the door and blew him a kiss. Ted did a little dance. *Man! I was looking forward to this weekend, but had no idea it would end up this way. The Monsignor would shit his pants! And to think he had Harlan Jensen to thank for it!* Ted couldn't wait to see Nancy at school in the morning. Her fragrance lingered in the air as he spent a very sleepless night.

Brad, the man who had botched the plan to kill Father Shanks, left Nathan's office with two pictures. He had time to spare before meeting a man he didn't know at a bar in Council Bluffs. He looked at the address. It was on Broadway. Brad wasn't familiar with Council Bluffs, but Nathan had given him a map. He drove across the river and immediately got lost. The city had a confusing street configuration, and he needed to be completely familiar with it. He drove to the points marked on the map until he was confident he could find the places from any direction.

He checked his watch. Still two hours to go before he met the man named Joe. Nathan assured him that Joe was competent and loyal, and would work as a team. Brad had his doubts; this wasn't a damned soccer team, but he knew he had to make it work or it was his ass!

Brad walked into Barley's Bar at fifteen minutes to eight. It was hard to miss Brad when he walked in. His jeans and work shirt labeled him as a laboring man. He stood six feet four inches tall and weighed close to two-eighty. He was an imposing figure, except for his face. Brad was thirty-five, but had the boyish face of a teenager, complete with spikey short hair. He looked around; the bar was larger than he had imagined from the outside. The room with the antique back bar was in an adjacent room; he clomped to a table at the back of that room where it was quiet and private. He took off his jacket and sat facing the door. Brad always had his back to a wall, as he had burned a few bridges in the past, and wanted to see any threat aimed his way.

The bartender walked around the bar and approached Brad. *SOB better not ask for my ID.* He didn't. Nothing pissed Brad off more than being asked for his ID. Brad ordered a draft beer, a Sam Adams seasonal, and they visited about the vintage back bar. Brad used to do some woodworking and was impressed by the old bar.

Halfway through his beer another man entered the room. Brad assumed it was Joe. He was wearing a muscle shirt, and was the scariest guy Brad had ever seen. He was short, and his narrow waist angled up to muscular shoulders, his large head sitting on them with no neck between. His most disturbing feature, however, was his eyebrows. More of a unibrow, thick and black, it shielded deep-set eyes and gave him an "I'm meaner than you" look. Brad motioned him to sit, not bothering to shake hands. After all, they weren't friends, and never would be.

"You Brad?" the short man asked.

"Yes, and I assume you must be Joe."

"Right. So what am I doing here?" Joe asked.

Brad studied the tattoos all over the arms. *Prison, maybe. Or just a guy who wants to look good at the gym?* "Nathan didn't tell you?"

"He called and said to meet you here. He had a job for us to do."

Brad pulled out his map and explained the plan to Joe. He sat impassively, never saying a word, not even asking a question.

"So what do you think?" Brad asked.

Joe sat mute for a minute. "So these guys are going to be walking along the street after they leave the hospital tomorrow. If I'm reading your map right, they will be a block over from where we are right now."

"That's right," Brad said.

"If it's going to be daytime, there's going to be people around. No cover, no place to hide, all open space. I don't like it," Joe said emphatically.

"I thought of that," Brad said. "I'll make sure they know I am following them. They'll cut off of Kanesville Blvd. and head for the cover of the cemetery. I'll force them to do just that. You," he pointed at Joe, "will be waiting at the top of the hill. That's when we take them."

"I still don't like doing this in broad daylight," Joe said, shaking his head.

"Nathan said they always dismiss patients late in the day. It should be dusk when we hit them," Brad emphasized.

"It better be," Joe said. "You said the white guy is a piece of cake, but the black guy has skills…So we take out the black guy first. Agreed?"

They agreed on the plan and decided to meet about noon the next day to go over the route and the plan again.

CHAPTER 24

S AM AWAKENED EARLY ON MONDAY. He went to breakfast and waited until eight o'clock sharp. He took out his cell phone and called Chief Marlowe.

"Any word on Whitney?...I see...I need a couple of favors...Do you know a man named Nathan Landry?...I figured that...Okay, I've got a lot on him and you get to bring him down. But you tell no one. Your ears only. You trust no one, understand...*especially* another cop...now here's what I need from you..." After spelling out his request, Sam hung up the phone and headed for the streets to try and find some information about Whitney.

"Mr. Hughes, you have a call on line one."

"Good morning, this is Jason Hughes." Jason was cheerful this morning.

"Good morning, Jason. This is Detective Larry Malone from Grand Island." Jason went white as a sheet. He also lost his ability to speak.

"Are you there, Mr. Hughes?" Malone asked.

"Uhh...Yes, yes, I am." Jason was flustered and the fear showed in his voice.

"Good. I believe you talked to my partner, Detective Worthy, on Saturday morning."

"Yes, and he said everything was fine," Jason said a little too quickly.

"Sure, just following up on his notes," Malone said. "Perhaps it's just his handwriting, but I was going over them and need to confirm some points. Max's notes don't match up with statements from your friends. I'm sure he got something wrong, but let's start from the beginning. Tell me what happened from the time you entered the gymnasium until you left for Omaha."

Jason was terrified. *What does he mean, don't match up? Oh shit, what did the others tell him? I thought this was over... Okay Jason, pull yourself together. Just repeat what you told the other detective.*

"Mr. Hughes, I would like you to relate the events of that day to me. Do you understand?" Malone let the silence have its desired effect.

"Yes, I was just composing my thoughts." Jason repeated the story exactly as he had told it to Max on Saturday. Malone knew this because Max was listening in, and was giving him nods as the details of the story progressed.

"Thank you, Mr. Hughes. Your account of the events that day is very concise. Perhaps one of your friends got his wires crossed. I'll visit with them and get things cleared up. Thank you for your time." Jason started to ask what the discrepancies were, but Malone had hung up.

"Good idea, partner," Max said smiling. "I'll bet he's shitting his pants right about now."

"Let's hope so," Malone said. "This is our last shot."

Five miles away Nathan's phone rang. He looked at the caller ID. He had a lot on his plate and wasn't in the mood for lunch. He answered, "Hi, Jason. Hey, buddy, got a problem. Can't make lunch today."

He listened to Jason's near hysteria. "Jason, you're getting off track. They're grasping at straws because they don't know anything. Don't worry about it. Trust me. It's under control. Stick to your story. They can't prove a damn thing." Nathan closed the phone.

Across the river in Council Bluffs, Sam walked past the cellar where Whitney was fighting for her life. It had been thirty-six hours since she had food or water, and she floated in and out of consciousness with no sense of time. She was bruised, her clothes were dirty and torn, and they were soiled from her body fluids. Her lips were cracked and dry, her mouth felt like it was full of cotton. Her hands were still bound. All the rubbing and scraping on the shovel had failed to cut her bonds. It had just rubbed her wrists raw. She was getting concerned about infection. *Why am I worried about infection? Stupid thought. Here I am, probably going to die in this hole, and I'm worried about infection? Maybe I'm delirious. I want my family. I want out of here.* The cramps started again in her back and shoulders from lack of movement. All she could do was endure the pain until the cramps subsided. She wanted to cry as she rested her head on the cold floor, but she couldn't summon any tears. she had to fight for her life but her desire to live was fading. She cursed Father Shanks, or whoever he was, hoping it would strengthen her will to live.

Sam went along Broadway Street and then Kanesville Boulevard talking to other homeless people. All were worried about Whitney. They told him about the bonfire vigil, feeling like maybe they had accomplished something. Sam knew better. It was just a way to vent, totally useless. But if it made them feel better, or gave them hope, who was he to criticize? He didn't know where to begin, either.

Sam walked along, the chill still in the air from the previous evening. Probably wouldn't get much above fifty degrees today. His cell rang. Sam answered.

"Sam, this is Mike." Sam was silent. The voice said, "Father Kelly."

"Sorry, Father," Sam said. "It didn't click for a minute."

"You're losing your touch, Sam," Father Kelly said. "Who else knows this phone number?"

"Good point...Maybe I *am* losing my touch."

"I did some research on your Father Shanks. No one seems to know anything about him. He isn't a priest in any diocese in Nebraska or Iowa. He's not a Jesuit, and I have checked with a couple of other orders, but nothing so far."

"So where else could he be from?" Sam asked, curious.

"Anywhere I suppose," Father Kelly said. "Anyway, one of my friends from Davenport said he thought he attended the seminary with a Marcus Shanks, but he wasn't sure. He's going to check with the seminary office and see if they have any records."

"So what do you think?" Sam asked.

"Don't know what to think until I have an answer, Sam," Father Kelly said. "In the meantime, I would be very wary of him."

"Thanks, Father. Call me back if you find out anything."

"God bless, Sam."

Sam mulled this over. *What the hell is going on? Could Father Shanks be the missing piece of the puzzle?*

Sam decided to go back to the shelter and have a talk with Father Shanks. He got halfway there when he saw the man following him. The same guy as the day before. Sam started to pick up his pace, but decided it didn't matter if he lost the man tailing him. The guy knew where he lived. But Sam stopped short. If Father Shanks was involved with Landry, Sam would be tipping his hand if he confronted him. Best to forget about him for now. Sam decided to go to the hospital and wait with John until he was discharged.

Whitney woke with a start! *Oh God, how long was I asleep? Is that water dripping?* She listened closely. Nothing. *It must have been a dream.* She started to drift off. *I hear it! I hear water dripping.* Whitney listened intently. She heard the drops fall about ten feet away. She rolled toward the sound. She felt a tiny splash hit her face. Water was dripping from above. A drop or two, then a small trickle. She positioned herself so the drops would fall in her mouth. She had to keep adjusting her position so the drops would fall in her mouth. *Water! Precious water!* She kept moving to catch the drops. It wasn't much, but it moistened her dry mouth. It seemed to last a long time, but then it stopped. *I got what? A half a cup? Less?* It didn't matter. It gave her some hope. She rested her head on the cold, wet floor. *Please somebody find me. Where are you, David? I need you and the kids.* She wanted to scream, and scream. She had done that several times before. Best to save her strength. Someone would find her. She knew it. She decided to stay close to where she heard the water, so she could catch it again.

The sprinkler wasn't set to go off for another two days.

Brad and Joe met outside of Barleys. They drove the route they expected Sam and John to take. They made note of buildings, dumpsters, fences, anywhere a person could hide. Joe was adamant they hit them somewhere in the open, a place where there was nowhere to hide. They planned their attack with precision. Brad was impressed with Joe's thoroughness. Brad had assumed he was just a hunk of muscle with a small brain.

They drove to the parking lot of City Hospital and started their vigil. Waiting was the tough part. But it provided them with an adrenalin rush, like the hour before the big football game. The anticipation was as rewarding as the kill itself.

Sam entered the hospital and took the elevator up to the fourth floor. The name tag on his uniform told Sam the officer on duty was Sgt. Valdez. The sergeant stood and greeted Sam, then told him there was a package in the room for him, courtesy of Chief Marlowe. Sam thanked him, and told him he could leave if he wished. He was going to stay with John until he was discharged later in the day.

"If you don't mind, I'll stay," Sgt. Valdez said. "Chief Marlowe said to stay with him until he left the hospital. In fact, I could even give you a ride back to the shelter. I'd feel better knowing you got home okay."

"Thanks," Sam said, "but we can manage. Besides, we have to go back to our lives sometime." Sam turned and entered the room.

John was joking with a man sitting in the chair beside his bed. John looked up, saw Sam, and said, "Hey, Sam, I want you to meet someone."

The man stood and extended his hand. "Steve Cantelli. I've heard a lot about you, Sam. John here calls you his guardian angel."

Sam shook Cantelli's hand. John chimed in, "Dr. Cantelli treated me after I was beaten," John said, adding, "He saved my life."

"I thank you for that, Doctor," Sam said with emotion.

"Well, I had best get moving," Dr. Cantelli said. "I'll get your discharge orders written up after I see a few more patients, John." He turned to leave, giving Sam a nod of his head.

"Nice guy," John said. "This is the first time I've seen him since my first stay here. He was interested in my progress, and I filled him in on everything that's happened since I left the first time."

"Was he surprised to see a policeman outside the door?" Sam asked, curiosity in his voice.

"No, he was concerned," John said. "He joked about saving me so someone could come in and try and kill me again. I know he didn't think it was funny, it was just his way of dealing with the situation."

"I think you and I need to stick close together for the next few days until this blows over," Sam said. "I'd prefer they kept you right here for a couple of days."

"FBI man going to save my ass?" John said, laughing.

"Not funny, John," Sam said, deadpan serious. "We both need to watch our backs." Sam walked across the room and opened the package from Chief Marlowe. He rummaged through it, pursed his lips and nodded his head before closing the box.

The clock moved slowly. Finally the silence was broken when Sam's cell rang.

"Sam, this is Mike Kelly. If, and I mean *if* I'm right, your Father Shanks is no more a priest than Satan himself."

"What do you mean? What is he if he's not priest?"

"Well, my friend Jonas from Davenport called me back. He called the seminary and inquired about Marcus Shanks. They wouldn't tell him much, only that he had left when he was just a deacon. He was never ordained a priest.

"Well, Jonas made some calls to other seminarians, and the story is that he was asked to leave. He was a troublemaker. A loner who didn't make friends. In fact, he was not well liked. Jonas told him that one of his contacts said he was actually afraid of him. At any rate, one story was that he was dealing drugs, another that he stole some money, and he was gone shortly after. Everyone knew he was asked to leave, but those things get swept under the rug, you know."

"You're sure about all this? This is the same guy?" Sam asked, not questioning, but needing confirmation.

"Yep," Father Kelly said. "I can send you his picture from his seminary days if you like."

"Please," Sam said, "I'd like you to do that."

"You sure you're going to be okay, Sam?" Father Kelly asked.

"I'll be fine, Father," Sam said. "A rattlesnake is only a threat if you don't know he's there."

"Be careful, Sam."

"Thanks, Father. I will." *The missing piece of the puzzle. Shanks is involved in this whole thing. And who better to know every move John makes. This may be the break I need.*

The black Ford Explorer cruised north along I-29, merged with I-80 West, and took the Omaha/Eppley Airfield exit. Marcus Shanks, aka Father Shanks, had some unfinished business in Omaha. When Nathan terminated him, he knew Nathan would never let him leave and start a new life elsewhere. There was too much to risk with him free. His cover was blown and wherever he went, he would be looking over his shoulder, if not for the police, for one of Nathan's cronies. He simply knew too much. That was why he had watched the car following him. He made a stop at a convenience store, got some chewing gum, and pulled back onto the interstate. After about five miles, he slowed his speed, and sure enough, the same car was behind him again. Nathan was having him followed. *There is no pickup waiting for me down the road. And if there is, I'm not leaving in it alive.*

Father Shanks had driven on, sweat starting to soak his undershirt. His Roman collar rubbed his neck when it began to get soaked also. *Where is this guy going to do the hit? Run me off the road? Wait until I get to the motel?* He was approaching the Rock City exit when he saw a rest stop. That was when he spotted the state trooper car parked in the rest stop. He cranked the steering wheel, almost missing the exit ramp, but gained control and parked next to the State Patrol car. He got out and walked briskly into the building. The trooper was on his phone, walking toward the door. Father Shanks waved his arms frantically. The cop ended his call. "Is there a problem, Father?"

"I don't know, officer," Father Shanks said fearfully. "I just said mass in Council Bluffs and am on my way to Mound City. This car pulled up very close behind me. I thought he was going to run into me. I sped up a little, and he did too. Then he passed me, almost forcing me onto the shoulder. He slowed back down but was driving down the middle of the road. I was afraid to pass him again, so I just stayed behind. That was when I saw your car parked outside. I exited so I could report him. I think he may have been drinking, and may cause an accident."

"You did the right thing, Father. Did you get his license number?"

"No, I'm sorry. I was too flustered. But I can tell you he's driving a newer Ford, gray, and it has Nebraska plates, probably Omaha."

"Okay, you go ahead, Father. I'll head out and see if I can catch him before he hurts someone."

"Bless you, officer. It was frightening." Father Shanks got in his car and watched the trooper get into his. Father Shanks merged back onto the freeway from the rest area, and sure enough, the gray Ford was parked on the shoulder about a half mile down the road. Father Shanks watched the Ford pull back on the Interstate behind him, and smiled when the red and whites lit up behind him. *Take that Landry! You're going to be one pissed dude when you find out I got away.* Father Shanks turned on his radio, hummed along with the tune, and took the next exit, not caring where it took him.

Now Father Shanks was back in Omaha. The last place Nathan would think to look for him. He smiled to himself, as he headed for the apartment house. Time to get even. Nathan had used him, mistreated a man of the cloth—he couldn't accept the fact he would never be a real priest—and he was going to make Nathan pay. He knew where Nathan's girlfriend lived, and he parked six blocks away in a motel parking lot. Now it was time to wait. And he had all the time in the world.

CHAPTER 25

T HE NURSE ENTERED JOHN'S ROOM, had him sign some papers, and went to get a wheelchair. John settled into the chair when she got back with it, and Sgt. Valdez walked out with them. As they reached the entrance and walked into the late afternoon sun, John said, "Wait! You forgot your package, Sam."

Sam shook his head. "I got all I needed from it." He offered to call a cab, but John resisted.

"I really need to walk, Sam. You can call a cab if I get tired, okay?"

They thanked the nurse, said good-bye to Sgt. Valdez, and began to walk along Kanesville Boulevard. They didn't see the two men watching from a car in the parking lot. They also didn't hear one of the men say, "Okay, that's them. Let's go get set up," as he steered the car onto Broadway.

Sam and John didn't talk much as they walked; they had done a lot of that in the room, and wanted to save their breath for a brisk pace back to the shelter since it was getting dark fast, and cooling off. They had walked a while, when Sam slowed down.

John looked back at him and grinned, "Look who's getting tired!"

Sam's murmur was almost inaudible to John. "Stop talking so I can listen. Just keep walking beside me."

John started to ask what was wrong, but stopped himself and kept his silence. They walked another full block before Sam spoke.

"Did you hear that dog back there?"

"Yeah. He was barking his head off."

"But not at us," Sam said. "He started to turn toward us, but he was barking at something behind the fence in the alley. Or someone." Sam had taken this route enough times to know nobody walked by that fence without the dog barking at them the length of it. Sam turned to look at John as if in conversation, and saw the figure out of the corner of his eye. It was not the same man who had followed him before. This guy was much bigger. They walked to the next intersection.

"Turn right on Second Street," Sam said. "Then let's step up our pace; we've got a visitor behind us."

John did as he was told. Suddenly he was scared. He looked behind them but saw no one.

"Keep going," Sam said. "Don't look back. He probably doesn't know we made him."

Sam stepped up the pace a little more. It was difficult for John. He had lost some strength in the hospital, and they were going up a steep hill. Sam could hear John panting, gasping for breath. Sam pushed him on as he saw the man turn the corner onto Second Street.

"Not much further," Sam said, his own breath coming in gasps. "There's a statue at the top of the hill with a wall and a hedge. We can hide there, then I'm going to find out who's following us." He grabbed John's arm and, as they reached the top of the hill, he pushed him to the right. "Run," Sam whispered, "and get behind the wall below the statue."

John turned and ran around the right side of the wall. Sam ran straight ahead and launched himself into the hedge. A shot rang out. John lay on the cool grass behind the statue, his hands over his ears. *What the hell? Sam? Oh God, what's going on?* John heard rustling in the hedge. Another shot. He kept his head covered, afraid to raise it up.

He heard footsteps running up the street. John's breathing was still labored, and now he was also sweating profusely, partially from the exertion, partially from fear.

There was more rustling in the bushes, and he started to look up, but changed his mind and covered his head in his hands, as if it would protect him from the bullet.

Someone knelt beside him. "Don't move." It was Sam.

The footsteps got closer, and a voice shouted out, "Police officer," as a man ran toward the statue.

"Show some ID!" Sam yelled above him.

The man stopped, pointed his weapon toward the ground, and said, "I'm going to reach into my coat pocket." His hand came out and something shiny raised above his head. It was a badge.

Sam said, "Okay, John, you can get up now. Show's over."

John tried to stand, but needed Sam's help. "God, I thought you were shot," John said.

"He wasn't expecting me to charge the hedge right at him," Sam said. "It forced him to shoot quickly, and lucky for me, he missed."

"How did you know he was there?" John asked, puzzled. The police officer was looking around, alert for any further danger, and listening to Sam's explanation.

"The man behind us was hanging back way too far. He was staying visible and following just fast enough to keep us moving. I figured he had someone up ahead, and the Black Angel was the likely spot to ambush us. The guy in the hedge shifted as we started to run and the rustle of the leaves gave away his position, so I charged right at it. Got lucky."

John was still shaky. Sam told him to sit, and he turned to the police officer.

"Sure glad to see you," Sam said. "What happened to our other friend?"

"He's back down the hill a ways," the officer said, "hands cuffed around a lamp post. What about the guy up here?"

"Not so lucky," Sam said. "We wrestled for the gun, and it went off. I checked for a pulse, but..." He shook his head.

"I better call an ambulance just in case," the officer said, taking out his cell.

Sam asked the officer how long he had been following him. "Last couple of days," the officer said, still panting, Chief Marlowe's orders."

Sam nodded, and asked if he could go and talk to the other man.

"Okay with me. Just don't get cute and rough him up or anything."

Sam walked down the hill, telling John to stay by the statue with the officer. Brad had given up his fight and sat on the ground, hands cuffed behind his back and around the post. The apprehension showed in his eyes as he watched Sam walk toward him.

Sam walked to the lamppost, approaching from behind Brad, keeping the post between them. Brad craned his neck to see what Sam was doing.

Sam squatted down behind him, and said, "Who sent you?"

Brad spat out, "I'll never talk. But you better know, there's going to be others, so you're as good as dead."

"Wants me that bad, huh?" Sam responded. "Is it Landry?" When he got no response he reached into Brad's jacket pocket. "Well, well, what have we here?" Sam pulled a cell phone from the pocket. The officer had disarmed him, but must not have noticed the cell. But then, he was in a hurry to get up the hill. Sam opened the phone.

"Hey, you can't take my phone!" Brad shouted.

"Not going to take it," Sam said, "just going to use it for a minute." He looked at the screen, and called the last number on the display.

Nathan answered on the first ring. "Well?"

Sam replied in a mocking voice, "Hello, Nathan."

"Who is this?" Nathan demanded.

"This is your worst nightmare, Nathan, and I'm going to bring you down," Sam said, with malice in his voice. He closed the phone and put it back in Brad's pocket. He rose to walk away and looked back at Brad. "Oh yeah, have a nice day...or maybe twenty years."

Sam and John stayed to answer questions. Chief Marlowe himself showed up at the scene. He asked Sam if he got his package. "Yes," Sam said, "thank you. I'll be in touch tomorrow. It's been a long day." The Chief told the black and white to give Sam and John a ride home.

"What was that you said about a black angel?" John asked on the way. John had never been in the back seat of a police car, and he noticed there were no door handles or controls for the windows. It was claustrophobic. The question was nervous chatter.

"The statue," Sam said, "the locals call her The Black Angel." The real name is the Ruth Ann Dodge Memorial. She was the wife of a Civil War general.

"She sure saved our butt tonight," John replied. "Or, rather, you did."

They were both silent the rest of the way.

The next morning Sam was up early. He knocked on Father Shanks's door. No answer. He turned the doorknob. It was unlocked. *Strange.* He opened the door and the room was empty. No clothes, no papers, nothing. Father Shanks was gone. *Son of a bitch! Shanks was the missing piece, and now he's gone. Shit! We may never know how he was involved.* Sam called Chief Marlowe.

"Chief, this is Sam Washington. I found out our good Father Shanks, who runs the shelter, was involved with Landry. I went to his room today and he's gone."

"A priest was mixed up in this?"

"That's the rub," Sam said. "He's not a priest. He's been impersonating a priest. It's my guess he's in this up to his eyeballs."

"Good God, Sam, what next?"

"Next, I need to come to your office. Can you furnish me a ride?" He didn't wait for an answer. "And any news on Whitney?"

"Sorry Sam, we don't have a clue."

"I'll be waiting by the front door," Sam said.

Sam and Chief Malone talked about twenty minutes. "I'm not sure I really want to do this your way, Sam," the Chief said, "but you can have until noon tomorrow."

"Thank you," Sam replied. "You can have Landry. I just want to get my name cleared."

As Sam opened the door to leave, the Chief said, "By the way Sam, what did you do with the gun you took from the shooter last night?"

"It should be somewhere at the scene. I may have tossed or dropped it when I went to help John."

"Okay, I'm sure it will turn up today."

Sam left. *One more place to go and it would be over.*

Chief Malone placed a call to the Grand Island Police Department. He asked if they had a missing person named James Wilson.

"Detective Malone here, Chief. What do you know about James Wilson?"

"First, Detective, what do *you* know about James Wilson?" the Chief asked. "There are some things we need to sort out before I release any information to you."

CHAPTER 26

S AM CALLED A TAXI TO take him onto Omaha. He usually walked, but his destination was almost ten miles from Council Bluffs. The address he gave the driver was about a half mile from his actual destination. He had to scout out the area before putting his plan into action.

As he walked to his destination he noticed a black Ford Explorer in the parking lot of a motel. It made him angry as it reminded him of Father Shanks, and how the man had deceived everyone. It was ironic in a sense. He did actually offer the homeless food and shelter, as well as comfort, and a sympathetic ear. On the other hand, God only knew what evil actually lurked in his mind.

Sam approached his destination with caution. He entered the apartment complex and went to apartment 2B. He had been in the building before, but never inside the apartment.

He knocked on the door. A gorgeous twenty-something wearing a sweatshirt and cut-off jeans answered the door, her blond hair and long legs catching his eye. Her looks didn't distract him. He planted a foot inside the doorway, and pushed her back, slamming the door behind him. She was too startled to react. He raised his hands and said, "I'm not here to harm you, I'm here to save your life." She turned to run and Sam saw she was heading for the cell phone on the table. He beat her to it, grabbed it up and blocked her path. "Please, just listen to me." She backed against the wall, shaking with fear. Sam kept his distance.

"You are in grave danger. An associate of Nathan's wants to harm you to get back at him. I don't want that to happen. Is there somewhere safe you can go?"

"Who are you, and what the hell is this all about?"

"It doesn't matter who I am. What matters is that you could be lying on the floor dead when Nathan shows up. The choice is yours. Cooperate and live, or possibly be killed.

She gave Sam a defiant glare, and said, "Go to hell! I'm going to scream my head off until the neighbors call the cops."

Sam calmly said, "Okay, have it your way." She didn't have a chance to scream. The Taser caused her to jerk, then she collapsed to the floor. Sam carried her into the back bedroom. He used duct tape to bind and gag her, and secured her to the bed.

Sam used her phone to call Nathan. "Hello, Nathan. This is not Nicole. If you care about her be at her apartment in thirty minutes." Sam closed the phone. He knew Nathan recognized the number. The phone rang as Sam started to put it down. The caller ID said Nate. *How sweet.* Sam opened the phone and said, "Thirty minutes," and closed the phone. Now it was time to wait.

Malone motioned for Max to pick up the phone and listen in as he talked to Chief Marlowe. Chief Marlowe wasn't revealing any information when he learned there was a warrant out for the arrest of James Wilson on possession of drugs.

"That puts a new perspective on things," the Chief said. "I would be harboring a criminal, at least an alleged criminal, if I told you I knew where James Wilson was at this time."

Max chirped in, "Well, obviously you do, so who are you kidding? And...why are you protecting Wilson?"

"This is a very strange situation," the Chief said. "I don't like your insinuation in saying that I am protecting him."

Malone took over. "Look, Chief Marlowe, the charges are bogus. We've been working on this case for six months now, and there is nothing in Wilson's background to indicate he has ever dealt drugs, or been involved with any form of diversion. We think whoever did this planted the drugs in case Wilson surfaced."

Malone went on to explain Wilson's strange disappearance, his wife's endeavors to find him, and their suspicions involving Jason Hughes, Nathan Landry, and Tom Meyer. He also explained that he felt Jason Hughes was the weak link, and they were putting pressure on him.

"Let's not spar on this issue," the Chief said. "The name Nathan Landry is enough to turn my stomach. If Landry is involved, there's every reason to believe Wilson may have some drug involvement."

"Are you serious?" Max asked with incredulity.

"Landry is dirty," the Chief said. "We found Wilson in an alley back in May, beaten half to death. The problem is, Wilson has amnesia, and doesn't have a clue who he is, or who did the beating."

"Jesus Christ!" Malone exclaimed. "So how do you know this guy is Wilson?"

"Another long story," the Chief said. "But trust me, he's Wilson. Can I get the FBI or Omaha authorities involved in this?"

"If you can find out who did what, and get Wilson back to his pregnant wife, you can get the God-damned U.S. Marines involved in it!"

"Give me twenty-four hours," the Chief said. "I'll need an address on Meyer and Hughes; I know where to find Landry."

"Coming your way, Chief!" Malone was emailing the information even as they said their good-byes. He stood, and gave Max a high five with a grin.

"So how are you feeling about this?" Max asked Malone.

"What do you mean?" Malone asked.

"You know," Max said with a grimace. "I thought you had some feelings for her."

"Oh. Naw. She was needy and I felt sorry for her. Sure, I almost let my feeling get in the way of my objectivity, but I got over that. Mary helped me with that."

"So when do we tell Susan?"

"I think we wait," Malone said. "If we tell her, she will set up camp in the Chief's office, and I'm sure he doesn't need that. Hell, she may even show up with that handgun of hers."

"Yeah, Annie Fucking Oakley," Max said with a laugh. "We better wait to tell her anything."

Whitney was desperately in need of water. She was hallucinating and having minor seizures. She knew she was about to die. Luckily, she was so weak she slept most of the time. She wanted to die. Her body was racked with pain, spasms, and she was delirious.

The morning passed. Chief Marlowe got the Omaha authorities involved, who in turn alerted the FBI. This was a kidnapping now. He gave them the information he had, and they were in contact with Malone within an hour. Unmarked units were dispatched to Landry's home and business. Chief Marlowe had convinced them to use surveillance only, not to approach the subject, as he needed time to nail him on drug charges.

Jason Hughes was called away from a meeting to an interrogation room by an FBI agent. Deputy Tom Meyer visited with another agent at the Douglas County Sheriff's Department. He agreed to accompany him to his office for further interrogation.

Sam checked the bedroom. The girlfriend was still immobile. He looked at his watch. Ten more minutes. Sam knew Landry would not come alone. There were windows in the kitchen and a sliding glass patio door in the bedroom. It was possible to get to the balcony outside the bedroom from the balcony below. *Damned*

corner apartment! Sam made sure the sliding glass door was locked, curtains open, and positioned himself so he could see both windows. Landry would have some trick up his sleeve, Sam was sure of that.

Sam didn't know if he would survive the day. He studied the beige walls. They reminded him of the paint in his former home. He envisioned his daughters and his wife, embracing the happy times they had shared inside those walls. He was so close to revenge he could taste it. He remembered a quote: "Sometimes the sweetest forgiveness comes in the form of revenge." No, that wasn't quite right. Hmm...*Sam! Get your head on straight. You've come too far to blow this now. Think! Time is running out.*

Nathan met two men a block away. He set up his plan. He approached the apartment door slowly. It was unlocked. He turned the knob and swung it wide open, stepping behind the door jamb. He peered out, and saw the overturned table by the wall on the left. It was made of very heavy, thick, and expensive wood. Would it stop a bullet?

Nathan entered the room, swinging his gun in all directions, but keeping his eye on the table. He fired two shots through the table.

"Nice try, Nathan," Sam said as he stepped from behind the wall opposite the table into the bedroom doorway. "Drop the gun."

Nathan still held the gun high, suddenly pointed it at Sam and fired. He missed. Sam didn't. He put a bullet into Nathan's shoulder, and his arm fell. "Drop the gun, Landry. The next one will be between your eyes."

Nathan complied. He ventured a glance over his shoulder. Sam told him to get back in front of the doorway. If someone was in the hall, Sam wanted Nathan between them so prevent a clear shot.

"Where's Nicole?" Nathan growled, as he bent and held his bleeding shoulder.

"She's fine," Sam replied, nodding to the bedroom.

"Nicole!" Nathan shouted.

"Forget it," Sam said. "She can't answer with duct tape over her mouth."

"If you've hurt her..."

"It's you I want, Nathan. I don't give a damn about her." *Where are the others? I know he wouldn't come alone. He always gets someone else to do his dirty work. Where the hell are they?* Sam was growing nervous. He checked both windows, but saw no movement. *Had the shots scared them off? Not likely.*

"I know you have people with you, Nathan. You're too much of a coward to come alone. Call them off and you live. I have nothing to lose anymore. You destroyed my life. You took my family away. All because of your damned drugs. You're worse than a drug dealer, Nathan. You're just pond scum who thinks he's somebody."

"So what do you want from me, *former* Agent Washington?" Nathan's tone was mocking as he sneered at Sam with fury.

"First, you can admit it was you who planted the money in my car," Sam said.

"Go to hell," Nathan spat out. A bullet whizzed past his ear. He ducked reflexively, grasping his shoulder in pain from the movement.

"Okay...Okay. I planted the money!" Nathan said, his voice raising an octave.

"And what about Sgt. Tredrow?" Sam asked.

"Who in the hell is that?" Nathan asked.

"The officer who was going to testify in my behalf," Sam said, his eyes narrowing.

"I believe he was killed in a boat accident," Nathan said with a smirk.

"By one of your men," Sam retorted.

"Actually, it was me," a voice said as a man stepped into the doorway behind Nathan. Sam turned his attention to the figure.

"Drop the gun, Sam," Father Shanks said. "I have no quarrel with you. My quarrel is with Nathan, here. Oh, and I took care of your backup men, Nathan," Father Shanks said with a mock grin, cocking his head.

Before Sam could react, Nathan grabbed his gun from the floor and fired two quick shots at Sam. Sam felt the bullet's impact before he collapsed to the floor, blood pooling around his head. He heard another shot before he passed out.

CHAPTER 27

*"H*OW IS HE, DOCTOR?" THE *woman asked.*
"I'm sorry. We tried, but he had lost too much blood."
The woman took her two daughters in her arms and explained that their daddy was dead.

James Wilson, no longer John Doan— although his memory was still blank—sat in the waiting room with Susan. She clung to him. Her touch felt good, although he was unsure of their relationship, and was having trouble coming to grips with the situation.

Malone and Worthy had left, trusting Susan to bring James back to Grand Island. He still faced drug charges, but there was little doubt the charges would be dropped. Susan put her arm around Sam's wife, Iris, telling her how sorry she was. His daughters sat beside her, still in shock over the situation.

The doctor came into the room, and said, "You can see him now, Mrs. Washington."

She rose, and slowly walked beside the doctor, leaving her daughters in Susan's charge.

She cautiously entered the room. Walking up to the bed, she reached out and took Sam's unmoving hand. "Oh, Sam," and a sob escaped. She took a deep steadying breath as she studied her husband's face. "I've been expecting this for a long time. I never stopped loving you, and..." Tears overcame her, and she fought for control. "I forgive you for abandoning us. I knew you had to clear your name—and you did. I'm so glad for that."

The tears rolled down her cheeks, and burst into a flood when Sam said in a raspy voice, "Iris, is that really you?"

"Yes, Sam, it's really me."

"Thank God. I thought I had died and was dreaming." His eyes were heavy and his voice weak as he said, "I love you, Iris. I'm so sorry about how I handled..." Sam's eyes drifted shut and he faded into unconsciousness. The doctor stepped up behind Iris, gently touched her arm, and said, "He will be in and out of consciousness for a while. You can stay if you like. He just needs rest."

"Can you get my girls so they can see their daddy?"

"Of course," the doctor said. He returned with Sam's daughters, Molly and Maddy, and left them with their mother. They hung back, unsure of the situation, but Iris told them to tell him who they were and tell him they loved them. They hadn't seen Sam for four years, but Molly remembered her father reading her stories and playing with her. The man in the bed looked older. She stepped up to the bed, took his hand, and told him she loved him. Maddy barely remembered him, but she managed to say, "I love you, Daddy." Iris took them by the hand, and they walked back to the waiting room, the girls still trying to comprehend what had occurred.

Down the hall, Whitney was visiting with her husband and children. James knocked on the door, stepped in and said, "Sam is awake. He's going to be fine."

"Oh, thank God!" Whitney exclaimed. "When can I see him?"

"Probably not until tomorrow," James said. "He's still recovering and in and out of consciousness."

"And how are you doing, John—er...James, now, isn't it? James Wilson. Soon to be a father. Can't think of a better ending. Actually, a better beginning." Whitney looked at the doubt and worry on his face. "Don't worry, James, you'll get your memory back. Thanks to Sam. We all owe him a debt of gratitude."

"Thanks to you, too, Whitney. You never gave up on me. Take care, and..." James's emotions threatened to get the best of him, and he took a deep breath. "Know that I'll never forget you."

James returned to the waiting room. A priest was holding Susan, who was sobbing. He wasn't sure what was going on. She finally gathered herself together, and said, "James, you remember Monsignor Kelly."

"Uh...I guess," James said, extending his hand.

"You will, James," Father Kelly said. "We'll get you back into your own environment and it will help your memory. I'll get you back on the church finance committee and you'll become a pain in my ass again." He chuckled as he clasped James's hand with warmth.

Iris Washington came back into the waiting room. She told them she had decided to call a neighbor to watch the girls so she could stay the night with Sam. Susan was quick to object. "James and I will watch them. We'll take them to the motel and they can swim. But first, we need to go shopping and find them some swimsuits and new clothes to wear tomorrow to see their dad." Iris, uncomfortable leaving her girls with a stranger, thanked Susan but insisted the girls stay with the neighbor.

Sam awakened during the night, and was able to speak a little with Iris. He apologized over and over, telling her how sorry he was at having abandoned her and the girls. He tried to explain how he had been so consumed with hate that he wasn't himself, couldn't think of anything but restoring his good name, but he so regretted all he had missed.

"Monsignor Kelly stopped by the house a few days ago," Iris said. "He told me he had seen you, and you were well, but he was concerned about you. He gave me a cell number to call, but I was afraid you didn't care about us anymore. And, truthfully, I didn't want to put the girls through any more hurt."

"Iris, I hate all the hurt I've put both you and the girls through. If you will have me back, I promise I will never abandon you again." "It's going to take a while, Sam, but I want to give it a try." She held his hand and he drifted off.

The wheels of justice had moved swiftly. Chief Marlowe had raided the meth lab that Tomas was running. Joe, of course was dead, and Tomas was nowhere to be found. At least they confiscated the equipment and the lab was shut down. Sam's information had been right. He had done his homework. This was going to put Landry out of business, not that it mattered anymore, since Landry was dead.

Sam was responsible for figuring out James's identity. James' intuitive knowledge of drugs had tipped Sam off that he might be a doctor, or some sort of medical practitioner. It was a shot in the dark, but it had hit the mark. In the package the Chief had left at the hospital were photocopies of five years' worth of the yearbooks from the University of Nebraska Medical Center and Creighton University. He looked through the College of Medicine, College of Nursing, and College of Pharmacy...and there it was. John's picture above the name, James Wilson, in the yearbook from the University of Nebraska Medical Center. Sam was thankful James wasn't involved with Landry; he never would have forgiven himself for digging so deep.

The FBI had cooperated and Jason Hughes was in custody. "He sang like a canary," the agent told Chief Marlowe. The agent explained how Hughes and Landry had approached Wilson over a shouting match they heard between their teacher friend and a student. Wilson had seen the argument too, and told other parents he was personally going to get the teacher fired.

"Hughes didn't know why it was so important for Landry to defend this teacher, Bingham. Hughes claimed he thought they were just going to ask Wilson to calm down and back off. Hughes claimed Wilson pushed Landry and Landry went ballistic. Beat the hell out of Wilson. The last thing Hughes saw was Landry driving away with Wilson in the trunk of his own car,"

"What about Deputy Meyer?" the chief asked.

"Hughes claimed Meyer never knew anything about it. He also said Landry told him that Wilson was hospitalized and released, and everything was fine. But then those persistent detectives from Grand Island, Worthy and Malone, got too close. They were relentless and would have eventually broken Hughes. You speeded up the process." The agent looked disgusted. "Christ, all of this over a stupid argument."

"Actually, Landry was becoming more and more paranoid. He was close to cracking," the chief said. "Sam Washington, your former agent, almost had Landry once, and Landry had him watched day and night after he got out of prison. He saw to it that he got into a shelter run by a crony of his posing as a priest. Father Shanks, the name his crony used, ran the shelter and kept tabs on Sam.

"When Wilson got out of the hospital, this Father Shanks got him assigned to the same shelter. Both were threats to Landry, both were under one roof. You have to admit, Landry may have been paranoid, but he was smart, too."

The Agent shook his head. "Well, it's over now. I think my boss wants to talk to Sam once he recovers a little more and is up to visitors."

"Tell your boss to treat him with the respect he deserves," Chief Marlowe said. "Sam Washington spent the last two years of his life living as a homeless man, all the while compiling the most complete case file I have ever seen. He has a list of Landry's dummy corporations, drug operations, and off-shore bank accounts, complete with account numbers. And you better not forget that tape recording where Landry admits to planting the money in Sam's trunk. The FBI owes him an apology, back pay, his record expunged, and his job back if he wants it." Chief Marlowe saw the agent nod in agreement. "I'm trusting you to see that this gets done, but right now I need to go to the hospital and give Sam my thanks."

Chief Marlowe went to the hospital, but had trouble fitting into Sam's room. Sam's wife and girls, James and Susan Wilson, and Monsignor Kelly were all in the room. Sam was still exhausted, but happy to have the company. Malone and Worthy had been by the day before to wish him well, and thank him for finding Wilson; Sam didn't remember their visit, but was glad to hear of it.

The Chief opened the door, and was about to back right out due to the crowd, but Sam spotted him. "Hey, look who's here. Come in, Chief. Meet my family and friends." Iris introduced everyone to Chief Marlowe. The chief engaged in some small talk before saying he had some things to discuss with Sam, but would come back later.

"No, you won't," Sam said. "You have to fill me in. Last thing I knew I was lying in a pool of blood on the floor, and Landry and Father Shanks were both standing there with guns. I need to know what happened."

"Well…if you say so," the Chief said, hesitating only a moment. "These folks may as well know the whole story too."

The chief moved a little so he didn't have his back to anyone in the room. "You obviously confronted Landry. His girlfriend said you had tased her and tied her up. She said you used her phone to get Landry to come to her apartment. Now you have to fill in some details, Sam; I'm only assuming what went on next."

Sam took up the narrative. "I waited for Landry. All I wanted was a confession that he had planted the money in my car. I told him I wanted to hear him say he planted the money. He laughed at me, raised his gun, and I shot him in the shoulder. Oh, by the way, thank you for the package, Chief. It saved my life."

The chief narrowed his eyes. "The package had a Kevlar vest, the photos and records you requested, a tape recorder, and a Taser. There was no gun."

"Huh—really? I don't remember where that gun came from, then," Sam said, a twinkle in his eye. "Anyway, Landry dropped his weapon, and admitted he had planted the money in the trunk of my car. I asked him if he killed the police officer who was going to testify on my behalf. Suddenly Father Shanks appeared in the door, gun trained on Landry, saying, 'No, it was me that killed the officer.'"

"It stunned me. I screwed up, let my guard down, and Landry stooped and grabbed his gun—clearly, I'm out of practice that I didn't remember to have him kick his gun away!—and I heard two shots. Next thing I knew I was on the floor lying in my own blood." Sam smiled at the chief. "Now it's your turn."

The Chief continued. "One of the neighbors had called 911, reporting gunshots. When the officers arrived at the scene, your Father Shanks, or whatever his name is, was found in the room with you, dead."

"What about Landry?" Sam asked. "Please don't tell me he got away."

"We found him near the stairway, shot in the head."

"Jesus," Sam said. "Oh—sorry for the profanity Father, and girls." Sam was silent for a minute. "So who shot Landry?"

"That's a mystery, Sam. You were shot in the chest and side of your head by Landry. He used a 9 mm. We picked the bullet out of your vest. Father Shanks was also shot with a 9mm, presumably by Landry. Ballistics will confirm that. Landry was shot in the shoulder with a .45, your gun. But the bullet in his head was from a .38. Most likely a revolver, as there were no shell casings at the scene.

"One of his own do it?" Sam asked.

"Not probable. Two other men were found dead outside the building. Throats slashed. Very professional to catch both of them from behind. We think it was your Father Shanks. He wanted Landry to himself. The man, Brad, who we arrested after the attempt on your life, told us that Landry had sent him to kill Father Shanks, but Shanks got away. We think it was revenge on Shanks's part, but Landry got him first."

"So who killed Landry?" Sam asked, hoping for an answer.

"We don't know," Chief Marlowe said. "We'll figure it out. Or not. I imagine he had plenty of enemies."

"What about Whitney?" Sam asked. "I heard you found her and she's on another floor in this hospital. What happened to her?"

"Father Shanks grabbed Whitney from the hospital parking lot after he stabbed the orderly. Dirk Medley, the orderly—oh, did you hear he'd recovered?" The chief smiled to have good news to share with Sam. "Dirk told us he had called Whitney after he recognized Shanks, and apparently Shanks heard him make the call. After he stabbed Dirk, he caught her in the parking garage, tied her up, and put her in the storm cellar next to the shelter."

Sam shook his head. "You know, I walked past that cellar every day. I had no idea. How did you find her?"

"Father Shanks did one last act of kindness. He called 911 shortly before he confronted you and Landry, and told them where she could be found."

"I read once that it was possible Judas may have made his peace with God before he hung himself," Sam said. "Thank God Father Shanks had a change of heart!"

"Oh, you're going to appreciate this, Sam," the Chief suddenly interjected. "The shelter was owned by a corporation called NALCO, and Landry held all the stock in the company. Landry bought the shelter and hired Father Shanks to lure you there so he could keep tabs on you."

"I'm surprised he didn't just kill me. But then, he had me where he wanted: homeless and helpless. Or so he thought," Sam said.

"One of his few mistakes. Anyway, Sam," the Chief said, "I just wanted to thank you and fill you in. I'll leave you with your family, and we'll talk later." He started for the door, stopped, turned around, looked at Sam, and said, "Oh, by the way, we found that gun from the park," and gave Sam a broad wink.

Susan and James decided it was time to take their leave. James shook Sam's hand and promised he would keep in touch. He thanked Sam for his friendship. Susan bent over and kissed Sam on the cheek. "Thank you, Sam. We'll never forget you. In fact, James and I have been talking." She patted her belly with a smile. "We'd like baby James's middle name to be Samuel, if that's all right with you?"

"I would be honored," Sam smiled, a bit overwhelmed as he reached out to shake James's hand.

Susan hugged Iris and the girls, then turned back to Sam. She said, "James's aunt was a nun. After his parents died, she always told him he had a guardian angel who would watch over him. I guess I never imagined his angel was black." She smiled and left.

Sam's ex-Agent In Charge of the local FBI came by the hospital. He assured Sam that he would be exonerated of any wrongdoing, and he had spoken to the Bureau Chief about Sam's eligibility for duty again.

Sam's parents came to Omaha and visited Sam in the hospital. Monsignor Kelly had kept them informed of the sequence of events. They encouraged him to take up his law practice again. Maybe help the homeless. Sam smiled and said, "I'll think about it."

CHAPTER 28

Two weeks later Sam left the hospital and went home to his family. He still had to schedule another surgery to repair his ear and scalp from the bullet wound. In the meantime, he had plenty of time to think about his future. The whole experience had changed his outlook on life. For now, he just wanted to be a husband and father again.

Tomas was sleeping when his cell rang. He had gone back to Mexico to visit relatives, and was irritated that Nathan was calling him before he was even back in the country.

"Hello," Tomas answered.

"Tomas, this is Audrey Landry. Nathan is dead. You work for me now." Audrey watched out the window as the sanitation truck whined to life, smashing the contents of her trash container. She smiled as the .38 revolver became part of the waste for the landfill.

ACKNOWLEDGMENTS

First, and foremost, I would like to thank my wife, Arlene. I could not have accomplished this work without her patience, dedication, and support. Her enthusiasm kept me going when words failed to come, and her praise encouraged me to continue when they did.

To my family and friends: I appreciate your wholehearted support.

My editor, Carol Weber, kept me on the right track. She was critical when necessary, yet supportive throughout. All in all, she was a joy to work with. We shared a few emotions, but I only remember the humorous ones. Thanks, Carol.

To my cover designer, Victorine E. Lieske, a *New York Times* best selling author; *How to find Success Selling eBooks.* I appreciate her creativity and willingness to work with a novice in designing a striking cover.

Craig Hansen, my formatter. Craig re-worked his schedule to meet my timeline, which a month ago I thought was unattainable.

Cliff Carle, a creative writer and editor who gave me my start.

Gina Barlean, author of several books, who introduced me to Vicki and Carol.

The Nebraska Writers Guild for their dedication to Nebraska authors.

Others responsible for this book include: Sergeant Trent Hill, Amy Hill, and Officer Jimmy Olson of the GIPD who gave me technical advice. The Council Bluffs Area Chamber of Commerce.

ABOUT THE AUTHOR

This is the first novel for Ben Wassinger. Ben is a native of Grand Island, Nebraska, a graduate of the University of Nebraska, College of Pharmacy. He has been a practicing pharmacist since 1967, and now specializes as a pharmacist consultant to long term care facilities. Up until now, he jokes that his writing has been confined to "one liners" on the labels of prescription bottles.

Made in the USA
Charleston, SC
09 November 2014